con

D0357658

HUNTING MIDNIGHT

"Sets the standards on erotica-meets-paranormal . . . Will have you making a wish for a man with a little wolf in him." —*Rendezvous*

"Amazing . . . Red-hot to the wall." —*The Best Reviews*

"A roller-coaster ride of hot passion, danger, magick, and true love." —*Historical Romance Club*

CATCHING MIDNIGHT

"A marvelously gripping mix of passion, sensuality, paranormal settings, betrayal, and triumph . . . Dazzling . . . A sensual feast." —*Midwest Book Review*

"Holly has outdone herself in this erotic tale . . . A must-read." —*Affaire de Coeur*

"A wonderfully passionate read." —*Escape to Romance*

ALL U CAN EAT

"Amazing! . . . A must-read. There are no excuses for missing out on this book." —*Romance Junkies*

"The sensuality level is out of this world . . . It's light-hearted, deliciously naughty, and simply perfect fun." —*All About Romance*

THE DEMON'S DAUGHTER

"A sensually erotic novel, and one of Ms. Holly's most entertaining." —*The Best Reviews*

"Thoroughly engrossing . . . An exceptional book . . . A must-have for fans of more erotic romance." —*Booklist*

STRANGE ATTRACTIONS

"A sizzling, erotic romance . . . Readers will enjoy this wild tale." —*The Best Reviews*

"A different kind of erotic story." —*Sensual Romance*

PERSONAL ASSETS

"For a sensual and sweeping examination of contemporary relationships, with the extra zing of some very hot erotic writing, you can't do better than *Personal Assets*." —*Reviews by Celia*

BEYOND SEDUCTION

"Holly brings a level of sensuality to her storytelling that may shock the uninitiated . . . [A] combination of heady sexuality and intriguing characterization." —*Publishers Weekly*

"Emma Holly once again pens an unforgettably erotic love story." —*Affaire de Coeur*

More praise for Emma Holly and her novels

"Emma Holly is a name to look out for!"　　*—Robin Schone*

"A sensual feast."　　*—Midwest Book Review*

"A wonderfully passionate read."　　*—Escape to Romance*

"Fans of bolder romances will relish [Emma Holly]."
—Publishers Weekly

"A wonderful tale of creative genius and unbridled passion."
—Affaire de Coeur

"Ms. Holly is a rising star who creates tantalizing tales . . .
Delicious."　　*—Rendezvous*

"Steamy sex, interesting characters, and a story that offers
a couple of twists . . . A page-turning read."
—The Romance Reader

"The love scenes were an excellent mixture of eroticism
and romance, and they are some of the best ones I have
read this year."　　*—All About Romance*

"I was captivated . . . and fascinated . . . Powerful erotic
overtones . . . that will fulfill readers' desires for Holly's
signature erotic love stories."　　*—Romantic Times*

"A winner in every way."　　*—Romance Reviews Today*

"With an author like Emma Holly . . . a sizzling erotic
novel is guaranteed."　　*—A Romance Review*

Books by Emma Holly

Upyr Books

KISSING MIDNIGHT

COURTING MIDNIGHT

HOT BLOODED

(with Christine Feehan, Maggie Shayne, and Angela Knight)

HUNTING MIDNIGHT

CATCHING MIDNIGHT

FANTASY

(with Christine Feehan, Sabrina Jeffries, and Elda Minger)

Tales of the Demon World

DEMON'S FIRE

BEYOND THE DARK

(with Angela Knight, Lora Leigh, and Diane Whiteside)

DEMON'S DELIGHT

(with MaryJanice Davidson, Vickie Taylor, and Catherine Spangler)

PRINCE OF ICE

HOT SPELL

(with Lora Leigh, Shiloh Walker, and Meljean Brook)

THE DEMON'S DAUGHTER

BEYOND SEDUCTION

BEYOND INNOCENCE

ALL U CAN EAT

FAIRYVILLE

STRANGE ATTRACTIONS

PERSONAL ASSETS

Anthologies

HEAT OF THE NIGHT

MIDNIGHT DESIRE

BEYOND DESIRE

KISSING MIDNIGHT

EMMA HOLLY

BERKLEY SENSATION, NEW YORK

THE BERKLEY PUBLISHING GROUP
Published by the Penguin Group
Penguin Group (USA) Inc.
375 Hudson Street, New York, New York 10014, USA
Penguin Group (Canada), 90 Eglinton Avenue East, Suite 700, Toronto, Ontario M4P 2Y3, Canada
(a division of Pearson Penguin Canada Inc.)
Penguin Books Ltd., 80 Strand, London WC2R 0RL, England
Penguin Group Ireland, 25 St. Stephen's Green, Dublin 2, Ireland (a division of Penguin Books Ltd.)
Penguin Group (Australia), 250 Camberwell Road, Camberwell, Victoria 3124, Australia
(a division of Pearson Australia Group Pty. Ltd.)
Penguin Books India Pvt. Ltd., 11 Community Centre, Panchsheel Park, New Delhi—110 017, India
Penguin Group (NZ), 67 Apollo Drive, Rosedale, North Shore 0632, New Zealand
(a division of Pearson New Zealand Ltd.)
Penguin Books (South Africa) (Pty.) Ltd., 24 Sturdee Avenue, Rosebank, Johannesburg 2196,
South Africa

Penguin Books Ltd., Registered Offices: 80 Strand, London WC2R 0RL, England

KISSING MIDNIGHT

A Berkley Sensation Book / published by arrangement with the author

PRINTING HISTORY
Berkley Sensation mass-market edition / June 2009

Copyright © 2009 by Emma Holly.
Cover photo of "Couple" by Corbis Photography / Veer; "Big Ben" by Inspirestock / Jupiter Images.
Cover design by Lesley Worrell.
Interior text design by Laura K. Corless.

ISBN: 978-0-425-22339-0

BERKLEY® SENSATION
Berkley Sensation Books are published by The Berkley Publishing Group,
a division of Penguin Group (USA) Inc.,
375 Hudson Street, New York, New York 10014.
BERKLEY® SENSATION and the "B" design are trademarks of Penguin Group (USA) Inc.

PRINTED IN THE UNITED STATES OF AMERICA

10 9 8 7 6 5 4 3 2 1

To two amazing ladies,
Roberta Brown and Cindy Hwang,
for being so encouraging when I stretch my wings.

Bedford Square, 1922

Estelle leaned out from the tiny balcony off her bedroom, her face tilted to the sky over Bedford Square. Rain fell from a blanket of leaden clouds, the droplets cool and fresh as they struck her skin. She was fifteen. Gawky. Bookish. Almost too shy to know how to make a friend. Fortunately, none of that mattered on this stormy May evening.

Her life had changed forever today.

She'd met the most marvelous man this morning. To him she hadn't been invisible. To him she'd been a person worthy not just of notice but trust as well.

She'd noticed *him* at once. The schoolyard had been full, cliques of girls whispering to each other, boys running between them, screaming like lunatics. Estelle was neither popular nor bold enough to interest either group. Her banker father's desire to seem more successful than he was did not extend to kitting out his daughter in the latest styles. She wore last year's dress and last year's shoes. She wasn't growing anymore, he'd blustered when she'd dared to ask if she could have new things. Why shouldn't she wear what still fit? This he'd had the bottle to say after buying a real gold cigarette case for himself, the same as his biggest rival at the bank carried.

Other events had blotted out those annoyances this morning. She'd been leaning against her usual wall with her latest book, her I-don't-bloody-well-care demeanor protecting her from the chaos. A motion had caught her eye: a man, leading a small golden-haired girl into the schoolyard.

His presence had straightened her from her slouch, had brought her head out of her mystery. It was rare to see a father escort his daughter, and rarer still for him to be so youthful and good-looking. This one certainly didn't resemble any father she knew. He was tall and lean, with a dark-brimmed trilby pulled rakishly over one brow. As he parted the crowd, his strides were different from other men's, tension and grace in them, like a predator stalking antelope across the veld. The way his dark brown suit flowed with his movements was as much a testament to his fitness as his tailor's skill. Estelle's own muscles tightened as if she were secretly longing to run from him—though not, perhaps, to escape.

He must be a widow, she thought. *That's why his wife isn't here instead.*

Given Estelle's fascination, it took a moment for her to notice his daughter had been crying. Tears streaked her little cheeks as she clung desperately to his hand. Estelle could have told her she needn't fear her strange surroundings. The child was pretty, her clothes stylish and expensive, her flaxen curls shiny. Nary a wrinkle marred the perfection of her navy frock. She was like a doll from the very best department store. Odds were good she'd have a dozen tiny sycophants before the day was through, all vying to be her new best friend. Appearances mattered in a place like this, as did who one's parents were. No amount of Great Wars could level the youngest child's understanding of who belonged on what rung of the class ladder.

Estelle pegged this girl's father as a resident of considerably loftier reaches than her own.

A cynicism beyond her years had her burying her nose back in *The Mysterious Affair at Styles*. Books didn't care which year's footwear one was shod in. Books let one step into their characters' shoes instead. She was trying to focus on doing that when the sound of someone politely clearing his throat brought her head up again. Her breath whooshed from her as if a giant's hand had given her ribs a squeeze. The throat-clearer was the tall man in the trilby. His little girl was beside him, still clinging tearfully, but Estelle scarcely had a scrap of awareness to spare for her.

Up close, the man was shockingly beautiful. Beneath the slanting shadow of his hat, his hair was a darker gold than his daughter's and surprisingly poet-long. Hyacinths were not bluer than his eyes, which seemed to glow with their rich, dark hue. His mouth was cut to perfection, like stone buffed to the finest of smooth edges. Estelle couldn't help but lick her own nervously.

"Forgive me," said the man as if he hadn't just laid all her Rudolph Valentino fantasies to rest. His voice was deep and cool. "I'm sorry to intrude, but you have a wonderfully kind face. Do you think you might look out for my daughter, Sally? Just until she gets settled in her class. She's a little nervous about her first day in school."

He thought *she* had a kind face? Was something wrong with his eyes? Resentful was more like it. Or sulky. As if her mind wished to prove this, all the not-so-kind things Estelle had been thinking about his daughter flew through her head.

"Only if you wouldn't mind," the beautiful man added. "I know it's a lot to ask."

"*You* stay," pleaded his daughter, tugging his jacket sleeve. "You stay with me, Daddy."

He looked down at her, such love and patience in his expression that Estelle's throat went tight. She didn't think

either of her parents had ever looked at her that way. They
didn't look at her *any* way very much.

"You know I would, lovey, if I could."

"I like it better at home," Sally insisted. "Ben can teach
me to read when he gets back from boarding school."

The man knelt before her and squeezed her hands.

"I'll look out for her," Estelle said, before he could utter
whatever parental platitude he was searching for.

Clearly surprised to be interrupted, man and girl turned
their faces to her in unison. Estelle had the odd sensation
that she was being put to the test by both sets of eyes. She
felt dishonest, but couldn't she decide to be kind if she
wanted to? Was what this man saw in her necessarily a lie?

"I'll look out for you, Sally," she repeated, meaning it—
a bit to her own surprise. "I'm one of the big girls. You'll be
perfectly safe with me."

Sally bit her lip and looked at her father.

"You see?" he said, bracing her little shoulders between
his palms. "What could be better than having a lovely
young lady like this to show you around?"

"I *have* to stay?" Sally asked.

"You do," her father confirmed, that gentle smile lifting
his mouth as he rose.

"This is awfully decent of you," he said to Estelle.
"You've no idea what a load you've taken off my mind."

"'S nothing," Estelle mumbled, still off balance from
being called lovely.

Her shyness seemed to amuse him.

"I'm Edmund Fitz Clare," he said and held out his hand.
"I'm a professor of history at the university."

He must mean London University. That was the closest
one to here. But who would have guessed he was a *professor*? His clothes seemed too Savile Row for that. Conscious
that her thoughts were rude, Estelle shook his hand awk-
wardly, nearly dropping her Agatha Christie as she tried to

tuck the book out of the way beneath her other arm. "I'm Estelle Berenger."

He put his second hand over hers, easily swallowing it between his gloves. Within the supple leather, his fingers seemed very hard. "A star among women, to be sure."

She knew he was making a joke about the meaning of her name—Estelle, star, all that rot—but a flush washed through her exactly as if he were serious. What would it feel like to be a star among women, and to be one to a man like this? She wasn't worldly enough to know what that might entail, but trying to imagine caused her to grow hot so swiftly that all her clothes went prickly.

She could practically feel his smooth, cool lips on her neck.

So softly she almost didn't hear it, Professor Fitz Clare drew a sharpened breath. Perhaps the timing of the inhalation was only chance. Perhaps she was listening too hard to him. But if he'd guessed what she was thinking . . . what his inadvertently exciting touch had done to her . . .

She couldn't finish the thought. His eyes were darker than before, the faintest quiver widening his nostrils.

She yanked back her hand at the same time he released it.

"Well," he said. He turned up the collar of his coat, despite the mild morning temperature. His neck was pink, she noticed, as if he had a slight sunburn. "I should be getting back to my books."

"Bye, Daddy," Sally said forlornly.

"Bye, Sunshine," he returned.

As a pair, Estelle and Sally watched him hurriedly cross the street, loping toward the shelter of a waiting Model T. Considering how graceful he'd been before, his gait was oddly unsteady.

"The professor drinks," Sally announced sadly with the wise-innocent air of a child repeating something she's heard adults say. "That's why he sleeps all day."

The words rang false for Estelle. The professor hadn't smelled of liquor, nor had his speech been slurred.

"Perhaps he's a night owl," she said, giving Sally's soft curls a tentative stroke. "Even if he isn't, you probably shouldn't tell everyone you meet that he drinks."

"I shouldn't?" Sally asked.

"You shouldn't," Estelle said firmly.

Luckily, Sally believed her, and her first day of school unfolded exactly as Estelle foretold. Estelle gave Sally what help she needed to fit in: predictably, not much. The girl was bubbling with enjoyment by the time her father picked her up again. She remembered to thank Estelle without prompting, which Estelle couldn't help but be impressed by. That Sally's father's thanks were what really warmed her Estelle kept to herself.

Never mind that Sally—her chattiness irrepressible— had revealed her father wasn't married, that he'd adopted Sally and two older boys after they were orphaned in the last war. Estelle knew Edmund Fitz Clare wasn't thinking of her romantically. No matter how kind he seemed, Estelle was just a girl to him.

A lovely young lady, she repeated soundlessly to the sky. It was darker now, almost night. Lightning flickered yellow within the clouds, the sight exhilarating to her wound-up nerves. A dog bayed with longing down in the square, invisible beneath the trees. Estelle could have hugged the sound to her in delight. Wolves howled like that when they missed their companions—though of course no real wolf would be racketing around London!

She wondered if Sally's father would speak to her tomorrow.

"Estelle!" her mother called from behind her closed bedroom door. "Your father's home from the bank. It's time to come down for tea."

"In a tick," she responded, loath to lose the magic of her own daydreams.

Tea with her parents was a tiresome business, a pro forma family gathering not a one of them was interested in. Her father would grumble over Britain's monetary policy, how it kept men like him from advancing as they deserved, her mother would say "yes, dear," and Estelle would entertain herself by stabbing her fork into her toast points until her mother ordered her to stop. Watching a storm approach was much more thrilling, hearing the thunder rumble, seeing the power of nature snake inexorably closer. Estelle would have to change her clothes for tea, in any case. She was wet through, the rain spitting hard against her cotton dress. The clinging cloth made her more aware of her body, of its strength and femininity. Maybe she was becoming a woman. Maybe this day had been a part of it.

What came next unfolded without warning.

The mournful dog howled again, and then a flash filled the air above her balcony. Estelle couldn't believe what she was seeing: lightning blooming into being right in front of her. Fine hairs stood on end all across her skin. The electric burst was streaking toward her blinding as the sun. She was going to die, but she didn't have a chance to feel more than surprised.

Really? she thought in the millisecond left to her. *I'm supposed to go now?*

She could have sworn she heard someone growl *no!*

Thunder buffeted her ears just as a shadow leapt between her and the blazing light. She would have blinked if she'd had time. The shadow looked like a wolf at full gallop—a hallucination, she was sure.

As if to prove this, the lightning bolt pierced the phantasm, breaking into rainbow shards. One stabbed her right eye, ran down her arm and out her middle fingertip. She flew backward like she'd been thrown, sailing clear across the room. Her back crashed into the wall behind her bed, the plaster cracking beneath the flowered wallpaper. None of her limbs would move. Helpless to brace for the fall, she slid until she half sat, half slumped on the mattress. Smoke issued in gray tendrils from the soles of her shoes.

Her right ear felt like a burning coal had lodged in it.

"Estelle!" her mother screamed, but Estelle had lost her power to answer.

She was seeing pictures through her lightning-blasted eye. Knights on horseback. A diminutive, dark-haired woman with skin like snow.

Goodness, she thought. *Maybe I did die, after all.*

Paddington Station, 1933

Graham Fitz Clare was a secret agent.

He had to repeat that to himself sometimes, because the situation seemed too ludicrous otherwise. He was ordinary, he thought, no one more so, but he fit a profile apparently. Eton. Oxford. No nascent Bolshevik tendencies. MI5 had recruited him two years ago, soon after he'd accepted a job as personal assistant to an American manufacturer. Arnold Anderson traveled the world on business, and Graham—who had a knack for languages—served as his translator and dogsbody.

He supposed it was the built-in cover that shined him up for spy work, though he couldn't see as he'd done anything important yet. He hadn't pilfered any secret papers; hadn't seduced an enemy agent—which wasn't to suggest he thought he could! For the most part, he'd simply reported back on factories he and his employer had visited, along with writing up impressions of their associated owners and officials.

Tonight, in fact, was the most spylike experience he'd had to date.

His instructions had been tucked into the copy of *The Times* he'd bought at the newsagent down the street from his home.

"Paddington Station," the note had said in curt, telegraphic style. "11:45 tonight. Come by Underground and carry this paper under your left arm."

Graham stood at the station now, carrying the paper and feeling vaguely foolish. The platform was empty and far darker than during the day. The cast-iron arches of the roof curved gloomily above his head, the musty smell of soot stinging in his nose. A single train, unlit and silent except for the occasional sigh of escaping steam, sat on the track to the right of him. One bored porter had eyed him when he arrived, shaken his head, and then retired to presumably cozier environs.

Possibly the porter had been bribed to disappear. All Graham knew for sure was that he'd been waiting here fifteen minutes while his feet froze to the concrete floor, without the slightest sign of whomever he was supposed to meet. Doubly vexed to hear a church clock striking midnight, he tried not to shiver in the icy November damp. His overcoat was new, at least, a present from the professor on Graham's twenty-fifth birthday.

That memory made him smile despite his discomfort. His guardian was notoriously shy about giving gifts. They were always generous, always exactly what the person wanted—as if Edmund had plucked the wish from their minds. He always acted as if he'd presumed by wanting to give whatever it was to them. The habit, and so many others, endeared him to his adopted brood more than any parent by blood could have. The professor seemed to think it a privilege to have been allowed to care for them.

All of them, even flighty little Sally, knew the privilege was theirs.

Though Graham was old enough to occasionally be embarrassed by the fact, there really was no mystery to why Edmund's charges remained at home. Graham's lips pressed together at the thought of causing him concern. If tonight's business kept him waiting long enough to have to lie to the professor about where he'd been, he wasn't going to be amused.

Metal creaked, drawing his eyes to the darkened train. Evidently, it wasn't empty. One of the doors had opened, and a dainty Oriental woman was stepping down the stairs of the central car. Her skintight emerald dress looked straight out of wardrobe for a Charlie Chan picture. Actually, she looked straight out of one, too, so exotically gorgeous that Graham's tongue was practically sticking to the roof of his mouth.

He forced himself to swallow as her eyes raked him up and down.

"Hm," she said, flicking a length of night-black hair behind one slender shoulder. "You're tall at least, and you look healthy."

Graham flushed at her dismissive tone, and again— even harder—when she turned her back on him to reascend the stairs. Holy hell, her rear view was smashing, her waist nipped in, her bum round and firm. Graham knew he wasn't the sort of man women swooned over, not like his younger brother, Ben, or even the professor, whose much-younger female students occasionally followed him home. No, Graham had a plain English face, not ugly but forgettable. Normally, this didn't bother him—or not much. It just seemed a bit humiliating to find the woman who'd insulted him so very attractive herself.

That green dress was tight enough to show the cleft between the halves of her arse. His groin grew heavy, his shaft beginning to swell. The sight of her lack of underclothes was so inspiring he forgot he was supposed to move.

"Don't just stand there," she said impatiently over her shoulder. "Follow me."

Shoving *The Times* into his pocket, he followed her, dumbstruck, into a private compartment. She yanked down the shades before flicking on two dim sconces.

"Sit," she said, pointing to the black leather seat opposite her own. Her hand was slim and pale, her nails lacquered red as blood.

Graham sat with difficulty. He was erect and aching and too polite to shift the cause of the trouble to a different position. Hoping his condition wasn't obvious to her, he wrapped his hands around his knees and waited.

The woman stared at him unblinking—taking his stock, he guessed. She resembled a painted statue, or maybe a mannequin in a store window. In spite of his attraction to her, Graham's irritation rose. This woman had kept him hanging long enough.

"What's this about?" he asked.

She leaned back and crossed a pair of incredibly shapely legs, a move that seemed too practiced to be casual. Her dress was shorter than the current fashion, ending just below her knee. Graham wasn't certain, but from the hissing sound her calves made, she might be wearing real silk stockings.

"We're giving you a new assignment," she said.

"A new assignment."

"If we decide you're up for it."

"Look," Graham said, "you people came to me. It's hardly cricket to suggest that *you're* doing *me* favors."

The woman smiled, her teeth a gleaming flash of white behind ruby lips. Graham noticed her incisors were unusually sharp. "I think you'll find this assignment more intriguing than your previous one. It does, however, require a higher level of vetting." She leaned forward, her slender forearm resting gracefully on one thigh. The way her small breasts shifted behind her dress told him her top half wore no more undergarments than her bottom. Graham's collar began to feel as tight as his crotch. The space between their seats wasn't nearly great enough.

"Tell me, Graham," she said, her index finger almost brushing his, "what do you know about X Section?"

"Never heard of it," he said, because as far as he knew, MI5 sections only went up to F.

"What if I told you it hunts things?"

"*Things?*"

"Unnatural things. Dangerous things. Beasts who shouldn't exist in the human realm."

Her face was suddenly very close to his. Her eyes were as dark as coffee, mysterious golden lights seeming to flicker behind the irises. Graham felt dizzy staring into them, his heart thumping far too fast. He didn't recall seeing her move, but she was kneeling on the floor of the compartment in the space that gaped between his knees. Her pale, strong hands were sliding up his thighs.

"We need information," she whispered, her breath as cool and sweet as mint pastilles. "So we can destroy these monsters. And we need you to get it for us."

"You're crazy." He had to gasp it; his breath was coming that fast.

"No, I'm not, Graham. I'm the sanest person you've ever met."

Her fingers had reached the bend between his legs and torso, her thumbs sliding inward over the giant arch of his erection. She scratched him gently with the edge of her bloodred nails.

"Christ," Graham choked out. The feathery touch blazed through him like a welder's torch. His nerves were on fire, his penis slit weeping with desire. He shifted on the seat in helpless reaction. Her mouth was following her thumbs, her exhalations whispering over his grossly stretched trouser front.

"I'm going to give you clearance," she said. "I'm going to make sure we can trust you."

He cried out when she undid his zip fastener, and again when her small, cool fingers dug into his smalls to lift out his engorged cock. Blimey, he was big, his skin stretched like it would split. She stroked the whole shuddering length of him, causing his spine to arch uncontrollably.

"Watch me," she ordered as his head lolled back. "Watch me suck you into my mouth."

Graham was no monk. He watched her, and felt her, and thought his soul was going to spill out his body where her lips drew strong and tight on him.

He didn't want to admit this was the first time a woman had performed this particular act on him. He could see why men liked it. The sensations were incredible, streaking in hot, sharp tingles from the tip of his throbbing penis to the arching soles of his feet. She was smearing her ruby lipstick up and down his shaft, humming at the swell of him, taking him into her throat, it felt like. Her tongue was rubbing him every place he craved.

The fact that she was barking mad completely slipped his mind.

"Oh, God," he breathed, lightly touching her hair where she'd tucked it neatly behind her ears. The strands were silk under his fingertips, so smooth they seemed unreal. "Oh, Christ. Don't stop."

She didn't stop. She sucked and sucked until his seed exploded from his balls in a fiery rush. He cried out hoarsely, sorry and elated at the same time. And then she did something he couldn't quite believe.

She bit him.

Her teeth sank into him halfway down his shaft, those sharp incisors even sharper than he'd thought. The pain was as piercing as the pleasure had been a second earlier. He grabbed her ears, wondering if he dared to pull her off. Her clever tongue fluttered against him, wet, strong . . . and then she drew his blood from him.

He moaned, his world abruptly turned inside out. Ecstasy washed through him in drowning waves. She was drinking from him in a whole new way, swallowing, licking, moaning herself like a starving puppy suckling at a teat. All his senses went golden and soft. *So good. So sweet.* Like floating on a current of pure well-being.

He didn't know how long it lasted, but he was sorry when her head came up.

"You're mine now," she said.

He blinked sleepily into her glowing eyes. Was it queer that they were lit up? Right at that moment, he couldn't decide.

"I'm yours," he said, though he wasn't certain he meant it.

"You're not going to remember me biting you."

"No," he agreed. "That would be awkward."

"When I give you instructions, you'll follow them."

"I expect I will," he said.

She narrowed her eyes at him, her winglike brows furrowing.

"I will," he repeated, because she seemed to require it.

She rose, licking one last smear of blood from her upper lip. As soon as it disappeared, he forgot that it had been there.

"Zip yourself," she said.

He obeyed and got to his feet as well. It seemed wrong to be towering over his handler, though he couldn't really claim to mind. She handed him a slip of paper with a meeting place in Hampstead Heath. As had been the case with the note tucked into his paper, the directions were neatly typed—no bobbles or mistakes. He had the idle thought that Estelle would have approved.

"Tomorrow night," the woman said. "Eleven sharp. You'll know when you've seen what we need you to."

"Will you be there?"

He thought this was a natural question. Any male with blood in his veins would want to repeat the pleasures of this night, if only to return the favor she'd shown him. But perhaps he wasn't supposed to ask. She wrinkled her brow again.

"*I* won't be," she said, "but chances are our enemy will."

Hampstead Heath

The hinges on the window in Edmund's study were deliberately well oiled. If that weren't enough, both his housekeeper and his family had strict pain-of-death orders not to enter without knocking. With practiced motions, Edmund pushed the attic casement open, swung his long legs over the sill, and touched the chimney stack for balance on the sloping roof. From where he perched, he could see across Bedford Square's lush garden, straight into the windows of the handsome brick Georgian that, not long ago, had been Estelle Berenger's home.

She'd lived in *his* home for the last two years, ever since her parents had been accidentally flattened by a motorcar while out for an evening stroll. Sally had insisted they take Estelle in, her affection for the older girl having lasted since her first day in the local school. By human standards, Estelle had been old enough to live on her own, but she *had* been shocked by the loss, and Edmund hadn't minded Sally's pleas. He'd wanted to lend Estelle his protection; still did, though he knew he needed to prepare himself to let her go.

One more night, he thought. *One more night beneath my roof before she moves out.*

A pang tightened his chest, almost turning him back inside. He could listen to her sleeping for a few more hours, could forget all pride for the thousandth time by taking his private pleasure to the rhythm of her strong, young heart.

His obsession was pathetic, really; she was his daughter's best friend, a child compared to him, but he couldn't stop wanting her. He'd watched Estelle grow into a woman, had seen her beauty blossom long before she'd guessed it would. He remembered what he'd thought the first time he saw her: that this girl needed a friend as much as Sally did, and that she'd make a better one than those monsters in her schoolyard. She hadn't disappointed him even once. He *liked* her, damn it, and because he did, she called to every urge for pleasure he possessed.

Considering who and what he was, that meant she called to more than one.

"Hsst," hailed a voice from the mews behind the house. "Are you coming with me or not?"

Edmund shook himself, frowning at the tug of what had become a ridiculous attachment. He'd had five and a half centuries to grow up. Surely he could let one human girl live out her human life without regretting that his secrets kept them apart.

He'd bound them together quite enough when he'd got between her and that lightning bolt.

Silent as a shadow, he leapt from the roof to land lightly in the narrow lane below. His blood son, Robin, waited, the one he'd sired when he was mortal. They fell into step at a normal human walking pace. They'd speed up when they were farther from an area where they might be seen.

"All well with the family?" Robin asked in a teasing tone.

"Yes," Edmund said, though the question was enough to have him glancing back over his shoulder at the dark windows. Graham hadn't come home yet. Edmund couldn't hear his heartbeat among the rest. That made two nights in a row that his eldest had stayed out late.

Reading the gesture, Robin laughed under his breath, but did not comment. "Percy has a new passion," he said instead, speaking of the Fitz Clare descendant they'd made one of their own midway through the last century. "He wants to convert part of Bridesmere into an airfield. Apparently, he's gone barmy for aeroplanes."

"Well, I don't think I like that," Edmund said, stopping in his tracks. "The humans are bound to be at war soon, and airfields will be targets."

"You really think so? The dust has barely settled on the last struggle."

Edmund grimly shook his head and resumed walking. It was an aspect of their immortal nature—and their age—that their footsteps barely echoed off the pavement. "Their leaders are talking peace, but it's war their thoughts circle round. Now that this Hitler maniac is in charge in Germany, I doubt the Armistice will last another full decade. Treaty or no treaty, I'd be surprised if he isn't rearming now."

"So speaks the professor of history."

"Not just the professor. Aimery has been making noises about moving the Council out of Rome. They've weathered Mussolini's rule thus far, but he doesn't think our kind are safe under *Il Duce*."

"Does your brother think the humans have discovered we exist?"

Edmund's shoulders rose and fell. He had reason to be uncomfortable with this question. "There are always a few who know. In times like this, I'm not sure we want to find out what they'd do with that knowledge."

"Lord," Robin breathed, considering. "Where would Uncle Aimery move headquarters?"

"Switzerland, he says. Or possibly Canada. Whatever humans become embroiled in, he's hoping to keep our kind out of it."

"Lord," Robin repeated. "Our kind live everywhere. France. Germany. All the major powers."

"Exactly. And only some owe allegiance to my brother. I'm not sure Nim Wei will be as committed to keeping her broods from acting on their national loyalties."

"She hasn't given *you* any trouble, has she?"

Nim Wei was the second of the great *upyr* leaders, the first being Edmund's brother. Aimery ruled the shapechangers of their kind, Nim Wei the blood-drinking nests. With the exception of Rome, the world's principal cities fell under her jurisdiction. There were cultural variances between the two subspecies, rivalries, divergences in power, but for centuries they had shared the globe peacefully. At one point, Nim Wei and Edmund had been lovers. Though she'd offered to make him immortal, Edmund had declined. He'd feared her darker nature would stain his own less-than-snowy one. Over the years, Edmund and his brother had had their differences, but that decision they'd agreed on. While Edmund wasn't certain London's vampire queen had forgiven him for choosing another sire, she hadn't moved against him during his residence here.

"She tolerates me," Edmund said drily. "And I take care not to tread on any of her toes."

They'd reached the end of the streetlights. The rolling darkness that was Hampstead Heath stretched enticingly ahead of them. Thanks to local nature lovers, the eight-hundred-acre heath was now a huge preserve, home to foxes and rabbits and all manner of tasty things. Robin slapped his father on the back, his smooth, hard fingers squeezing his nape reassuringly. For a second, Edmund's heart nearly burst with love. Bonding with his wolf soul all those years ago had made him a pack animal. Family meant everything to him, both his mortal and immortal one. That Robin had forgiven his failings as a human father was a miracle he didn't think he'd ever take for granted.

Truly, his life had been blessed beyond his deserts.

"Come on," Robin said, his eyes glittering with starlight as he grinned. "Enough serious talk. Let's shake off this city and have a run."

Graham's instructions had been specific. Following them to the letter, he stretched out on his belly behind the brow of a hill that overlooked the heath facing Highgate Village. The ground was damp and cold, but he took the discomfort philosophically. A man did what he could for his country, even if he wasn't privy to the whys and wherefores.

His handler's talk of monsters was balderdash, of course. It was probably just a test, to see how obedient Graham was.

Sufficiently concealed for nighttime surveillance, Graham lifted his binoculars to his eyes. A half-moon hung over the heath tonight, enough for him to see by. Graham didn't recall when he'd first noticed, but his vision was sharper than most people's—a legacy, he presumed, from his dead parents.

He remembered them more than Sally or Ben remembered theirs, having reached the age of twelve before he lost them. Though British, Graham and his parents had been living in Belgium—his father was some sort of importer—and they'd been separated during one of the confused exoduses of refugees who'd fled the German invasion. Graham had learned only later, from a former neighbor, that his parents had been killed. He'd been in the Red Cross's care by then. The news had panicked and then numbed him.

He'd been older than so many who'd lost their families. *Old enough*, he'd decided. When he'd met Sally and Ben at the orphanage, it had seemed perfectly logical to take the pair under his wing. Sally had been four and Ben about nine, his undernourished arms nearly too skinny to carry the little girl—despite which he'd refused to relinquish her to anyone. Ben's illogical devotion had been a touchstone for Graham. He'd been hungry for someone to help, to belong with.

Sometimes Graham still felt that fierce protectiveness toward them.

Being here, for England, was a part of that.

Grimacing, he shifted on the grass. This morning, when he'd shuffled to the bath to piss, he'd found smears of lipstick on his cock. It had been sore as well, deep down, which made him wonder if his new handler hadn't done *her* bit for England a tad more forcefully than she ought. It hadn't been necessary anyway. He'd have done what she asked without the extra incentive. To tell the truth, he probably should have stopped her. Fraternizing with the upper levels couldn't be standard protocol.

Bugger, he thought as his cock began to thicken at the memory. He had to lift his hips to ease the throbbing. Ben was right. Graham did need a girlfriend. Graham would never admit it, but his younger brother had lost his virginity two full years ahead of him.

Bugger, he thought again and resettled his binoculars. He scanned the heath, but found nothing of interest. What the ruddy hell was he supposed to see that MI5 was interested in?

A fat white hare pelted around the banks of the fishing pond, drawing his attention. Two blurs of motion followed it, as if the hare were being chased by something too fast to see. Graham thought he heard low growls, but his ears weren't quite as keen as his eyes.

The creature's sudden squeal, on the other hand, carried easily.

Graham sucked in his breath. It looked like the hare was levitating, its hind and forelimbs stretched out oddly. He thought he saw . . . Were there shadows pulling it from either side, or did he have something in his eye? Graham had just time enough to blink when the hare appeared to rip apart in the middle, blood exploding into the empty air.

And then their air wasn't empty.

Two gray wolves faced each other, each gripping half of their slaughtered prize. Christ, the things were as big as ponies. They were bristling at each other, muzzles pulled back in threat from long, bloodied teeth. Graham's skin prickled with primal fear, though the wolves were too far away to sense him. The wind was blowing in his direction, and more low growls vibrated across the heath. The wolves tossed their heads. An instant later each caught its portion of their prey and gulped it whole.

Criminy, Graham thought, his pulse roaring in his ears. What was he seeing?

The wolves stopped bristling before he could begin to answer his own question. Like magic, the mood between them changed. They woofed at each other, softly, their tails wagging, and then they plunged together into the fishing pond. Graham didn't know what they were doing, but it wasn't taking a swim. The surface of the water churned like a boiling pot. It simply wasn't possible that two creatures, even that size, could affect a large pond that way. The banks had to be fifty yards apart. His heart was beating wildly when the wolves emerged again. Each held a fish flopping in his mouth, which they consumed as summarily as they had the hare.

Graham's brain struggled to make sense of it. Was this what his handler had meant by monsters? Lord, it had to be. He'd never seen wolves so large, or even heard of their breed in London outside the zoo. But still—why ask him to watch them? His job was to help uncover possible espionage against Britain.

As far as he knew, four-legged creatures weren't involved in that.

The wolves were playing now, chasing and pouncing on each other with a speed so great he had trouble following it. Graham dug the binoculars into his eye sockets, afraid to remove them long enough to rub his eyes. These animals couldn't be as fast as they seemed. No natural creature could.

Finally, the darker wolf pinned the lighter, his jaw closing gently on the other's nose. Light shimmered around their bodies like marsh fire. Graham's throat closed on a moan whose meaning he doubted he could have explained.

Both wolves dissolved into flickering stars.

Graham swore he hadn't blinked, but suddenly two naked men appeared. Their bodies glowed like pure white marble lit from inside. They were wrestling, one atop the other just as the wolves had been.

Graham thought he saw the subordinate man's lips cry "Uncle" a second before both began to laugh.

The moment they did, Graham recognized them.

The man on top was the professor, and his companion was his friend, Robin. Graham didn't know much about the man, but Robin had visited their home in Bedford Square a time or two—often enough to identify him on sight. The professor, on the other hand, couldn't have looked more different from his normal self, even allowing for his nakedness. Oh, his longish golden hair was the same, his features and his height, but everything else screamed that he was young. Gone were the seams of age around his eyes, gone the scholarly stoop of his shoulders. He was as young as Graham was, and every bit as fit. His stomach was a ruddy board. Graham had to avert his eyes from the swing of his sizable genitals. In Edmund's current state, Graham had no problem imagining women Sally's age swooning over him.

Before Graham could convince himself he'd gone crackers, the professor threw back his head and let out a soft, yipping howl. Moonlight glinted off his incisors, which were longer and whiter than an ordinary man's. Graham's spine shuddered in reaction. God in heaven, the professor *was* the wolf.

Even worse, he was the monster Graham's bosses were hoping he'd spy on.

The cold didn't bother beings like Edmund. He lay back on the dank, wet grass, panting from his fight with Robin, perfectly at ease in his naked skin. Out in the wild, packs rarely felt a need for clothes. Edmund realized he hadn't been this relaxed in a while. Estelle's imminent departure must have wound him tighter than he'd known.

Not that he wanted to dwell on that.

"How are you enjoying White's?" he asked, referring to a private club in St. James Street that another of the shapechanging vampires owned.

"It's comfortable," Robin said, his gaze on a distant hill. "Better than having to maintain my glamour in a human hotel. Plus, it's nice to know the locals won't have the nerve to mess with us on Lucius's premises. Coming and going's a right pain, though. The nests watch the exits day and night. I don't know what those bloodsuckers think we're going to do."

"Take over London, I expect."

"As if we'd want this heap of soot, no offense to your—" He broke off, rising onto his elbows. "Did you hear something?"

"Nothing out of the ordinary. Do you think you did?"

"I don't know. Do me a favor and put up your glamour. You're better at that than I am."

Edmund camouflaged them with his energy, the trick made easy by long years of passing for human. The natural sparkle of their skin faded, followed by them seeming to disappear into the landscape: chameleons blending in. Edmund thought he heard a distant gasp, though it could have been a scud of wind—a wind that wasn't blowing in the right direction to carry scents to him.

"Lord." Robin laughed breathlessly. "You have gotten good at that."

"Practice," Edmund said, vaguely embarrassed. He'd raised a full cloak without thinking.

"Practice, my arse. We're not even touching, and you erased my visibility. You've got to be a hair's breadth from turning elder. You'll be able to change humans in no time."

"I'm not making plans for that."

"Aren't you? I know your human family doesn't know what you are, but—"

"I want them to live their own lives. I'm going to let them go when that time comes."

Edmund's tone was sharper than he'd meant. The topic of elder status was an uncomfortable one for him. Few among their kind achieved the distinction, though Edmund's brother, Aimery, had. It had taken Edmund a damn long time to make peace with his younger brother's swifter rise. For that matter, it had taken him a damn long time to make peace with any number of his brother's superior qualities. Wishing his days of envy were behind him, he gritted his teeth as Robin fumbled in the dark for clothes.

"Blinking hell," the other *upyr* muttered. "Getting dressed is hard when you're invisible."

Edmund eased up on the glamour, only to find his son smiling angelically. He was pushing his arms into his shirt-sleeves. "You know old Auriclus has been talking about walking into the sun."

"I know," Edmund growled. The elder, who had founded

the shapechangers who knew how many millennia ago, claimed he was ready to let younger wolves direct their destiny. Auriclus was a bit of a prig, in Edmund's opinion, but he supposed the loss would be sad.

"If he dies, his power will be divvied up among the packs."

"Aimery will get most of it."

"You'll get some, Dad, and it might be enough to push you over the edge. You'll have to be careful not to influence your little family more than you have."

"I haven't done anything to them," he bristled. "Haven't even thralled them since they were kids—and that was only to keep them from running completely wild. They had more energy than human children should."

"Right," said Robin. "And I'm sure that energy was a coincidence."

Edmund sighed gustily. He'd never bitten his children, no matter how berserk they'd been. Taking their blood had seemed wrong to him. A bite marked a mortal, made him forever vulnerable to the biter's influence. Thankfully, he'd attained a sufficient level of power to curb their high spirits with will alone—or at least to curb them enough to keep from going insane.

It was, however, undeniable that his immortal aura was very strong. Being around him—day in, day out—couldn't help but affect Sally and Ben and Graham. They'd avoided virtually all the ailments human children were prone to. Only Sally had endured so much as a sniffle. Ben—who'd been born a daredevil—had once healed a broken ankle (which he'd gotten diving off a runaway go-cart) in less than a week. Luckily, the doctor who'd treated him concluded the injury had only been a sprain.

But Robin didn't need to hear all that. "Any effect they've soaked up from my proximity will wear off once they leave home."

This was true, not to mention exactly as it should be.

Edmund simply wished it didn't make him thoroughly depressed. Humans grew up so fast. He wasn't looking forward to releasing the apron strings. As it was, Graham already spent half his time away with that translating job of his.

His blood son had no trouble whatsoever reading his face.

"You're a sap," Robin said, laughing. "If your mortals do move away, I'm sure they'll come back and visit you."

Tottenham Court Mansions

⸻✦⸻

The old dear is off his feed again," Sally sighed. "Him and his 'delicate stomach.' He should just stop drinking. Then his stomach would be fine."

Sally stood elbow to elbow with Estelle in the brand-new galley kitchen of her brand-new flat. She was helping Estelle arrange the tea things on her chrome and glass tea trolley. Tottenham Court Mansions, as the well-equipped modern flats were called, weren't more than a five-minute walk from Bedford Square. Nonetheless, being here, preparing to entertain her first guests, had the power to make Estelle's fingers tingle with excitement. Even the hand that had been struck by lightning—which, oddly enough, was stronger than the other—was threatening to go numb.

Estelle had her own place now. Her own rugs and chairs and, most of all, her own privacy. She'd loved living with the Fitz Clares—too much, maybe—but at twenty-six this finally made her feel grown-up.

"I don't know why you always say he drinks," Estelle said, carefully unwrapping another of her Harrods pack-

ages. Estelle didn't cook, and the treats for tonight's celebration came from her employer's abundant food halls.
"I've never seen the professor take more than half a glass."

"You didn't used to see him stumble around in the
morning, trying to fix me breakfast before school."

"He hasn't fixed you breakfast since he hired Mrs.
Mackie as your housekeeper, so if he ever drank, maybe
he's stopped. I don't think you and Ben should call him
an 'old dear,' either. You make it sound like he's in his
dotage."

"Oh, Lord," Sally gusted as she balanced the last
Bakewell tart on the plate she'd made. "Don't tell me you've
still got that crush on him!"

Estelle blushed fire-hot and busied herself spreading
pâté on triangles of toast. The kitchen door wasn't soundproof. She prayed Sally's voice had been too low to carry.
Graham hadn't yet arrived, but Ben and the professor were
waiting politely in her living room. Thinking how horrified
she'd be if either of the men discovered what she felt, the
only cool spot on Estelle's face was the old spidery lightning mark around her right eye.

"He's been good to me is all," she said. "I don't like to
hear you speak ill of him."

Sally snorted, but said no more on that topic. Her cheeks
were flushed as well, but only from the cooker where the
kettle was heating up. On her, the color was roses and not
embarrassment. At seventeen, she'd grown into the beauty
her looks had promised as a little girl—though today she
was more Jean Harlow than porcelain doll.

Somewhat to Estelle's dismay, she liked to emulate
the platinum bombshell's habit of swanning about with
her perky breasts unbound. Whatever Sally claimed, she
wasn't small enough to get away with that.

"This place *is* darling," Sally said as a peace offering.
"I'm frightfully jealous, even if I'm still annoyed with you
for moving out."

"You'll move out one day, too. Once you stop cultivating that horde of followers and settle on a husband."

"Settle is right." Sally tossed her short blonde bob. "If I left home, it would only be to go to Hollywood to be a star. The old dear needs someone to look after him." She grinned to let Estelle know she was teasing.

As Estelle began to shake her head, a bustle at the hallway door told her Graham had arrived at last.

"Oh, goody!" Sally exclaimed, forgetting her carefully cultivated maturity. "Now you can see the present we all chipped in to buy for you."

She ran out, leaving Estelle to deal with the heavily laden tea trolley. She rolled it through the door in time to find Sally giving Graham a hug through the open flaps of his wet trench coat. Estelle pressed both hands to her mouth. A brand-new Hotpoint vacuum cleaner sat on the parquet floor in her entryway, a length of damp red ribbon draggling from its neck.

"Sorry about the bow," Graham said over Sally's head. "I tried to shield it with my coat, but it's lashing down rain out there."

"It's beautiful," Estelle said, her eyes welling up. She couldn't believe they'd bought anything so expensive for her. Overcome, she bent to kiss Ben—who sat closest—on the cheek. He, in particular, socked away every penny he earned at the garage, saving for the day when he'd start his own.

"Quick, somebody spill some crumbs," Ben joked, squirming away from her effusion. He was twenty-two and, especially around Sally, tended to guard his dignity. "Estelle wants to try her present out."

"The tea!" Estelle cried, reminded by the mention of crumbs.

"I'll get it." The professor pushed up from his chair, giving her a fond half smile. The sight of his long body unfolding itself was as arousing to her as ever. Estelle turned her eyes away, wondering as always how anyone could think him old. To her, he seemed as young as the day they'd met. "The kettle's still in the kitchen, I take it?"

"Yes, but—"

"You should see her kitchen!" Sally broke in excitedly. "It's got a refrigerator and chessboard tiling and the cleverest little fold-down table hidden in the wall!"

"A refrigerator?" Graham repeated, a shadow Estelle didn't understand flickering across his face. "One that came with the flat?"

"*And* a gas fire out here. Lord, what I wouldn't give not to have to fuss with coal anymore!"

"Hey," said Ben, his thumb jabbing his lean, hard chest. He wore an argyle sweater-vest and no tie, the most casually dressed of them all. "I'm the one who hauls it up to you half the time."

"And what about the other half?" Sally demanded, her fists on her tiny waist, her breasts bobbing enough behind her ruffled satinette blouse to make Estelle wince. "I have appearances to keep up."

"Hush," said Graham, before Ben could respond. "No arguing at Estelle's party." He smiled at her, his expression so like the professor's that it squeezed her heart. Estelle and Graham were nearest in age, and she'd always felt a special bond with him. "Your new home is lovely. I'm glad you found somewhere nice to live."

"Me, too." Estelle was unable to suppress a small, Sally-like bounce. "And the mortgage is so reasonable! I can't believe the building society wasn't asking for more."

"About that . . ." Graham's gaze cut to the kitchen where the professor was clinking cups.

Estelle flipped her hand at him. "You're sweet to be concerned, but it's unnecessary. Between what Harrods pays me and what my parents left, I'll be able to save as well as Ben."

Remembering her hostess duties, she collected Graham's dripping trench coat and hung it in her new closet. Unexpectedly, Graham followed her. When she turned back from shutting the door, he was looking down at her in concern. They were separated from the others by the arm's length of wall that demarcated the entryway. Graham was the only Fitz Clare who wasn't some shade of blond, and the faintest shadow of brown whiskers darkened his square jaw. Sometimes Estelle forgot how tall he was, how solid and masculine. To her surprise, he feathered his fingers over her cheek beneath the lightning scar. The Fitz Clares rarely acknowledged her old injury; rarely noticed it, as far as she could tell. She'd had it almost since she'd met them, after all.

He lowered his voice confidentially. "If you do ever need help, I've got some money put away."

Graham was a bit of a worrier, but the offer touched her. She was about to thank him, and soothe him, when a buzzing in her right ear warned her she'd better not. Sometimes that ear, the one the lightning had burned through, acted up queerly.

A woman like you shouldn't be in debt to a monster, she thought she heard Graham's voice say. Naturally, this was only a hallucination. Estelle rubbed her temple and shook it out.

"Oh, isn't he the sweetest!" Sally cried, ignoring the fact that Graham probably hadn't wanted her to overhear. "*Some* people are so generous."

Since she was giving Ben a pointed look, Estelle knew exactly what she was getting at. Sally's favorite hobby was comparing her middle brother unfavorably to the older one.

"For shame, Sally," Estelle scolded. "You have reason to know how generous Ben is."

"Those are *loans*. And I always pay him back . . . mostly."

"Tea," announced the professor, before the row could escalate. "I see the table in the dining room has been set. Shall we eat in there?"

The dining "room" was more like a dining nook, seeing as it was only separated from the living room by a hint of an arch. Its walls were painted milky blue, and its windows were the curved, gridded sort modern builders called "sun catchers." This evening all they caught was rain, but the view of the double-decker buses still entertained. Inside, the decor was as different from her parents' dark Edwardian furnishings as it could be, and for that alone Estelle loved it. She nearly burst with pride as her favorite people in the world took seats around her table. Tiffs aside, nothing had ever given her more pleasure than being with the Fitz Clares. They loved each other more than any family she knew. She had no doubt that any one of them, Sally included, would lay down their lives for any of the rest.

Assuming, of course, that Ben and Sally didn't strangle each other first.

"Let Estelle sit at the head," Ben said. "She's the lady of the house."

Sally pouted, but she gave way. The others, per usual, did their best to ignore them both.

"To the lady of the house," Graham said, toasting her with his tea. "May this be the first of many evenings she shares with us."

"Hear, hear," the professor echoed from the table's other end. "Health to everyone."

Estelle was so emotional she couldn't speak. She beamed at all of them through her tears, certain she was the luckiest woman in London.

Edmund could have eaten the tasty-looking tarts if he'd been in his canine form. His wolf digested solid food admirably. Since that wasn't possible, watching Estelle glow with happiness would have to serve as his sustenance.

Of all his adopted brood, only Graham was as reserved as she. To witness her open joy made him almost happy to part with her.

Humans have to grow up, he told himself. *That's simply the way life is.*

Estelle had grown up beautifully. Her skin was smooth as cream, her figure strong and feminine in the smart wool suit she'd worn to her job. That Garbo woman Ben and Sally were perpetually going on about did not have more lambent gray eyes than she—their beauty undiminished by the strawberry-colored scar that rayed around her right one. The eye itself was undamaged; enhanced, in fact, had she but known it. Estelle had a disturbing resistance to his glamour, hence her refusal to think of him as an "old dear." Edmund knew people occasionally stared at the lightning mark. To his mind, ignoring them lent her loveliness dignity, said her confidence didn't depend on appearances.

On top of which, those soft, full lips of hers were enough to make a male of any species sweat.

More than sweat, actually. He squirmed in his chair, struggling to turn his thoughts to safer topics. He was too late to stop his gums from stinging where his fangs were trying to emerge, or his mouth from watering. The thought of biting her, of taking just a sip of her hot mortal essence was abruptly irresistible. Old Auriclus would have been ashamed of him. Their founder didn't think the members of his packs should crave any food beyond what their wolves could catch. Too bad Edmund couldn't help his attraction. For some unknown and very inconvenient reason, Estelle's move into her own home had intensified his desires.

Controlling his response required such concentration that he only shook from his fog when Ben and Sally pushed back their chairs and started pulling on rain gear.

"Charlie Chan," Sally said as if this explained everything. "*The Keeper of the Keys* is playing at the Imperial. If Ben and I hurry, we can catch the next showing."

At least these two were in harmony over their cinema addiction.

"Straight home after," Edmund said, cupping Sally's cheeks to press a gentle kiss to her brow. As always, her simple mortal fragility touched his heart. "No dawdling."

"No, sir," Ben agreed.

Edmund nodded, knowing he'd keep Sally safe, however crazy she drove him. "Are you joining them?" he asked Graham, realizing only then that his eldest hadn't said a word to him all evening.

Graham looked at Estelle and then back at him. "I thought I'd stay and help Estelle clear up."

"I can do that," Edmund said. "You've been keeping late hours. Why don't you go home and catch up on your sleep?"

Graham set his jaw in the stolid way that was purely him. The boy's stubbornness surprised him, but, at the moment, ferreting out the reason wasn't his priority.

With an idle corner of his mind, he noticed that Graham's barriers to being read were more opaque than usual.

"Go on," he said, catching Graham's troubled dark brown eyes. The contact allowed him to put a subtle mental push behind the suggestion. Now that his children were adults, he tried to thrall them as seldom as possible, but— dangerously attracted to Estelle or not—he had matters he preferred to settle with her alone. "I have a few small things to say to Estelle."

"Oh!" Sally gasped from the door, looking as if she wanted to stay now, too. "Is it about *your* present for her?"

"Don't be a nosy puss," Ben said.

"But I like presents, even when they're not mine."

"All of you out," Edmund ordered, fighting back a sigh. "Estelle and I can manage on our own."

It took a few more "buts" and hugs and pushes, but at last he and Estelle were left to themselves.

"Well," said Estelle, hugging her elbows as if she were cold.

He stared at her for a moment, simply enjoying her: her warmth, her nerves, the way she'd coiled her long ash brown hair back from her lovely face. Short hair might be the fashion, but he was glad she'd never cut hers like Sally. He was even glad for her little crush on him—though he told himself he'd never trade on it. He'd known about it without Sally's help, of course. No human could completely hide her thoughts from him, not with the power he'd amassed over the centuries. But Estelle couldn't begin to know what a relationship with him would be like. That being so, he'd guard her innocence with every ounce of strength he had.

At the moment, that innocence had her kicking the knife edge pleats that finished off the bottom of her skirt.

"I'm sure I don't need another present," Estelle said.

Edmund laughed, the sound bringing a delightful rush of blood to her cheeks. "Maybe *I* need to give you one."

"But—"

"Shh," he said, allowing himself the treat of taking her hand. Her fingers curled slightly over his. "It's only a telephone. I've arranged to have one wired for you here, so you don't have to share the one in the lobby. Sally would never forgive me if you weren't able to reach us any time of the day or night."

Estelle pursed her mouth wryly. "You mean Sally wants to be able to reach me."

"I mean I want you to be able to call. No matter what the reason. Even if it's only that you're lonely. I know you're a grown woman, but I like to think of you as mine to take care of, just as much as Sally or Ben or Graham."

He hadn't precisely meant to, but he'd surrounded her hand in both of his. Generally speaking, he was careful not to invade her privacy, but touch unavoidably increased his gift for reading minds, especially when the contact was with her scarred hand. He felt her thinking that he was always so proper with her, always the father of her closest friend. She didn't want him to be that way anymore. Her body was warming, growing liquid and tight deep within her core. She wanted him to treat her like the adult she was, wanted to know what kissing him would be like. The detail with which she imagined this was more specific than he expected.

Estelle had been kissed before, and not tepidly.

He felt hackles he wasn't wearing rise up at the back of his neck, the wolf inside him ready to growl. As far as it was considered, it had saved her life when it jumped between her and that lightning bolt. If that didn't make her its private possession, the wolf didn't know what did. Caught between both sides of his nature, desire slammed through him like an explosion.

"I know you put in a word with the building society for me," Estelle was saying. "I expect they wouldn't have given me the loan without your backing."

Edmund had done more than put in a word. He'd bought the blasted building, then set the mortgage at exactly what she could afford. He couldn't have said so even if he'd wanted to. His fangs had just punched out to full length, the second erection she'd inspired in ten seconds. Her smell was all around him, the heady thump of her strong, young heart. At that moment, the inedible Bakewell tarts couldn't have been less appealing. Out of respect for his brother and his brother's respect for Auriclus, Edmund had been denying himself his kind's favorite vintage for quite a while. That restraint turned around and bit him now. Blood was what he wanted: blood and a bout of hard-driving, endless sex. Preferably at the same time.

He'd dropped her hand in self-defense, his fingers digging hard into his palms. His head was spinning worse than if he'd been sundrunk.

"Anyway," she said, "I just wanted to thank you."

She laid her hands on his shoulders and went to the balls of her feet. She was a tall young woman, just a few inches shorter than he was. His heart thundered in his chest, though it didn't have to beat at all. His fangs had never ached this badly in his life.

He knew the only thing that would ease them was plunging into her vein.

"Estelle," he gasped as her soft human lips brushed his cheek glancingly. Her neck was so close. Her pulse. Heat swept over him like a bad fever.

She dropped back onto her heels, only to discover the grip he'd taken on her biceps prevented her from stepping away. It took all the self-control he had to force his fingers to release her.

"Excuse me," he said, knowing his elongated teeth were garbling the sound. "I need to use your facilities."

This was hardly a smooth excuse, but it was all he had. If he stayed here another instant, she was going to see what she'd done to him. Obviously startled, she pointed him in the right direction, and he stalked off.

The bath was sleek and shining, tiled all the way to the ceiling in celadon and cream. The tub was large enough for two, and the toilet had its own compartment. Edmund had enjoyed selecting the streamlined fittings, imagining Estelle using them. Now he could have cursed for what his extravagance revealed to him.

He was in love with Estelle, and probably had been from the moment he laid eyes on her. Why else would he torture himself this way? Why else would he care how capacious her hot water supply was?

He snarled silently at the mirror above her pedestal washbasin. He only wished that—as popular belief averred—his kind didn't cast reflections. His glamour had fallen, and his image glared back at him glazed with lust. His fangs were so long they verged on cutting his own lips. He didn't want to check the state of his cock. It felt large enough to need its own telephone exchange.

Whatever he wished, this arousal wasn't subsiding with a few deep breaths.

"Damn it," he muttered to himself, ashamed but knowing what he wanted to do—what he had to do, if it came to that.

He winced as he eased the clever zip to his trousers down. Humans and their inventions never ceased to amaze him. He slid his hand into his smallclothes, almost afraid of what he would find.

It was as he'd feared. His erection was enormous, his penile skin blazing hot. For an *upyr*, this was a sign of rare arousal. His kind tended not to waste resources on warming themselves, not needing warmth to be comfortable. He eased his cock free and fought a moan. Without even trying, he'd homed in on the sound of Estelle's heartbeat. The familiar rhythm worsened his painful state. He was addicted to this, to her, as badly as if he were the drunkard Sally thought.

He closed his fingers around his root and pulled them slowly up his thick, pounding rod. He didn't have to rush this. He was already too close to orgasm for pleasuring himself to take long. He let his energy seep through his skin, let it play along hungry, straining nerves, touching himself the way he longed to touch her. He'd play with Estelle like this, inside and out. Along her clit. Deep through her passage and into her womb. He'd make her weep before he slid inside her.

And then he'd pump and pump until they both caught fire.

Feeling twanged through him, making him twitch within his own hand. The sensation was near enough to climax that he tightened his fingers to prevent it, sealing up the tiny passage through which his ejaculate would flow. To his relief, his feeling of imminence faded. He needed a good climax, a deep one, or the lust that wracked him would not lessen. If that meant he had to take longer, then so be it. The thought of Estelle waiting, wondering what he was doing, only made him more excited anyway.

Because of that excitement, the milking motions of his fist wanted to speed up. Doubting he could stop himself, he gripped his balls and tugged them down to hold off spilling.

His head fell back with ecstasy.

Faster was definitely better. Faster drove the pleasure deep inside his cock. His fingers found his foreskin, and his buttocks tightened in reaction. He'd always loved rubbing that hood over his penis head, though he didn't usually dare when Estelle was near his vicinity. His kind were sensitive and—like humans—even more so when they were uncut. Now pleasure stabbed him from the tight, circling massage. His slit was leaking with excitement, the *upyr* version of pre-ejaculate. Reckless, he released his balls to fist his lower shaft in tandem to the ever-quicker stimulation he was working around his crown.

A sound escaped him, tiny but sexual. Visions of Estelle, almost too erotic to bear, rolled through his head: her on her knees before him, her lips squeezing his penis where his fingers were . . .

A knot of feeling gathered underneath his shaft, his longed-for climax preparing to spring free.

Estelle, he thought. *Estelle.*

In his mind, her tongue was rubbing greedily against his glans, her long hair spilling loose down her back. His fangs stretched an impossible fraction farther as he pictured her. Jesus, he was going to cry if he didn't come.

His climax rose like an ocean shoving at a dam. He needed . . . wanted . . . Fearing he'd scream if he didn't, he turned his head and bit his own shoulder.

In all his life, he'd never done this when he masturbated, never having lost control so thoroughly. If he'd known how good it felt, he might not have managed to refrain. His kind loved mixing sex and biting; it was their ultimate pleasure. Now it propelled him over the edge.

Blood rushed into his mouth as his cock convulsed. He did moan then, in spite of knowing he needed to keep quiet. He felt like he was coming in slow motion, the contractions deep and powerful. Fluid shot from him in hard pulses, the emissions evaporating almost as soon as they hit the air. He let them fly with gasping abandon, knowing he'd feel guilty more than soon enough.

The bliss went on and on, and then he was able to sigh with relief at last. His fangs were sliding back into his gums, his cock hanging long and lax. Hard as it was to credit, his knees were actually trembling.

"Christ," he muttered, hoping the lorry that had just hit him had done its work. He wasn't sure he had the strength to do that again.

A tentative tap at the door caused his heart to jump into his throat.

"Professor?" Estelle asked unsurely. "Are you well?"

He must have been in here longer than he thought if she was asking. Estelle was nothing if not polite.

"I'm fine," he said and cleared his throat. "I just . . . lost track of time thinking."

He didn't know if she believed him, but she left after another hesitant pause. He covered his face as her quiet footsteps receded.

Laugh or cry? he asked himself but chose neither. He couldn't keep doing this, not with her anywhere near him, not when the longing he felt for her was clearly worsening.

Edmund had let loved ones down too many times to count. This family, and Estelle, had given him a chance to redeem himself. No matter what it cost him, he wasn't going to muck that up.

Limehouse

The note was folded inside Graham's *London Times*, the same as the initial one. He peered at the newsagent, but the old fellow in the cap seemed no more knowing or furtive than he'd been before.

The missive (which Graham opened only after he'd rounded a corner) contained the address for a Chinese restaurant in Limehouse, along with the time 11:45 p.m.

Graham's palms immediately went clammy. He didn't want to do this: *this* being, in essence, the betrayal of the man who'd raised him from the time he was a boy. Graham loved the professor. That sentiment hadn't been extinguished by discovering he was a monster.

On the other hand, Graham didn't see how he could avoid the meeting. He'd made promises to his country, to his handler—to himself, for that matter. Perhaps X Section could provide some explanation that would ameliorate the horror of what he'd seen. They'd told him precious little up till now. Maybe the professor's . . . condition wasn't as bad as it seemed.

And if it was, better to face the truth head on. Graham had Estelle to think of. He didn't like how the professor was "helping" her. Edmund had seemed possessive the other night, pushing the others out the door so he could remain on his own. Estelle had been Graham's friend nearly as long as the professor had been his guardian. Surely he owed her, too.

With thoughts like these battling in his head, Graham was a wreck by the time he stepped from the taxi into the insalubrious neighborhood of Limehouse. He could smell the docks and the brewery and another sweet, cloying scent that set his teeth on edge. An opium den was operating somewhere nearby, perhaps in the very building he was girding himself to enter.

If it was there, he couldn't sense it once he'd stepped into the pungent clouds of frying food and tobacco smoke. The lateness of the hour didn't prevent the restaurant from being packed with Oriental men. Graham confronted a sea of foreign faces and workmen's caps. Above the noisy tables, cheap paper lanterns did little to dispel the dark, closed-in atmosphere. The surrounding walls, shiny and lumpy from numerous coats of paint, were a shade of deep bloodred he didn't think he liked.

Graham shoved his right hand into his coat pocket, palming the folding knife he'd stowed there just in case. He knew how to use it, though he'd be buggered if he wanted to. Sadly, Chinese was not among the languages he spoke. If it had been, he suspected the bursts of laughter that were discharging around the room would not have sounded as threatening. As it was, he couldn't help thinking they might be laughing about him. As the only white man there, he stood out like a sore thumb.

When he spotted his handler in the far back corner, the relief that flooded him was almost sensual.

She had the small table to herself, her pale face lifting like a flower as he moved through the busy restaurant to her. She rose for him, as a man might have. She wore a traditional Chinese costume, a snug black gown with gold-embroidered dragons to hug her mouthwatering curves. Graham found himself kissing her smooth, cool cheek without thinking twice.

"Good," she said, gesturing him to the battered bentwood chair across from hers. "I like a man who's punctual."

His genitals had been swelling from the moment she caught his eye, but at this his cock thrust out forcefully, instantly ready to take her.

"Aren't you sweet," she said with a husky laugh—reading his flush, he supposed.

A waiter materialized before Graham's slow tongue could answer. He bowed deeply to Graham's companion (well-nigh worshipfully, Graham thought) and took an order in rapid-fire Chinese from her.

"Sesame noodles and shark fin soup," she explained once the man was gone.

Graham nodded as if he agreed this choice was important.

"So," said his handler, her slender arms stretching toward him until both her hands covered his. Her fingers were long and slim, but it wasn't only their beauty that affected him. The simple touch of her flesh sent chills racing down his skin and shooting out his cock, as if her body were electrified. "Tell me everything your guardian has done or said since we last spoke."

The lingering sore place in the center of his shaft throbbed like a heart. The discomfort was disturbingly sexual. It hadn't occurred to Graham that pain might arouse him.

"You already know what he's done," Graham gasped. "That's why you sent me to Hampstead Heath."

His handler narrowed her exotic eyes. "I know what he's *been* doing. I'm counting on you to fill me in on the rest."

And there Graham was, at the moment of decision.

"What is he?" he asked, delaying desperately. "How can he do the things he does?"

"He's a vampire, one who's learned to change his shape to that of a beast. His kind feeds off humans as if they were their personal cattle. If England doesn't figure out how to stop him and his ilk, the country will be overrun."

Graham licked dry lips, remembering the glint of Edmund's sharp white teeth. The image couldn't keep his tone from being dubious. "A vampire?"

"A vampire," the woman confirmed. "Worse than any fiction Mr. Stoker could dream up." She'd released one of his hands to slide her own under the table. By leaning forward, she managed to grip him where he was bulging thickly against his trousers, the action hidden by shadows he hoped. When her fingers kneaded him, impossibly strong and expert, they increased the odd throbbing pain that had been plaguing his organ's shaft. The manipulation felt so perversely good, he had to struggle not to cry out.

"God," he choked, his hand reflexively cupping hers closer. She was going to make him come if she kept this up, and he wasn't remotely convinced he cared.

"God has nothing to do with it, Graham. These things are minions of the fiend. They *must* be stopped, and *you* have to help us."

His reflection was trapped in her eyes, and he couldn't look away from it. Beneath his own tiny figure, glints of fire appeared to flare and sink in her irises. Somehow, falling into her gaze made phrases like "minions of the fiend" seem less ridiculous. He swallowed, but his voice came out like rasping sandpaper. "What do you need to know?"

"Where he's been. What powers he demonstrated. Who he cares about."

After that, the words spilled from him as if being pulled in an endless chain. He didn't know how to stop himself from telling her everything. The more he said, the easier continuing became. She seemed particularly interested in the fact that the professor had made himself and his friend Robin disappear, insisting he repeat the details twice.

"Cloaking," she murmured. "That's a very senior power."

Graham wouldn't know and wasn't sure he wanted to. Despite the clear necessity of doing so, he didn't relish talking like a crazy man. He was grateful to turn the conversation to new topics.

At first, his mention of Estelle didn't pique his handler's attention. When he shared his theory that the professor was attracted to her, however, and likely had been for some time, her focus sharpened like a knife.

"You think he subsidized the mortgage for her flat?"

"At the least. She isn't paying half what it ought to cost. I'm worried that he's going to take advantage of her gratitude. Maybe we could warn her she's in danger. Send her somewhere out of the city."

"No," his handler said, the decisiveness of her response surprising and unsettling him. He'd have thought she'd be more concerned for Estelle's safety. He opened his mouth to say so, but she silenced him by patting his hand. She'd removed her grip from his erection, and—Lord—he wished she'd put it back.

"We don't want to let your guardian know we're on to him," she explained. "He hasn't hurt her thus far. I expect he'll continue to restrain his evil impulses. His kind are capable of, well, *he'd* call it affection. You and I might term it *obsessive protectiveness*. Your friend will be safe with him for the time being. You can trust me on this."

His head seemed to float upward as he looked unsurely into her eyes.

"You can trust me, Graham," she repeated. "You can trust me on everything."

He knew he ought to agree, that it would be easier if he did. Certainly, he could pretend he believed her. It wouldn't hurt X Section's mission if, on his own, he watched over Estelle closer than before.

Satisfied with whatever his face was showing, his handler leaned back in her chair. As if this were a secret signal, the waiter reappeared with the food. To Graham's surprise, the plates were set in front of him.

"Enjoy," said his companion. "The cooks here are skilled."

The dishes did smell delicious, especially the sesame noodles. Still, Graham hesitated to dig in.

"Aren't you hungry?" he asked.

The corners of his handler's lips curved in a catlike smile. "Thank you for inquiring, Graham. I had a bite earlier."

Harley Street

꧁꧂

The naked vampiress nudged the parlor's heavy silk drapes aside. She wished to look out on the lovely terraces of Georgian homes, to remind herself what she was fighting for. Inside the parlor, none of the electric lights were lit. As if to compensate, the vampiress glowed a bit, the pale phosphorescence extending half an inch from her skin. Her glamour tended to be imperfect when she was relaxed. Had anyone been looking up from Harley Street at this hour, they would have thought they had seen a ghost. Part of her wanted to be seen. She'd never gone unnoticed when she was mortal.

"What time is it?" she asked her partner.

Frank was naked, too, sprawled in an elegant Victorian chair that seemed too delicate for him. He was a big blond man with the noblest face she had ever seen, like a warrior-angel from a Renaissance painting. His build was strong and long and substantive: her physical opposite. She liked that. It added spice to their lovemaking.

With a quiet sigh for being asked the same question yet again, Frank clicked open his engraved silver pocket watch.

This watch, which he always carried with him, contained a few nuggets of raw iron covered in her blood. Contrary to the disinformation some humans swallowed, the silver had no effect on him. The iron, however, allowed him to share her gift of not being mind-read against her will. The female vampire was youthful compared to some, but that skill she excelled in.

"It's four and twenty past," he said.

So they had two hours before they had to scurry back into the Tube where, unbeknownst to humans, all three of London's nests had their home. If they waited longer, the stations would be thronged with workers and trains. According to their fearless leader, the justification for *upyr* living belowground was security; bunkers were difficult to attack. The female vampire had a different theory. She believed the true reason for the choice was to herd them all together under the queen's control.

She's turned us into rats, she thought—though, apart from the occasional seepage issue, their subterranean accommodations were luxurious.

"Would you like to own a house like this someday?" Frank asked from the shadows.

What she'd like was not to be reminded it wasn't hers. The owner—a young, virile doctor—lay sleeping like the dead upstairs, relieved by her and Frank of a pint of his human blood. The vampire licked her lips in spite of her annoyance. Somewhat to the good doctor's surprise, he'd been as interested in Frank biting him as he'd been in shoving his prick inside her, his reaction too marked to write off as mere bite-bliss. As soon as the pair had noticed, they'd made him fuck Frank until it must have hurt to come anymore. The doctor would remember none of it tomorrow, just think he'd overindulged in liquor.

Then again, he might feel a frisson of forbidden interest the next time he met a tall Teutonic male. The vampiress and her partner had only revealed the truths that were there.

"I can feel you thinking," Frank reminded her. "Why don't you come here and share that memory with me?"

Her heart began beating before she turned. She loved him, more than she loved herself, a miracle she'd never thought to see. He'd forever be the prince of her.

He smiled at her approach, revealing fangs that were swiftly lengthening with desire. His cock was rising, too, so unbelievably thick it never failed to stir a tremor inside her womb.

She suspected Frank's unusual size was the reason their queen had chosen him to be *upyr*.

"Oh, Frank," she said as she swung her knees to either side of him in the chair. "Do you really think this plan will work?"

He eased her over his massive girth with a soft, low groan. This was the first time tonight that they'd made love alone. "I think it has a chance."

She bit her lip at the tantalizing slowness with which he was obliged to spear her. "It has to work. I don't think I can stand living like this much longer."

He kissed her, his big hands steadying her head for his tongue's deep drive.

"I mean it, Frank," she gasped when he released her. "We deserve to run our own lives."

"We will," he groaned, but she knew he wasn't thinking about what he said. He was too caught up in the pleasure of being able to move at last. Frank was a man of ferocious needs, and his careful entrance had loosened her. With only a bit more work, he'd be able to pump the way he preferred.

And then he surprised her by sharpening his gaze on hers. "You were hungry tonight, with the doctor. Didn't you bite the Fitz Clare boy again?"

"I thought you wouldn't want me to. You don't like when I bite the same human more than once."

In a maneuver too quick to counter, he flipped her backward and onto the floor. Clearly in the mood for this male-superior position, he braced straight-armed above her, his bunching biceps too big to wrap both her hands around. Just thinking about the differences between them made her well up with cream. He growled at that, letting loose a minute before she was ready. His hips slammed into her hard enough to draw delighted whimpers from her throat. The evidence that he was hurting her, just a little, was like catnip to a lion in rut. She splayed her legs with abandon, a change that didn't entirely please him.

Naturally, that was part of their game as well.

"I think we . . . have to . . . ignore my preference this time." Growling with frustration, he clapped one hand around her upper thigh, tilting her for a more comprehensive penetration by his heroic cock. Frank always got excited when he was overwhelming her. "You need to bite him every chance you get. From what you say, Graham seems to have . . . some resistance to your thrall."

"Not much. He's been living with a near-elder. Some of Edmund Fitz Clare's powers were bound to rub off."

"I don't know. It was midnight when you bit him. Your powers were at their strongest. He . . . shouldn't have been questioning you."

Frank stopped speaking, the needs of his body demanding his full energy. She clutched the shifting muscles of his broad, hard back. Her true love was about to come. She could feel it in the tension of his hips' accelerating swing. It was his greatest charm: that every orgasm felt like life and death to him.

"Not yet," she whispered, knowing he would hold off for her.

He gasped for control and looked into her eyes. His were glowing the flame-hot blue of intense desire. Tortured by his need for release, his mouth stretched in a silent snarl as his fangs lengthened.

She thought she could delay him just a bit longer.

"Graham asked for my name tonight," she confessed. "Before he left. He said he needed something to call me."

"And did you . . . tell him what we agreed?"

She nodded, and his pale blue eyes flared white.

"No turning back then."

"No. No turning back."

She pulled down his head and bit him, piercing his lower lip so he would cry out and go over. The taste of him made her clit explode. The orgasm that resulted shook her against the doctor's Persian carpet. Though Frank was coming, he was still desperate for sensation. He thrust into her that much faster, shooting memories into her mind as forcefully as he was shooting ejaculate.

They both enjoyed the long parade of victims: those they'd simply played with like tonight's doctor; those they'd broken the rules to kill ever so carefully. They weren't supposed to expose themselves to human notice, or to have any more reality than as the subject of an idiotic film at the cinema. The vampiress's resentment added power to her orgasm. She moaned with pleasure, her body convulsing strongly as Frank sank long white teeth deep into her vein.

"I love you," she sighed after he'd licked away the last sweet drop.

Collapsed and satiated, Frank echoed the declaration straight into her mind.

Bedford Square

I'm just saying you could attend the university, too. You're not too old yet, and I know the professor wouldn't mind paying."

Ben should have known Sally wouldn't drop this argument just because they'd reached their house. She followed him up the stairs, so intent on making her point that she nearly trod on his heels. He tried to ignore the way his skin hummed at her closeness. He didn't know why, but since Estelle had moved out, he'd been deviled by hard, hair-trigger erections—of the sort he hadn't had since he'd first discovered what his spanner and nuts were for. Admittedly, for years now he'd had an infuriating and very involuntary thing for Sally, but his recent sensitivity to her, even when she was being a pill, was getting tiresome.

It was as if Estelle's departure had been a catalyst, as if someone had pumped an invisible aphrodisiac into the atmosphere of their home. Ben wouldn't have chosen to react this way. Sally didn't need any more advantages over him.

He stopped at the closed door to his bedroom and turned to have it out. "My going to school or not isn't about who pays—or how supposedly old I am."

Sally flounced at him, hands on hips, breasts jiggling behind her pale pink sweater with sufficient energy to turn his cock appallingly stiff. The innocent white lace that edged her collar absolutely lied about her true nature. Sally's tits were a weapon she used without shame against weak-willed men.

"If you're afraid you're not smart enough . . ." she said.

"Sally, you're the only member of this family who thinks I'm not intelligent. No." He took her fluffy little head in his hands, his thumbs stretching inward to shut her protesting mouth. Her big blue eyes widened. "I love working at the garage. I love taking cars apart and making them run again. Every morning I feel happy to get out of bed."

"You could be happy at school as well."

"*You'd* be happy if I was there. *I'd* be completely aggravated at wasting my time. Hell, you only want to go yourself because you think the parties would be fun."

"That isn't—"

"Enough, Sunshine. I'm not discussing this with you again." He slipped through the door to his room before she could stop him, closing it firmly behind himself. He heard a huff outside and then silence. He wrenched off his sport coat with a sense of escape. He couldn't remember getting the last word with her before. It felt good: satisfying . . . at least until an incredible burst of heat exploded in his groin.

He moaned and clutched the suddenly agonizing bulge of his erection. Jesus, something had to be wrong with him. He'd never itched like this before, never ached like he was going to die. He was rubbing himself in instants and then tearing down his zip. He had to come, had to get his hands on bare skin. He dug frantically through his shirttail and then his smalls. His cock was pounding like a military band. He fisted the shaft and prayed he could pump the bloody thing to release fast enough.

Sally stood outside Ben's door, a hundred rapier comebacks hovering on her lips. She didn't think he was stupid. She simply wanted the best for him.

He ought to know that, she thought, tapping her shoe impatiently. Why did everyone keep accusing her of being unfair to him?

Anger whirled up inside her, followed by something deeper and darker that she didn't care to identify. Whatever it was made her reckless. Ben couldn't just slam the door on her. Never mind he hadn't actually *slammed* it. She wasn't finished speaking to him. She grabbed the knob and turned it before she could consider what was polite.

When she shoved it open, the sight that met her eyes almost bugged them out.

There wasn't much to Ben's room. A large iron bedstead. A desk with greasy engine parts strewn on it. Certainly, there was nothing to block her view of the prodigy thrusting from his groin. Her adopted brother stood no more than a yard away, his shirt torn open, his plain corduroy trousers shoved to his narrow hips. He gaped at her, his . . . his manhood gripped in his hand like he was about to beat someone to death with it. She'd never seen a man's erection before, and yet it didn't take more than a second to identify what it was. It was long enough to stick past his fist. Caught between his fingers, the head was a good bit bigger than she expected; shiny, too, as if its skin was extremely stretched.

"Oh, my Lord," she breathed, both hands pressed to her mouth.

He flushed crimson and spun away from her. "For the love of God, Sally, can't a man have some privacy?"

"But you were—" She gasped and went hot all over as a

possibility occurred to her. "Ben, were you excited by our argument?"

She thought he must have been. His shoulders were knotted with tension, one arm positioned as if he might still be holding himself. His thick, streaky blond hair stuck up more than usual. His ribs were moving like a bellows with his hard breathing.

"Don't be stupid," he said. "These things happen sometimes to men. It doesn't mean anything."

"But if you're . . . aroused because of me—" Her voice was husky and strange, the words a challenge to push through her thickened throat. She felt thick other places, too, places she probably wasn't supposed to know about.

"Just let me touch it," she said, unable to stop herself.

"*Sally*," he groaned, as if the mere suggestion were killing him.

"I'll never ask you for another favor as long as I live."

"Sally, we're like brother and sister."

"*Like*, Ben, but not the same. Please, Ben. Please, please, please."

This was hardly the first time she'd begged a favor of him, but she couldn't remember wanting any of the others quite so much. She stepped to him, winding her arms around him and pressing her face to his shirt-covered back. He was so warm she didn't ever want to let go.

"Ben," she crooned. "I really, really want to."

He twisted in her hold, his face angry. "Don't blame me if you don't like it."

She couldn't imagine that, not after her first wondrous contact with that rigid warmth. His skin was silken under her hand, very slightly loose, with hard, thick flesh beneath that jumped like it was skittish when she stroked it. Curious to see what would happen, she tightened her fingers.

"Oh, God," he said and crashed his mouth down on hers.

Sally's insides seemed to melt and run out of her. The kiss was hot and greedy, his tongue reaching deep as his hands streaked over her back and pulled her close.

"I need you," he groaned against her lips. "I need you so much."

She wasn't sure exactly what he meant by that, only that she wanted to give him everything. Her insides squirmed as his hips jerked his penis in and out of her grip. His testicles were hidden, but she could feel them swinging within his smalls. She wished she had the nerve to cup them. Sally had teased a lot of boys, but she'd never experienced a lust this potent with other males. She wanted to strip naked and fling herself wide for Ben. She wanted him to ravish her.

"Yes," she panted. "Please take me."

His chest rumbled with a growl like nothing she'd ever heard. As before, a rush of hot wetness escaped her sex. She thought he'd argue. That would have been the sensible thing, but apparently he'd gone just as crazy as she had.

"Turn around," he said. "Hold on to the foot rail and pull up your skirt."

She gripped the end of his metal bed frame without hesitation, only trembling a little when he yanked her new silk panties down her legs. Then he really shocked her. He went to his knees and licked her, not her bottom but the twitching place between her legs, shoving her knees apart with his shoulders so he could get to it. This was not an activity she'd even imagined, but she could tell he'd done it before. He wasn't at all afraid to delve into her private folds, even to tug at them with his teeth. She wouldn't have thought that would feel so good. Caught by surprise, she cried out when his tongue dragged over her most sensitive place.

"Push out your bum," he said hoarsely. "I want you open all the way for me."

He didn't wait, but forced her torso down onto the bed. What his mouth did then was wicked, latching onto that special place and sucking. She didn't have the slightest urge to object, but rocked up the way he'd demanded and squirmed closer to his tongue. This was better than chocolate. Better than shopping. She was making sounds she didn't recognize as coming from her own throat: desperate mewls of longing that he met with hungry growls. She heard something else as well: his fist slapping hard up and down his cock.

Evidently, his desires were too pressing to ignore.

The second she realized that he was pleasuring himself, she teetered over into orgasm, the first one she'd been given by any hand but her own. It was hard and deep, like a stab of pleasure into her womb.

The instant it finished, she wanted another one.

Ben gasped her name and jolted to his feet. "I can't stand it," he rasped. "I'm going mad."

He was behind her, crowding her with his hard, lean body before she could decide if she ought to let this go further. The bare muscles of his chest were a strong persuasion, but the second he wedged the pulsing smoothness of his tip where his mouth had been, decisions became pointless. The head of him was broad and warm, parting her desire-sleeked folds to slide over what lay between. He teased her with himself, then found the dip in her and wiggled the head inside.

The way he had to work to do that thrilled her beyond measure.

"Oh, yes," she moaned, her back arching instinctively.

While one of Ben's hands steadied his erection, the other had curled over her shoulder. She felt his fingers tighten, and then he pushed forward from his pelvis with an inarticulate moan, stopping only when he butted up against her barrier.

The impediment seemed to surprise him. "Sally . . ."

"Don't stop," she pleaded, reaching back for his hip. She didn't have the presence of mind to be insulted by him not expecting her to be a virgin. "What you're doing feels nice."

"Nice!"

She guessed that wasn't the correct thing to say, but she couldn't worry about form right now. Rather than lose him from the place she most wanted him to go, she dug her nails into his hip. Her insides positively ached to be filled with him. "Take me, Ben. I need you, too."

"Damn you," he said, but since he was plunging into her as he cursed, that was fine. She felt a sting of heat, and another, and then his motion in and out of her turned as smooth and easy as if that hard, long part of him were oiled. She was just getting used to it, just feeling that delicious gathering inside her when he sped up.

"Sally," he said, his exhalations ragged and short. "Shit. Shit."

He fumbled around her under her skirt, finding the swollen peak of pleasure at the front of her. He rubbed it in a hard, sweet circle even as his breath exploded out of him. She knew, with an incredible tingle of excitement, that he was having his orgasm. He kept thrusting as he jetted inside her, each penetration jabbing her deliciously. The release must have been good for him. Even when his hips stopped rocking, it took a moment before he recovered enough to speak.

"Oh, God," he breathed, full of wonder. "I want to do that again."

The words were magic. She gasped and tightened around him, and suddenly he wasn't fading in her anymore but hardening. He groaned, but it was resignation, because he began to move again.

"Come on, Sally," he urged. "You can do it. Come for me."

His thrusts grew more insistent, driving deeper, stronger, until he stretched her every bit as much as before.

She couldn't pretend she didn't like that.

"More," she begged, writhing her front against the bed

because his thickness felt so good. "Please don't stop this time."

He made a sound that told her he wouldn't. He went on for her, and on and on, until she thought she'd die from the pleasure. His second hand slid urgently underneath her sweater, so he could cup one breast and caress it. His hand was calloused and big, completely surrounding her. She felt strangely comforted by his hold, though it certainly aroused her, too. Her nipple seemed to sing between his pinching fingers, just as her pleasure bud was singing beneath the quick, rotating pressure of the other ones.

"Sally," he groaned, her name hot against her ear. "I love your tits."

His crudeness packed an unexpected sensual punch, jolting inside her like another touch. She came and didn't want to let him know it, trying to keep the part of her that held him relaxed. She wasn't ready for this to end yet.

"You're holding back on me," he growled, sensing at least partially what she was doing. "I don't think I can let you get away with that."

As it happened, he had the power to enforce his will. He performed some new trick with the fingers that had grown so busy between her legs, finding a spot that was more sensitive than the rest. Helpless against his probable years of experience, she gasped and drenched him with hot fluids.

"*Now*," he ordered, and bit the straining muscle beside her neck.

She couldn't disobey him. Something about being bitten, about being ordered, rendered that impossible. In that moment, to be obedient to him was what she lived for. Her body tightened and tugged at him, ecstasy shooting outward from the center of her sex. She almost couldn't stop coming; the contractions were that intense.

His body bucked up close as if to savor what her insides were doing.

"Oh, God, it's too good," he moaned as every muscle in his body tensed.

She knew what that meant this time: He was about to spill. He confused her by pulling out of her with a grunt and shoving two fingers into her instead. She came around them, too close not to, and then he made up for her disappointment by going over himself with a lack of inhibition that delighted her. His broken groan was music, the frantic grind of his cock against the crease of her inner thigh amazingly intimate. His second hand was pushing his shaft as close as it could go. He was making free with her body, using it for his pleasure as if it didn't matter what she thought. Sally didn't know why, but that excited her terrifically. She tightened on his fingers yet again as his seed hit the coverlet in hammering spurts. Finally, both of them were replete.

A luxurious glow bathed her afterward, one he seemed to share. He nuzzled her hair, rubbing the side of his face against hers.

"Sweetheart," he murmured. "Oh, Lord, sweetheart."

The unfamiliar tenderness in his voice shocked her back to her normal self.

Oh, God, she thought. *What have we done?* What if the professor discovered it? Or Graham? They'd never understand what had happened. Sally wasn't sure she did herself.

"Are you all right?" Ben asked, easing off her so she could rise and turn around. "I'm sorry I forgot to pull out of you that first time. You felt so incredible I lost my head."

He gave her just enough room to shake her skirt back down. She knew his words meant something, but they wouldn't sink into her mind. His shirt hung open, creased and askew, to frame the rippling muscles of his torso. His skin was sweating, flushed, his dark gold chest hair matted against his skin. Sally tore her eyes from the tempting line that ran down from his navel. Sharing a house as they did, she'd caught glimpses of him and Graham partly dressed. She simply hadn't noticed how impressively Ben's shoulders tapered to his waist these days. He was lean, but he was undeniably a grown man. She squelched a fleeting wish that he'd been *more* naked when he took her.

She couldn't afford to want things like that.

His face tightened when he saw her expression. "You're sorry."

His voice was dead now, not tender in the least.

"Aren't you?" she asked pleadingly.

He released her arms and stepped back. "I won't tell anyone, Sally. Ever. You don't have to worry about that."

She touched him, but he shook her off. "Ben—"

"It's my fault. I should have known better. You don't have to blame yourself."

"I asked you to, Ben," she said, forcing herself to be fair.

His gaze searched hers, not quite as hard as before. "We'll forget it," he said softly. "It'll be like it never happened."

She took his hand. She couldn't stop herself. As gently as if he were made of glass, she lifted it to her mouth and kissed his perpetually scraped knuckles. She didn't think she'd ever touched him this way before. Maybe she shouldn't have just then, but she didn't want him hurting because of her.

"It's all right," she said as softly as he had.

"Sally," he cautioned when she would have drawn away and left.

He bent and handed her her panties. They were in one piece. Evidently, he hadn't ripped them when he tore them down. Stepping into them, with him watching, turned her cheeks to flame. She felt worse than inexperienced; she felt like an idiot.

After that, she couldn't get away from him fast enough.

* * *

Their parlor-library in Bedford Square was nothing like Estelle's modern living room. Sally thought it must resemble the men's club the professor sometimes went off to, with heaped bookshelves and oversized leather furniture that had reached the perfect state of broken-in comfiness. It was Sally's nature to love new things, but she hoped the professor would never redecorate. This room was where she came when she was upset. It always comforted her, even when she hid in it alone.

Hiding was out of the question tonight. When she hugged the doorway molding and leaned inside, she found the professor sitting in his favorite chair—the most broken-in of them all—reading a newspaper. His choice of the moment was the Sunday *News of the World*, while *The Daily Telegraph* and *The Financial Times* waited in a stack on the floor. As ever, Sally marveled at the speed with which he read. She'd never known anyone for absorbing so many little bits of type so fast. The skill came in handy, she supposed, when he had to grade those giant piles of student essays. On the mantel, above the flickering coal fire, American jazz tinkled softly from the wireless.

The professor must have felt her eyes on him, because he lowered his paper with a rattle and smiled at her. "Hullo, Sunshine."

"Hullo, Daddy."

His smile broadened. The grin made him look young enough that she could maybe understand why Estelle was carrying a torch for him.

"You haven't called me Daddy in a while." He waved her past the piles of unshelved books that their housekeeper was forever threatening to tear out her hair over. "Come sit with me. I found that novel you've been meaning to lend to Estelle, the Dashiell Hammett about the bird."

Sally discovered *The Maltese Falcon* on a footstool.

She picked it up and retreated into the corner to Graham's favorite spot, a wide, brown leather armchair that didn't squinch up his knees. The cushions smelled of his cologne and swallowed her when she curled up, creating the illusion that she was safe. She'd felt like a woman when she was with Ben, but now she wished she could be a child.

She didn't open the mystery novel. She wasn't in the mood to read about that clever, lying Brigid O'Shaughnessy, who fell in love with Sam Spade and had to die in the end.

"You're not going to your club tonight?" she asked her father. She had the vague idea that important people belonged to White's, and that—although he was not a peer or a politician—the professor's brains were much respected there.

"No," he said. "I thought I'd spend the evening at home with my family."

She should have known Ben would end up down here. Just as she had, he hesitated at the door when he spotted the pair of them. She saw he'd changed into a fresh shirt and that, for the moment, his unkempt gold hair was combed.

She couldn't quite look away fast enough. It wasn't fair that his lips were so beautiful, or that the cleft in his chin begged to have feminine fingers laid in it.

"Ben," the professor greeted him pleasantly. "I've been meaning to talk to you about the funny noise my Minerva has been making."

The Minerva was his saloon car, a shining black yacht of an auto whose stuffy dignity made it rather wonderful to ride in. Royalty were ferried about in Minervas, and so was Sally Fitz Clare.

"I'd be happy to look at it," Ben said.

This seemed to give him permission to enter. He came in stiffly, picking his way across the cluttered floor. To her surprise, he didn't take the farthest seat from her. Instead, he lowered himself—also stiffly—to the carpet beside her chair. Then he laid his head on her knee, like a dog who fears it won't be forgiven for its misdeeds.

Sally's throat choked up. She knew if she didn't breathe just right, she was going to burst into tears.

"Well, that's disturbing," the professor said.

"What is?" Sally asked, only a bit hoarsely.

Her father seemed to vacillate before answering. "A friend of mine, an . . . experienced civil servant, has been discovered dead in his home. Apparently, he's been lying there for the last five days."

"Is that all it says?"

The professor lowered the paper, his expression a cross between amusement and offense. "You don't think that's enough to disturb me?"

"I don't mean that!" Sally cried. "I'm very sorry you've lost your friend. I simply wondered how he died. You know Ben and I love bloody mysteries."

At the moment, they could also use a distraction.

"If it's blood you want, I'm afraid you'll be disappointed. There wasn't any at the scene, though the paper claims he was exsanguinated."

Ben lifted his head from her knee. "Exsanguinated?"

"That means—"

"I know what it means," Ben snapped at her, evidently still capable of being irritated. He turned back to the professor. "That's queer, don't you think? How could a man lose all his blood, and not have it splattered about?"

"Maybe he was murdered somewhere else," Sally theorized. "Was his throat slit like a grinning mouth?"

Ben nudged her leg, and belatedly she remembered they were discussing their father's friend.

"Good Lord," the professor expostulated. "I don't believe I should be reading this to you."

"Reading what?" Graham asked, appearing at the parlor door in his wet trench coat. His employer must have kept him working late tonight. He looked wan, Sally thought, which wasn't easy to do when you were the size of a small mountain.

With a grimace of reluctance, the professor handed him the newspaper. Sally wouldn't have thought it possible, but Graham turned paler.

"Martin Walser is dead?"

"Did you know him, too?" Sally asked.

"I . . . used to. My employer had dealings with him. I spoke to him a few weeks ago."

The atmosphere in the parlor had taken on the strangest tone. The professor was watching Graham's reaction, as if it mattered very much to him. Graham met his gaze, his expression just as serious. Something passed between them that Sally couldn't interpret.

Graham's fist tightened on the rolled tabloid. "The paper says Walser was drained of blood."

"So it does," his father returned.

"It says his neck was savaged as if wild animals had been at him."

Sally's eyebrows shot up at that, but the professor's calm was unruffled. "You know how sensationalistic the *News of the World* can be. It's hard to imagine wild animals had been at Walser in his own parlor."

"Then he *was* murdered somewhere else," Sally said.

Neither Graham nor the professor looked at her.

"I have reports to write," Graham said after a pause. "Don't set a place for me at supper."

That was humorous, in a way. The professor was the one who usually ate alone in his study.

Oh, this isn't good, Edmund thought. Not Walser's suspicious death, and not Graham turning away from him.

His eldest knew something. How, Edmund couldn't guess. He was as careful as he could be about keeping his identities separate. The fact that Martin Walser had been privy to more than one of his secrets was doubly upsetting. Edmund could have cursed himself for exclaiming over the article. As soon as he had, Ben and Sally were destined to read it, whether he told them what was in it or not.

At the moment, though, they weren't his biggest concern.

Graham had lied when he claimed to have met Martin Walser through his employer. It wasn't a bad improvisation. Walser's connections were wide ranging. He probably did know the American industrialist. The thing was, Edmund knew who Walser really was, or, rather, who he'd been: a highly placed director within MI5, the man to whom Edmund had been entrusting Graham's safety.

Walser had been bringing Graham up slowly, as Edmund requested, but he'd had immense faith in him. *That boy of yours is a natural*, he'd liked to crow, considering it a reflection on his own genius for recruiting him. *Graham can walk into a room and know exactly which minor party official is worth digging deeper on. Holds his mud, too. I don't think I've ever seen him panic.*

This was high praise coming from a man who'd been with His Majesty's Secret Service from its humblest beginnings.

If that man was dead, and in such a manner, Edmund couldn't count on his eldest being safe anymore.

Graham closed the door to his room and tried to breathe evenly.

Martin Walser had been a drab little man with a dry sense of humor, more aged clerk than case officer. Graham had been under the impression that he didn't run many agents and that he'd only been running Graham because Graham wasn't important. Graham had liked Walser for his steadiness and because he was incredibly organized. He'd read every word of every one of Graham's reports and could recall whole paragraphs at will.

Now he was dead. *Exsanguinated.*

Graham shuddered, the sweat he'd managed to forestall while he was in the parlor breaking icily across his back.

He wanted to believe his guardian knew nothing of the murder, but the professor's fathomless blue eyes had been too knowing for that.

Harrods

❧❧❧❦❧❧❧

Graham stood in the shadows of Hans Crescent, opposite the staff door to Harrods. Estelle was late getting off of work, which made him uneasy—though he knew her boss, one of the store's section managers, could be demanding of her time.

He took some comfort that it wasn't raining, just misty and cold. He shook his wristwatch clear of his coat sleeve and checked the time. Eight o'clock. The last customers had been ushered out an hour ago. Estelle's fellow employees had, for the most part, disappeared into the Knightsbridge Underground Station. When Graham squinted up the store's grandiose terra-cotta front, the upper floors where the offices were housed were dark. She should have been out by now.

He forced himself not to pace the mist-dimmed street. The first rule of surveillance was not to draw attention to oneself. The second was to keep one's eyes and ears open. Graham did that when a series of hasty footsteps gritted down the pavement in his direction.

The feet belonged to two hulking men. Though dressed in the famous green uniforms of the store's doormen, they didn't look nearly sharp enough. Their coats didn't fit properly, for one thing. For another, their faces were—by Harrods's standards—unacceptably unshaven.

Lest he be seen, Graham shrank deeper into the dark. The men were looking back over their shoulders as if searching for watchers. When they found none, they laughed low and guttural to each other. Graham's heart rate accelerated at the sinister sound. With one last backward glance, the pair disappeared into the staff entrance.

Bugger that, Graham thought, immediately striding into action. He wasn't letting those brutes sneak in there alone.

The upside to being kept late typing "deathly urgent" correspondence for her boss was that Estelle got to leave alone. She never took the lifts when she was by herself, but enjoyed a leisurely circuit of the store's levels, savoring each department's astonishing array of stock.

Sally would have laughed to hear her supposedly sensible friend sighing over the latest china patterns from Paris.

The ladies department was Estelle's favorite, and she liked to save it for last. It hadn't been modernized, and the original rococo plasterwork swirled over its ceiling and walls—like Marie Antoinette herself might stroll up to shop. The railed light well in its center was equally exquisite. Some nights Estelle simply looked up it and lost her breath.

Tonight she was lucky. Harrods's army of cleaners had already finished this area. The few lights that remained on created the impression of being underwater, shifting and mysterious. Estelle smiled at the beautiful backless dance frock one of the headless mannequins had on. Sally would have adored that shimmering bias-cut pink satin. She rather adored it herself . . . at least until a chilly prickle gripped her shoulder blades.

"Is someone there?" she asked, turning instinctively in a circle.

"Just me, Miss Berenger," said a voice she didn't recognize.

A shape emerged from the shadows, a tall, hefty male. The sight of the familiar uniform reassured her only for an instant. Her hand flew to her throat to cover her racing pulse.

"I don't believe I know you," she said tightly.

"That's all right." The figure grinned at her with tea-stained teeth. He was advancing toward her as she retreated. "I know *you* just fine."

She was so amazed when his beefy arm lashed forward that she didn't bother to shield her face. His fist slammed into her eye, undeflected and as big as a ham hock.

He hit me, she thought, stunned by the utter impropriety. *A man hit me!*

That was all the brainwork she had time for before crumpling to the floor.

Unconscious then, she had no idea the stranger who had punched her would drag her to the light well's rail. Or that he'd curse her deadweight as he tried to heft her body high enough to roll her over it.

Had she seen Graham's heroic entrance, she probably would have enjoyed it, though maybe not the first man's partner getting the drop on him from behind. She could have warned Graham the iron mongery was only two departments back. The fireplace poker the man coshed him over the head with took him out handily. Graham toppled like an oak behind a bin of ladies lacy underthings.

Their opposition taken care of, the first attacker snapped for his partner to come help him. "Woman weighs a ton," he grumbled. "Females shouldn't be allowed to grow this tall."

Rather than assist him, the second man peered over the light well's ornate railing. "You sure the fall will kill her? It's only one story. Maybe we should snap her neck."

"I *hate* breaking necks," his henchman grumbled with a small shudder. "It makes a god-awful noise. Let's dangle her by her ankles so she'll drop on her head."

Edmund was preparing a lecture on the fall of Rome, when a horrible icy feeling crawled like river muck across his skin. He wouldn't have been surprised to see some flame-eyed specter looming over him. Instead, he knew—without knowing *how* he knew—that Estelle was in grave danger.

Harrods, he thought incoherently. *I must go rescue her there.*

Since he was working in his attic study, he shoved directly out the casement and started leaping across rooftops. Not a single thought of discovery was in his head. In truth, he wasn't thinking much at all, only that if he didn't reach Estelle in time, his life would be a misery.

That he should have realized the depth of his feelings sooner flashed through his mind. He wouldn't even be able to walk into the sun. His mortal children would still need him.

Don't think about that, he ordered himself, his right heel cracking someone's rotted rafter as he pushed off from it. The world was streaking past him like bleeding paint, the cold wind tearing at his clothes and hair. He grunted as he crossed the open space of Hyde Park in a few long bounds. Vampires couldn't fly, but he was coming close. The Harrods dome rose before him, the six long stories of windows. Finding Estelle in there would be like searching for a needle in a haystack.

Landing on the nearest roof across the thankfully empty street, he narrowed his supernatural senses, focusing harder than he ever had in his life. He heard a human talking about dropping a woman on her head.

Without hesitation, he gathered himself and dove toward the sound.

It wasn't a pool he plunged through but a thick window. Glass broke as if it had exploded, the shreds it tore in his face healing in instants. Hundreds of tiny pieces pushed out from his skin and fell tinkling.

Somewhat to his amazement, he landed on his feet.

Two big men turned to him with their jaws hanging. It was they who had been arguing about how to kill Estelle. She sagged unconscious in their hold, but even as Edmund steadied his footing, she murmured wordlessly and came around.

Edmund's heart exulted that she was alive, joy rolling through him in heady waves. The waves faltered when he realized what her being conscious meant.

Bugger, he thought, stealing Graham's favorite curse. If she was watching, he wasn't going to be able to tear these men apart the way they deserved.

"Professor," she said dazedly.

"Fight!" he shouted back.

He didn't expect her to do it so well.

She blinked and swung her right arm at the nearest man—the arm the lightning had run through the night his wolf saved her. A bit of muscle memory must have been blasted into her with his power. She caught her attacker's jaw with a sweet right hook. It was textbook, straight out of the boxing ring. What wasn't textbook was the way her little fist sent the big man sailing at least ten feet into a mannequin.

The other man took one look and tried to run.

Edmund caught him, of course, whipping his ankle out from under him and smacking him against the floor. It wasn't quite an accident that his head struck the carpet hard enough to knock him out. Edmund had a feeling he wasn't going to wake as quickly as Estelle.

"Good Lord," she said, staring from her clenched right hand to the other man. She was weaving on her legs like she'd been drinking.

Suspecting she had a concussion, Edmund caught her before she fell.

"My," he said, trying to make light of it. "That's quite a pop you put behind that punch."

"I couldn't have . . . it isn't possible . . ."

"Yes, well, beginner's luck does happen."

"My funny arm," she said, the words slurring. "I hit him with my funny arm."

"It wasn't funny to him, I'm sure."

She straightened herself by gripping his shoulder. "Edmund. What are you doing here?"

"Walking you home, what else? Someone left the staff door unlocked."

"Right," she said and rubbed her forehead.

"Do you have a headache, love? Let me check your eyes."

Thralling her was tricky. One of the brutes had socked her in the left eye, the one that wasn't resistant to his power. As gently as he could, Edmund lifted the puffy lid and peered into her pretty gray iris. She let him do it without flinching. A wonderful, homey tug inside his chest told him he'd established the connection.

To his amusement, even thralled, she was concerned with doing the right thing.

"Shouldn't we call the police?" she asked.

"Oh, I don't think so. I'm not supposed to be here. What if they mistook me for a burglar?"

"They wouldn't," she said with a heat that delighted him.

"You know what I think?" he said, still holding her gaze. "I think I should drag these nasty fellows out to the rubbish bins. Either someone will find them and call the police for us, or they'll wake up and count themselves lucky."

She thought for a moment, logic obviously difficult for her just then. "Very well," she surrendered. "It's not like they're *real* doormen."

"You have an admirable loyalty to your employers."

"Damn right," she said. "My boss may be a wanker, but I love Harrods almost as much as I love you."

The back of Graham's skull pounded like the devil, voices coming and going through the throbs of pain. The voices were familiar. Comforting. Was he at home?

He reached up, found the corner of a wooden cabinet. As he struggled to pull himself onto his knees, a heap of women's French-style brassieres fell onto his head.

He had just enough self-control not to let out a yelp of surprise.

Past the cabinet which had hidden him, Estelle and the professor stood talking. Estelle's attackers lay at some distance on the floor, neither of them stirring. The professor patted Estelle's arm and stepped away from her. He bent, heaved one of the unmoving men onto his shoulder in a fireman's carry, then grabbed the other by his wrist and dragged him along behind.

"The employee lifts are that way," Estelle said, pointing.

She seemed not to notice the feat of strength Graham's guardian was performing.

"Thank you," said the professor, not even out of breath.

Graham watched until they disappeared into the next department: the millinery, he thought.

He stood then, his knees about as steady as gelatin. The room rotated once around his head and stopped. He wasn't certain he could make sense of this.

Estelle had not appeared to be in danger or afraid—dazed, maybe, but not afraid. If Graham hadn't known

better, he'd have said the professor saved her from her
attackers. He remembered what his handler, the beautiful
Nim Wei, had said: that a vampire's affection could mani-
fest as obsessive protectiveness. Was that why Edmund
had saved Estelle? And who the buggering hell were those
men? The professor's enemies? Or—his chest hurt as the
notion came to him—had the professor hired the toughs
himself so he could play hero?

Graham didn't know how to find the answer, not with
his guardian conveniently dragging the evidence away.

As Edmund expected, there were rubbish bins in the
delivery yard. Three of Harrods's trademark green and
gold vans sat empty on the macadam, awaiting the next
day's outbound packages. Edmund sensed a security guard
patrolling in the distance but not nearby. He laid down his
unconscious burdens more gently than they had earned,
then took a moment to examine them.

He'd already gleaned one important fact from carrying them out of the store. They smelled of someone he had
once known intimately.

"What are you looking for?" Estelle asked as he knelt
down, frowning, beside the bodies. Despite being lightly
thralled, her curiosity was intact.

Edmund tugged down both men's ties, opened their col-
lars, and pulled them back from their beefy necks.

That's what I'm looking for, he thought. A set of neat
double punctures marked each man's carotid artery, recent
to judge by the bruising. He lowered his head and inhaled,
not because he was hungry but to confirm he'd noticed
what he thought. The pleasant, faintly musty scent of books
whose pages had turned yellow filled his nose.

He hadn't been mistaken. Every *upyr* had his or her own
distinctive smell, and this was Nim Wei's personal per-
fume. His long-ago lover and would-be maker had bitten

these men. Without a doubt, Estelle's attackers were the human servants of the mistress of London.

His fangs did lengthen then, his instinctive reaction to a threat against someone he loved. He forced himself to relax when Estelle bent over his shoulder, her warm, slim hand resting on his back.

"What are those?" she asked, one finger pointing at the bites.

"I don't know," he lied. "Perhaps a gang marking." He rose and offered her his arm. "I should take you to your flat. You'll want to rest after your ordeal."

She tucked her elbow through his with a sweet, shy smile. His thrall had lessened her inhibitions. For once, she wasn't hiding how much she liked his kindnesses. Edmund's heart, experienced though it was, actually skipped a beat. He hadn't forgotten what she'd said at the store: that she loved Harrods almost as much as she loved him. Being under an *upyr*'s influence might be a little like being drunk, but *in vino veritas*, as people said. Edmund would take the declaration any way he could get it.

When he stole another look at her, her head was tilted back. She was peering at the cloudy heavens with her one good eye.

"London is so beautiful tonight," she sighed. "I think I've never appreciated how the mist makes the buildings look magical. It's like an angel sprinkled every scrap of light with rainbows."

Edmund chuckled to himself. Forced by her injury to rely on her "funny" eye, Estelle was seeing the world as he did: in breathtaking, enhanced detail. It was a good thing she'd probably discount it later as the effect of having been in shock. Edmund would hate to have to thrall this memory away.

Feeling unusually light on his feet, he led her to the nearest Tube station. His skin tingled all over when her hand squeezed his forearm. He knew she didn't really require more support to get down the stairs. His examination of her eyes had reassured him she was not concussed. No, Estelle was holding him tighter because she wanted to.

"Let's go home," he said for the simple pleasure of uttering the phrase to her.

Blackfriars
Underground Station

⚜

The bodies were left on her doorstep, outside her customary exit from the maze of passages that descended deep under London to her personal nest.

The corpses had been gutted more like cattle than human beings. Worse, they'd been gutted here. The spray had turned the tunnel's concrete into an abattoir, blotting out any scent the murderer had left.

Nim Wei looked left and right but sensed no trains coming. Illuminated by the safety light outside her nondescript steel hatch, a silvery mist swirled like a snake through the lower reaches of the Tube's tunnel. The District Line ran straight here, its metal ribs narrowing in perfect artist's perspective to disappear as an ink black point.

Satisfied she wasn't going to be run over, Nim Wei stepped onto the gore-slicked tracks. She'd seen too many fashions come and go to suit anyone but herself with her choices. Tonight she was dressed like a pirate, her red silk blouse tucked into black trousers. Polished leather Hessians rose to her knees, while a red and white gypsy kerchief covered her straight black hair. In a pinch, she could have passed for a bohemian—assuming bohemians had heaps of money and skin like snow.

At the moment, she would have been satisfied to pass for nothing at all. She didn't think it a coincidence that this gift had shown up here.

Someone was trying to draw trouble to her door.

She tossed the bodies through the hatch as quickly as she could, each one landing inside with a heavy thump. The blood she couldn't do much about, though she smashed the safety light to render the stains less obvious to passing subway cars. The last thing she needed was some constable poking around here.

To her dismay, she recognized the humans once she was back in her own tunnel. She couldn't recall their names, but she believed she'd bitten them about a year ago: big, ruthless brutes she'd thought might come in handy as daytime muscle. She'd lost track of them, which could happen if you'd had as many servants as she did. Humans who didn't work close to their master—and thus prolong their lives—did have to be replaced frequently.

She saw these two had been rubbing their old bites with iron. Raw iron was toxic to *upyr* kind and counteracted the healing power she would have sent into the wounds. This behavior kept the signs that she'd claimed them fresh. Nim Wei wouldn't have wanted the reminder, but some human servants relished the knowledge that they were owned.

"What have you been up to?" she murmured to the open, staring eyes, bereft now of their divine spark. She knew she hadn't given them any jobs, and if she hadn't ordered them to do whatever had gotten them into trouble, she couldn't guess who had. Nim Wei was a very powerful elder. Her control over her servants would have been extremely difficult to override.

Perplexed, she stripped the closest body of its blood-soaked coat. She found nothing in the pockets, but from the corpse's arms a partial answer came. Dozens of needle tracks darkened the veins inside the dead man's elbow, from old and healing to as fresh as the day before.

So, she mused. *You found a compulsion stronger than the one I exercised.*

That, or someone else had found it for him.

Nim Wei shivered, not chill but presentiment. The door behind her back had a lock a bomb could not have broken through. All the same, she felt less secure in her little kingdom than she had a minute earlier.

Tottenham Court Mansions

Had Estelle ever been this happy? Maybe when she was a child, before she realized her parents weren't particularly enthralled with her. Or maybe when she first moved in with the Fitz Clares. Despite the accident that had led to it, that had been a lovely time, one in which she'd felt warm and safe and part of the fun. That emotion hadn't been quite like this, though, not quite this dreamlike and wonderful.

All through the Tube ride with Edmund's side brushing hers, all through their arm-in-arm walk to her flat, she'd wanted to kick up her heels and break into song. Her body felt so good, so easy and sensual.

The only bad part was reaching the entrance to her building.

Estelle took one step up the front stairs before turning back to her escort. Edmund was still on the pavement, and his face was slightly lifted, his pure, stark beauty an arrow to her heart. Had there ever been eyes as blue as his? Or as kindly and tender?

"You saved my life," she said.

His hand rose to mold her cheek, his fingers cool at first and then warm. "Estelle."

His voice was lower than usual, startling her into reexamining her assumptions. Maybe his kindness *was* more personal tonight. Unless she'd lost all her feminine powers of observation, longing colored his tone.

"I wish you'd come up," she said, forcing her gaze to hold his directly. "You could have a cup of tea."

His gaze dropped to her mouth, lingering for a moment before seeming to fasten on the pulse at her neck. Estelle imagined it was beating rapidly enough to catch his attention. Edmund licked his lips and looked into her eyes again. He was breathing faster. She could tell by the way his chest went shallowly in and out. For the first time that evening, she realized he wasn't wearing an overcoat. His shirt and tweedy waistcoat were all that kept him from the cold night air.

"I *could* help you with your eye," he suggested, as if he, too, were searching for excuses not to go. "Find something cool to put on the bruise."

Estelle didn't know why this caused her to blush.

"Yes," she said firmly. "Let's do that."

He knew he shouldn't come in with her, not in his present state—nor in hers. She was feeling grateful, and shaky, and not yet over being thralled. Both their emotions would be more volatile than was ideal.

You saved her, the wolfish part of him insisted. *You've earned the right.*

His body was so tense when they stepped into the cage of her building's lift that he couldn't tell whether arousal had coiled his muscles or sheer terror. *Arousal*, he decided as she unconsciously stroked her neck. *Oh, by heaven, it was arousal.*

She was in profile to him, her hot mortal scent filling the confined space. She smelled like she might be excited, too. He struggled to prevent his fangs from descending, but his gums were throbbing dangerously. His cock was erect already, shoving out his trousers in hard demand.

It had done that the moment she'd taken the seat beside him in the subway car.

"Oh," she said, laughing suddenly. "We forgot to tell the lift to go up."

He grabbed her hand before it could reach the mechanism, yanking it back beside her shoulder as he pressed her body into the wall with his. His strength ensured he could keep her pinned as long as he wanted. Considering the way she felt beneath him, that could be forever.

"Professor!" This was a delicate, feminine exclamation: fear mingling with attraction. The wolf in him savored it. Edmund's incisors ached a little more.

"Call me Edmund," he growled. "I'm not *your* teacher."

He didn't give her a chance to comply or indeed to say anything at all. He lowered his head and kissed her—not hard, not fast—but as deep and thorough and skilled as a man with five hundred years of experience could make an oral invasion. She tasted delicious, her tongue the sleekest, most suckable morsel he'd ever known. Unprepared for his onslaught, Estelle began to squirm.

He'd been aroused already, but when her hips unwittingly undulated under his, every cell in his body vibrated with pent-up lust. Eleven years was long enough to wait. She was his, and he was going to claim her. Nothing could stop him now.

Grunting, he shoved her higher against the wall, lifting her off her feet atop the steely bulge of his cock. She clutched his back and moaned, her thighs trying to part inside her narrow skirt. Edmund knew she must want to wrap her legs around his waist. Unthinking though it was, the telltale movement snapped the rein he had on himself.

In one hard, complete descent, his fangs rode down, their points as sharp as daggers. It nearly killed him, but he had to wrench his mouth from hers before she was cut.

"Edmund," she moaned pleadingly.

He didn't set her on her feet; that was asking too much. He did, however, reach back for the mechanism of the lift. It amazed him that he recalled how to operate it, his mood simultaneously crazed and grim. He had to stop this, and he had to stop it now. "Estelle, I'm taking you to your flat."

"Oh, yes," she sighed, utterly mistaking him. "I want to be alone with you there."

In his head, he laughed at himself. She was perfectly right to assume he wasn't stopping, though he was trying. She'd almost died, and his relief that she hadn't was too powerful to overcome. Lost to desire, he slammed her against the wall partway down her hall, actually bunching her skirt above her long, stockinged thighs. That her neighbors might come out meant nothing. The sultry warmth he found between her legs made it impossible not to mimic the act he had so long wanted to perform. Grinding his hips at hers through their garments, he licked her neck in substitution for the bite he craved. The thrumming of her pulse sang a potent siren song to him.

He could almost taste her blood through her skin.

If only to distract himself, he kissed her swollen eye, sending his healing power into the bruised tissues. He would soothe any hurt she had, including the growing ache he sensed in her womb.

"My door," she pleaded, not helping him at all by rolling her pelvis sharply into his. "My flat's right here."

All the vampire gifts in the world couldn't keep his fingers from shaking as they turned the key she gave him.

She shut the door behind them. He'd stepped away from her to enter. He had a brief chance for sanity. Naturally, Estelle wasn't having that, not with her inhibitions lowered by his thrall.

"Take off your clothes," she said. "I want to see what I've been feeling under them."

"Estelle—"

"Very well then. I'll take off mine."

She began to, and suddenly his hands were moving, too, racing over buttons and tugging cloth. He had to remind himself not to strip too fast. Thralled or not, she would notice. They were in her living room, the electric lights bright as day as each new piece of them was revealed. He couldn't look away from her, nor she from him. The world might have emptied but for the two of them. She was down to her slip, he to his underthings. As if the evidence of his erection was too much for her, her eyes closed for a moment, her thick ash brown lashes shadowing her flushed cheekbones.

"All right," she said, lifting them again. "I'm ready."

He knew she meant ready to see all of him. He hoped it was true. His heart beat in his throat as he pushed his underthings down his legs.

Her intake of breath could have been mistaken for a gasp of horror, except her hand immediately reached out to him. His hardness throbbed heavily in reaction. He wanted her hand on him almost more than anything.

"Finish undressing," he said hoarsely. "Then you can touch all of me."

Without hesitation, she peeled her slip over her head.

She was so lovely naked he could have cried.

No biting, he snarled silently to himself, praying he could obey. Her body was a goddess's—strong but curving, with breasts so round and perfect Venus herself would have envied them. Her legs could have run a Grecian marathon. Her pubis bore a triangle of silver-brown, which she covered shyly with one hand. Her other hand attempted to hide one breast, but her bosom was too generous for that. Her nipples were the color of persimmons, puckered with arousal and large enough to fill the space between his fangs.

No biting, he repeated, rather ruining the edict by lick-ing his upper lip. His mouth was swiftly filling with saliva. *No biting, no matter what*. He wasn't going to take her blood and make her his servant.

"Edmund?" she said. "Are you all right?"

"Come here," he said in what could only be termed a growl.

She came, hesitating for the first few steps and then run-ning into his arms.

"Oh, God," he said, hugging her nakedness tight to his. "Oh, God, I've wanted you so much."

She was kissing him, stinging little nips along his neck that made his eyes want to roll back inside his head. Fear-ing this was a bit too stimulating for his resolve, he tried to push her back.

"You promised I could touch all of you," she said.

He held her shoulders in lust-tensed hands. Her gaze met his steadily. Her left eye no longer showed signs of injury. He pushed a tiny flare of power into her. "Tell the truth, Estelle. Is this really what you want?"

Her expression changed, such compassion in it that it startled him. "That you could ask that, and of me! This is what I've wanted since I was fifteen."

"*Jesu*," he moaned, reverting to the favorite oath of his mortal years. Wrong though it would have been, her words made him wish he'd taken her when she first wanted . . . and every blessed night thereafter.

Maybe if he had, his control wouldn't be so close to shattering tonight.

Her lips and hands slid down his torso as he closed his eyes in defenseless bliss. She kissed the points of his nip-ples, skated over the dip of his navel. Her thumbs caressed his hip bones as if admiring their prominence. He held his breath to prepare himself, but when her fingers touched his rigidly erect penis, his whole body jerked, shaken by the flood of desire. Undaunted, she knelt on the carpet and pressed a kiss to his hardness's underside. Her soft lips whispered over the strongest pulse.

"This," she said as he shuddered from head to toe. "This is what I want."

He struggled with all his might not to ask for a different kiss, not to plead with her to suck him. Her hand slid up his shaft, her thumb finding just the spot he wanted beneath the rim. *Please*, he thought, biting his lip until it bled.

"All right," she said. "I think I can do that."

He could have sworn he hadn't uttered the plea aloud, but—as if it were the most natural act in the world for a neophyte—she tipped the head of him into her mouth. He groaned at the pleasure of those soft, satiny tissues closing tight on him. Her tongue was wet, her cheeks pulling at him firmly, but that was only the beginning of his agony. She still had her hand on him, her right hand, her funny hand that the lightning had blasted through. A clean right hook wasn't the only muscle memory she had absorbed. As she sucked, she began to pump him with the exact strength and speed he used on himself. She—or her hand—knew all his sensitive places and was taking care to put his preferred pressure on every one.

It was enough to turn any man into a monster.

"Estelle," he gasped with the last of his will. "Not so fast."

She let him go and looked up at him. "Your eyes—" she said unsurely.

As insane as he was with lust, he expected they were glowing.

He couldn't do anything about that now. He held out his hands for hers and lifted her to her feet. "Couch or bed, Estelle? And choose what you really want, because we'll be staying there for a while."

She gnawed the cushion of her lower lip hard enough to whiten it. "Bed. And please hurry."

He didn't need to be asked twice. He carried her there

and tossed her lightly onto the covers, barely noting how her room was furnished. The bed was big and firm, and that was really all that mattered. One small lamp burned beside it, dim enough to hide a multitude of supernatural sins. He felt more than half wolf—and all feral—as he crawled onto the mattress over her.

"You have to tell me what you want," she whispered, deliciously shy again. "I've never done this before."

She was killing him without even trying. Angling his head so she couldn't see, he ran the curve of his fangs over her left breast. Her nipple bumped them tantalizingly. He was going to be her first lover. He was going to own this moment for the rest of her life.

"I want you," he said, the confession bursting out of him, "and I have since you were fifteen."

Estelle thought she must be dreaming. Edmund wanted her. Edmund was in her bed. Edmund was—oh, Lord!—sucking her breast so hard she felt the tug of it, real as day, between her legs. She groaned because she couldn't help it, arching up at him wantonly. He shifted to her other nipple and inspired an even louder cry.

He eased back then but kept his hand around her breast, pointing the aching tip toward his mouth. He watched her reaction as he flicked his tongue over and around the tightened bud. His tongue seemed very wet, very red, very *pointy*. The sight of it teasing her nipple had to be one of the rudest things she'd ever seen.

She couldn't hide one blush of what it did to her.

"Oh, Estelle," he said with a laugh as low and masculine as any she'd ever heard. "How you make my mouth water!"

Mine, too, she tried to say, but he'd just slipped his hand between her legs and robbed her of the power to think, much less utter a word. He was pushing her folds apart, was sliding his middle finger up to the knuckle into her wet opening. His thumb found the part she thought was her clitoris. Her neck arched off the pillow at the first firm pressure he put on it. He knew how to rub this button better than she did.

"I'd like to suck you here as well," she heard him say from a distance, though his mouth was against her ear. His thumb and finger moved with devastating skill, drawing helpless cries from her. "You're lovely and wet and warm, and your little clit is very swollen. But maybe we'll wait until you're more comfortable with me."

She grabbed for his arms when he moved again, but he was only shifting between her legs. His weight seemed to settle naturally into the cradle of her hips. Her heart banged faster behind her ribs.

"Don't be afraid," he said, one palm stroking her hair away from her face. "I know what I'm doing. I won't hurt you."

He held himself above her without effort, his torso utterly male and gorgeously lean—too perfect to look away from. His skin was the gleaming white of buffed marble, his disk-shaped nipples copper in that field of snow. He didn't have more than a dusting of hair on his chest. What there was glinted in the muted light from her bedside lamp like twenty-four-karat gold. Taken altogether, he looked like something out of an obscene jewel box.

"Enjoying the view?" he asked with a slanting smile.

"Oh, yes," she breathed. "You don't look at all like I thought a naked professor would."

He choked out a laugh. "Estelle, now might not be the best time to admire my—"

But he stopped complaining and closed his eyes when she began running her hands up and down his arms. She didn't feel guilty for delaying his taking her. She knew he enjoyed her touch. Hadn't he begged her to kiss his cock earlier? In any case, she couldn't help it. His biceps fasci-

nated her. They didn't give when she squeezed them. For
that matter, he didn't give much of anywhere she stroked.

His were a warrior's muscles: graceful and merciless.
She had no trouble picturing him swinging a broadsword
or controlling a stallion with nothing but the power of his
long, hard thighs. Without warning, her vision flickered like
a film through a projector. Edmund sat at a massive desk,
scratching numbers into a book with a sharp quill pen. He
wore a rich velvet doublet that matched his eyes. His expression was so altered from what she was accustomed to—so
dissatisfied with life and bitter—that he seemed a different
man. A towheaded boy around the age of five ran in.

Father! tattled the child. *Thomas hit me with his—*

Not now, Edmund cut him off. *I'm working on the
accounts.*

She saw the boy's face fall, saw his small heart break, as
only a child's can.

"Are you well?" Edmund asked.

Estelle drew a more even breath than she'd been taking
while she had this strange vision. She didn't want her mind
playing tricks on her, now of all times. Edmund's body
hung warm and eager above hers, his rather astonishing
erection pointing like a torpedo toward the ache between
her legs. *He* was where she wanted her attention. *He* was
what deserved it.

She wet her lips and thrilled to the way his gaze focused
on her mouth.

"I'm well," she said breathlessly. "I'm simply struck
speechless by your pulchritude."

"My pulchritude!" He laughed, a beautiful, rich male
sound. He dipped his head to murmur against her cheek.
"Verily, Estelle, you are a pearl beyond price."

She flung her arms around his back, overwhelmed with
gratitude for his affection. She must have said it aloud and
not realized, because he responded.

"Estelle," he said, low and throbbing. "You know I feel more than affection."

He brushed his lips across her forehead and repositioned his hips.

"Oh!" she gasped, because the shift had placed his tip against her. Abruptly, she could think of nothing else.

"Use your hand," he whispered. "Put the head of me where it needs to go."

She reached between them, her right hand surer than her left. A sound broke in his chest, a mix of torment and delight. She pressed his wide, sleek crown just inside her gate.

"You feel like silk," she whispered. "Like hot, hard silk."

"*Estelle*," was all he could manage.

He pushed farther, groaned, and stopped. The heavy muscles of his thighs were trembling—and not, she thought, with weakness. His eyes opened slowly and held hers. Their blue was as bright as flames. "Do you want to feel this, Estelle, or would you prefer I took the pain away?"

This struck her as an odd question. She slid her hands up his back to his shoulders, curling her fingers over the muscles there. "I want to feel everything."

He nodded, drew a breath, and then shoved into her without warning. She felt a few seconds' pain, but it didn't matter. He was in her, stretching her, heating her, sliding deeper and deeper, until it seemed as if their bodies would be locked together by the sheer length of him. The earth-shattering wonder of his penetration overcame any passing discomfort. She arched beneath him, digging her heels into the bed to try to help him in all the way.

That made him swear, but she didn't think he was angry. His glowing eyes seemed to grow hotter as he ran one hand down her writhing side.

"Wrap your legs around me," he said, his voice gravelly,

"the way you wanted to before. Use your strength to pull me in."

She used her strength until his pelvis was snugged to hers, until his . . . testicles were squished with a strangely pleasant intimacy against her bum. Her thighs strained with her instinct to keep him forever exactly where he was. His cock was throbbing inside her, thick and vital and strong. She could feel herself throbbing, too, could feel the hot, wet longing creaming from her walls.

"Estelle," he sighed and kissed her so hard and deep she thought her mouth would take on the imprint of his teeth. Despite his fervency, his positioning was very careful, very precise. His tongue reached to hers and sucked it, drawing and twining until he seemed to lick lower things.

This, she thought, *is what it's like to be kissed by a master of the art.*

A second later, he tore free with a ragged moan.

She touched his face, hearing pain in his cry. He turned his head to kiss her palm. Emotion flowed like a shadow across his face, regret so deep it frightened her—all the more because she didn't understand its cause. When he shook it off, her unease remained. He caressed one of her thighs to relax it.

"Leave the rest to me, love. I'll take us up the mountain."

"You don't want me to help?"

"Help as you wish. Just trust me to please both of us."

"I do. You've already pleased me."

His grin was wolfish, a trick of the light sharpening his eyeteeth. "Not yet, my star, but you'll learn the difference soon enough."

She thought she learned it as soon as he began moving. His hips rolled into her in steady waves, the hot, hard length of him stroking every inch of her inside. His aim was flawless. He bumped the pulsing swell of her clitoris with every thrust. She especially liked the flaring rim of his organ's head, which he used to increase the pressure everywhere he slid. All too soon, Estelle cried out in a kind of panic. She knew she was going to come.

"Yes," he soothed. "Have your appetizer now."

She had it—and quite a few more besides.

Embarrassing though they were to her, her uncontrolled responses seemed to ease some concern in him. Satisfied she could take what he wished to give, he pushed her left leg higher and worked himself into her faster. He hadn't spilled yet, but the growling noises that rumbled from his chest suggested he wanted to. His beautiful features had twisted into a snarl. He flung his head back as she came again, his veins dark against his throat.

"Am I clamping down on you too tight?" she panted, once she was able to speak again.

He shook his head, sweat glistening like diamonds on his brow. He wasn't perspiring nearly as much as she was.

"It's perfect," he said. As if to prove it, he grunted and drove deeper. "*You're* perfect."

"That's good," she said. "Because I'm not certain I can help myself."

He echoed her broken laugh with a groaning one. She ran her hands up his laboring chest, wishing he weren't holding his upper body off her the way he was. His arm muscles were so tight they seemed carved from stone. He looked like pleasing her was torturing him.

"You can let go, Edmund," she said shyly. "If you want to."

"Not yet." His jaw clenched stubbornly. "I want this to be good for you."

"But—"

"Shh," he said. "Hold on tight."

She didn't think it was what he meant, but she clapped both hands around his thrusting bottom cheeks. Lord, his rear bits were sexy, tight and hard and almost too narrow for the rest of him. His arse provided the ideal grip for pulling herself up while he was plunging down. They both cried out at how good that felt.

"Yes," Edmund gasped, ramming into her so hard he had to brace one arm on the headboard to forestall them crashing into it.

Estelle's next orgasm gripped her violently, her sex contracting in a greedy fist around him. Edmund growled through his teeth, making her glad he'd explained this felt good to him. Her funny ear buzzed just as he shoved deeper. *Lord*, she imagined his voice saying. *You'd think the lightning struck her pussy, too.*

"More," she pleaded, wanting to hear real sounds and real voices. "Finish me again."

He couldn't speak. His body was taking over, as she wanted it to. She matched his rhythm—strong, deep—as though their needs were identical.

The stimulation was too much for him.

"Ah!" he cried, pushing his upper body even farther away from her. He had one arm on the headboard and one on the bed, both corded tight with strain. He looked like he was trying to flee even as his hips hammered desperately closer. His eyes were screwed tightly shut, his head lashing from side to side. His lips were pressed together in a hard, grim line. She felt another orgasm gathering inside her, almost too huge to bear. She fought a scream as the nails of her right hand pierced the flesh of his bottom cheek. Blood welled in the little cuts.

He roared. The sound had no other name. A sort of despair rang in it, but ecstasy soon drowned that. His hips slammed into her like a wall of pure muscle, grinding, holding, as his first burst of seed shot from him. She hadn't known she'd be able to feel it. The hot, forceful jets triggered her pleasure: an orgasm so complete, so electric and hard and lengthy that it put all the rest to shame.

Best of all, he was clutching her close at last, groaning as he shoved the whole front of his body tight over hers. She felt all his muscles, all his hair and sweat. His mouth latched onto her neck, and he was licking and suckling it like a starving child. His hips shoved into her and shoved into her, spilling, shuddering, striving ever closer until she couldn't tell his tremors from her own.

His hungry noises were a song she wouldn't soon forget.

"Oh, God," he said, pulling suddenly from her neck. He touched her skin in alarm. "Oh, *God*." This time the exclamation was heavy with relief. "I didn't bite you."

Estelle laughed throatily, her body glowing from the immense climax. Strictly speaking, she wasn't convinced she'd stopped coming. Luscious little aftershocks were pulsing through her sex and clit.

"Edmund," she purred, spearing both sets of fingers into his thick gold hair. "You can bite me any time you want."

Edmund woke to the silvery light of a sky anticipating dawn. This was not a usual sight for him, no more than the naked woman who was curled up and sleeping at his side. He'd forgone spending all night with a woman since taking on his new family. Curious little humans didn't need to wander into their father's room to find his latest paramour. Smiling at the pleasant change in his circumstances, Edmund ran the back of his fingers up Estelle's long, smooth spine.

Estelle. Beautiful, miraculous, amazing-in-bed Estelle.

He could have cursed her for not having hung a single shade inside her flat. Curtains simply weren't going to do the trick, even if he leapt up and closed them now. He was going to have to leave her, and within minutes. Though Edmund's power endowed him with a certain immunity to the sun, the current human fashion for tanning didn't include broiling like a lobster in a quarter hour—or beginning to smoke in twice that time.

Unable to resist, Edmund pressed his lips to Estelle's shoulder. Maybe she would wake if he kissed her well enough. Maybe they could burrow under the covers, and—

A fullness in his mouth warned him to stop right there.

Belatedly, he realized he'd woken with his fangs half down and his cock more than half turgid. His erection swelled as the scent of her teased his nose. He was hungry in more ways than one.

You can bite me any time you want, she'd said.

He groaned in his mind and rolled out of the nice, warm bed.

Clothes, he told himself. Clothes and a note to apologize for leaving without goodbyes. He hastened to her living room to find the first. The sooner he got out of here, the better . . . and not only on the sun's account.

He curled his lip at whatever imp of Satan had inspired her to speak those words. How nice to be given permission to perform an act he'd been fighting for eleven years! Edmund's branch of the *upyr* had rules. If a mortal refused their bite, they had to respect the decision. Of course, the mortal had to know there *was* something to refuse, information few among his kind cared to volunteer.

Auriclus's children weren't exempt from enjoying the traditional vampire meal. Human blood offered pleasures no other food could equal. It strengthened them more than sustenance taken by their wolves, and it was—generally speaking—erotically enjoyable.

You can bite me any time you want.

His cock almost refused to be shoved into his trousers as he remembered her purring that.

You can bite—

"Enough," he said quietly.

Wincing, he drew his zip tab carefully up. Incredible discomfort—not to mention moral issues—aside, he couldn't be sorry he'd bedded Estelle. He fully intended to keep bedding her for as long and as frequently as she welcomed him. He couldn't deny, however, that restraining his desire to savor *all* her charms was going to be hell on him.

He remembered the note at the last instant, dashing it off and dropping it by her pillow in a burst of speed she never woke to see.

Dearest Estelle,

    Thank you for an evening I'll remember all my life. I hope your dreams were as sweet as mine.

    Please forgive the early departure. I had a class to prepare for. I await only your permission to repeat the pleasures we shared last night.

My utmost respect,
Edmund Fitz Clare

Estelle ran her fingers across the exquisite calligraphic script. As mash notes went, it lacked a little in the "love forever" department. On the other hand, considering Estelle shouldn't have been sharing her bed with any man before marriage, maybe "my utmost respect" struck exactly the right tone.

She laughed aloud to the empty bedroom, unable to be vexed with him. Her body felt wonderful: relaxed, rested, and quite deliciously womanly. Grinning, she reread the line where he said he awaited only her permission to do it all again.

She flopped back against the pillows and stretched her toes. How surreal this was! She'd slept with the professor. She'd had sex with him, to be precise, and the experience had surpassed, to a mind-boggling degree, all her fantasies. She had to fan her face just remembering the things he'd done.

Estelle hadn't ever dreamed she'd say it, but Sally's father was a tiger in the sack.

She couldn't have been more surprised if she'd walked out her front door and found herself in a Dali painting, where formerly everyday objects had been transformed into dreamscapes. Edmund Fitz Clare had been her everyday object. What he was now, she couldn't venture to say.

But that question paled beside practical considerations. For the first time this November, the day had dawned sunny. Her beautiful bay window flooded the room with light. She and Edmund had been so engrossed in each other, they'd forgotten to close the curtains—not exactly appropriate when one was sleeping nude! Clearly, if she was going to entertain a lover, she needed more substantial window coverings.

The City

❧❧❧❧❧

Nim Wei sensed Edmund's approach the moment he entered her tunnels. Centuries had passed since she'd bitten his mortal neck. Nonetheless, the bond she'd forged with him still held. His scent, his taste were as familiar as her own. Not even his being changed by another elder had eradicated her attunement to the essence that was him.

Fortunately for her pride, her former lover had no idea of this.

She dismissed the lawyer she'd been consulting about the acquisition of a property in Spain and returned to her own quarters. Her rooms were her sanctuary: rich, dark, grand yet intimate. She liked to think of them as a cross between a church and a seraglio. Polished black granite formed their groined arches and doorways, while tapestries in jewel-bright colors defied the march of centuries. Her power was responsible for that. Her power kept the signs of age from all these furnishings.

Nim Wei swiftly changed her clothes, fluffed the pillows on the medieval-style bishop's chairs, and poured herself

a glass of blood-spiked French Cabernet. Her kind could
drink undiluted wine, but preferred that it have a kick. Both
halves of this vintage were nice; both were French, for that
matter. She was lounging by the fire, seductive in her long-
sleeved, low-cut black velvet gown, when Edmund burst
through the door.

He had an interesting burden caught in his grip.

Her honor guard for the night, a delightful curly-haired
vampire named Giuseppe, hung unconscious by the scruff
of his neck. Nim Wei was glad to see Edmund had been
obliged to fight his way to her, but less glad to note how
forcefully his beauty could still strike her. Anger had
always improved his looks. From the way her body was
responding, he was very angry now.

Without bothering to greet her, he dragged Giuseppe
onto her Turkish carpet and dropped him, face-first, with
an unapologetic thunk.

He made her wish she'd invited the talented Italian in;
let Edmund walk in on that tableau instead.

"We need to talk," he said, his voice excitingly harsh.

Nim Wei smiled over her wineglass. "You only had to
send a note. I wouldn't have barred the door."

He stared at her, disbelief warring with his rage. "What
the hell is wrong with you? It's been five hundred years
since you and I slept together. Don't you think it's a bit
ridiculous to be attacking the woman I'm bedding now?"

Nim Wei's heart began beating very carefully. She set
her goblet on the dark carved table beside her chair. "It
would be ridiculous, if it were true."

"Your scent was all over those men," he snarled, his
hands fisted at his sides. "The men who tried to kill Estelle
were your servants."

"Calm yourself," she said softly. "You are very close to
crossing a line."

His image disappeared from in front of her. He was

rushing her. Attacking. The presumption astonished her, so much so that he managed to grab her neck and slam her up into the black fireplace surround. Lifted off her feet, the carving of a struggling slave dug into her back. Edmund's face was barely recognizable, his fangs run out, his blue eyes afire.

"Touch her again," he said, "and you die."

She hadn't worn long sleeves for nothing. She pressed the point of the knife she'd slipped from her forearm sheath through the second buttonhole of his tweed waistcoat. The hilt was silver, but the blade was iron. Edmund grunted as it pricked him but did not let go.

"Edmund," she said as calmly as she could. "You'd be wise to set me down."

"Promise me you won't harm Estelle."

"Edmund, it would break my unbeating heart to kill you, but if you force me, I will."

His grip tightened on her throat. She was an elder and greater in power than he, but for an instant, she thought he might succeed in snapping her neck out of sheer anger. His eyes glittered with emotion, their rims gone red. Nim Wei very much doubted those tears had risen at the thought of destroying her. They'd risen for Estelle, for the woman he was accusing her of attacking.

"Think of your family," she said, knowing his mortal brood were a weakness for him. "Would they want you to kill a woman on a suspicion?"

He lowered her reluctantly. To her dismay, she was shaking when her feet touched the ground. If she'd been alone, she would have rubbed her abraded neck. To give herself time to mask the reaction, she poured a second glass of wine and held it out to him. "Why don't you tell me what this is about?"

"As if you didn't know!"

"Humor me. In case I am innocent."

He frowned at her, then took the goblet and tossed its contents back. "*Jesu*," he coughed. "How much blood did you put in that?"

At least he didn't pretend he was too goody-goody to enjoy it. She smiled and gestured him to her high-backed chair's partner. He sat with the same reluctance that he'd ceased strangling her. She waited for the story, and he told it: the young mortal he'd quite obviously fallen in love with, the attempt on her life at Harrods, the human servants who reeked of Nim Wei. She recognized the men's description as those she'd found gutted outside her tunnel door.

"Please," he finished, "for the sake of whatever you used to feel for me, leave this woman alone."

Nim Wei stiffened at the cold slap of shock. He still believed she was responsible, though she'd heard him out and had refrained from killing him herself! He believed she was that childish, that conscienceless, and—hardest of all to swallow—that much in love with him. He'd always believed the worst of her, and perhaps some of what he believed was true. That, however, didn't keep her pride from rushing like ice water through her veins.

She gripped the lions heads at the ends of her chair arms, curling her fingers into their mouths so she could rise smoothly. "I see I shouldn't waste my breath trying to convince you."

"Nim Wei—"

"Do *not* repeat yourself," she warned. "You have insulted me in too many ways to count. I assure you, you will not find killing me—despite your wild declarations—quite as easy a feat."

A flicker of doubt crossed his angry features, satisfying but far from sufficient recompense. "Forgive me if I've—"

"Leave," she ordered, pointing toward the door. "Before I forget the respect I owe your brother, Aimery."

That insulted him, as she'd known it would. Prideful

soul that he was, he hadn't taken his younger brother's rise to power easily.

"As you wish," he said, offering her a belated bow.

Her fangs were throbbing with irritation by the time he left.

"Frank!" she roared with both voice and mind. The big German vampire was her head of security and had just the deviousness she required. He'd help her sort this stupid tangle out, help her discover who among her people had the temerity to try to set her at odds with Edmund Fitz Clare.

She paced back and forth in front of the fire as she waited for him to answer her summons, her body heating with more than one sort of frustration.

Frank could help her with that as well. The man was hung like a stallion, and twice as eager in bed, especially when she added a lash of pain to the mix. Stopping, Nim Wei tapped her nails against folded arms. Frank had better be prepared to prove himself tonight. He had a good deal to make up for, considering how easily Edmund had breached her private rooms.

Old boy, Edmund said disgustedly to himself. *That was not your finest hour.*

He'd headed out to confront Nim Wei the moment dusk descended, having spent the day waking intermittently to worry about Estelle. A vampire with insomnia was a marvel he hadn't thought to see; their kind required considerable determination to stay awake when the sun was up. Edmund simply had been unable to rest, knowing he hadn't guaranteed Estelle's safety yet.

You haven't guaranteed it now, he thought, bending low to get through the hatch that led into the Blackfriars tunnel. Nim Wei was a short little thing; Edmund not as much. He was lucky the nestling he'd cornered in that alley had known about this door, and luckier still that it had been left unlocked. Had it not been, Edmund would have been obliged to find another entrance . . . or send a note, as Nim Wei said.

On the other hand, that might have been better, everything considered. The delay would have given his temper time to cool before he out and out attacked London's vampire queen. He rubbed his aching temples with both hands. Nim Wei had told him nothing of use at all, including whether she'd been behind the plot to kill Estelle.

He'd never trusted her, not completely, even in the early days. With Estelle's safety to consider, he didn't think he ought to start now. All the same, hadn't Nim Wei's hurt over his accusations seemed genuine?

He shook himself. Lesser actresses than Nim Wei had been known to feign insult. Blood still stained the concrete around this door, the scent naggingly familiar. When he'd arrived, he'd been focused on chasing down Nim Wei, but the smell *could* have belonged to the men he'd dragged out of Harrods. He knew the police hadn't found them. The newspapers would have said.

The wail and clatter of an oncoming train warned him to get out of there. He ran at near bullet speed to and out of the nearest underground platform.

He slowed again on Queen Victoria Street, only a block away from St. Paul's. Martin Walser had maintained a dead drop near the cathedral, where his small circle of agents could leave messages. Now that he was dead, maybe Edmund should check it. The MI5 director had played his cards close to his vest. Edmund wasn't certain how much of X Section business his colleagues were aware of.

His colleagues weren't around, in any case. London's financial district—"The City," as it was known—was abandoned at this hour. The pigeons scarcely bestirred themselves to coo as Edmund strode up the street across from the churchyard. Wren's masterpiece could be seen for miles, the graceful dome as much a part of Edmund's consciousness as the faces of his children. Though Nim Wei's passages had been a maze, he suspected the chamber where he'd found her lay directly, if deeply, under St. Paul's foundations. The vampire queen probably enjoyed the irony. In her long life, she'd seen too many gods rise and fade to be troubled by Christian ones.

Untroubled himself, Edmund stepped into the red telephone kiosk Walser had used for his drop. When he opened the hidden compartment beneath the phone, a message fell out: a tightly rolled piece of paper no bigger than a cigarette.

Since no one was about, Edmund opened it where he was. His quick *upyr* mind made short work of the simple substitution code.

ESTELLE BERENGER'S LIFE IS IN DANGER.
PLEASE ADVISE.

Edmund nearly dropped the paper in surprise.

This came from Graham. He recognized the neat block letters. Who was Graham leaving this for if he knew Walser was dead? The section director's replacement? And how could Graham be certain there would be a replacement soon enough to suit the urgency of this note?

Damnation, Edmund thought. What in Hades was going on?

On impulse, he lifted the receiver. The phone was tapped, of course, but Edmund knew how to disengage the switch. He did so, then gave the exchange directions to connect his trunk call.

After an interminable wait, during which he was humiliatingly tempted to bite his nails, his sister-in-law picked up. Her greeting came in Roman-accented Italian. The connection was clear, fortunately, only crackling over the line a bit. He waited for the operator to hang up.

"Gillian?" he said. "Is my brother there?"

"Edmund!" Gillian's cry of pleasure was as warm as her recognition of his voice was swift. "How lovely to hear from you!"

Edmund ran a finger under his collar. "I know it's been a while."

"No, no. Any time you call is wonderful. We know you're busy with"—she hesitated—"with your family."

Perhaps she didn't intend it, but this was a handy reminder that she and Aimery were his real relatives.

"Hold on," she said, her voice firming up again. "I think I hear your brother coming up the stairs."

Edmund heard a kiss and a laughing murmur: his brother greeting his wife in their palazzo. Edmund told himself Aimery *was* family to him, no less than Sally or Graham or Ben. Aimery was simply going to be his family a lot longer. Edmund's mortals were a treasure he didn't want to miss a minute with.

"Edmund," Aimery said almost as warmly as his wife. He'd learned caution with his brother at a young age. "I hope you're well."

Evidently, Aimery knew this wasn't a social call.

"I'm well," Edmund said. "But there's trouble in London I think you might want to know about."

He told him about Estelle and the attack on her, knowing his brother would hear what she meant to him without him putting it in words. He didn't spare himself in his description of his confrontation with Nim Wei. He'd been rash, and as Council head, Aimery had a right to be apprised. He finished by sharing his suspicions that Graham might have discovered what he was.

"I'm not sure how much he knows," Edmund admitted. "Graham has never been an easy one to read."

"Oh, Edmund." Aimery's sigh contained a laugh, but not a humorous one. "You couldn't have adopted a dog?"

"Those mortals needed me," Edmund said as levelly as he could. *I needed them*, he thought.

"Well, don't go bearding the lioness in her den again, even if you get proof she was involved in hurting your friend. I'd like to keep my only brother with me for another century or two."

Edmund stifled his own sigh at that. Elder or not, iron knife or not, Nim Wei wouldn't have been able to dispatch him easily.

"I'll be more diplomatic from now on," he promised.

"Good." Aimery sounded genuinely tired. "I don't need any international incidents right now."

They turned to speaking of world affairs, which did much to unbristle Edmund's nerves. In this arena, Aimery trusted his older brother's opinions. He might not always follow Edmund's advice, but he respected it.

"Be well," Aimery said before ringing off. "You know we all love you."

And I you, Edmund mouthed, because the connection had been broken.

He felt ragged from the night he'd had—and it was barely eight o'clock. He had a class scheduled for nine, but he didn't think he could face the usual sea of bright young faces. He shrugged to himself philosophically. Someone else could cover the lecture. He'd duck into his office too fast to be seen and leave the notes on his desk. His absence would be forgiven. He was popular, well published in scholarly journals. The more generous alumni liked knowing someone of his caliber was attached to the school. Over the years, the university had grown accustomed to Professor Fitz Clare's unpredictability—the price they paid for brilliance, or so they thought. Edmund didn't mind trading on that misconception now and then.

He wanted Estelle tonight, with a hunger that went beyond the physical. He knew if he simply held her, simply assured himself she was all right, the pain that had been pinching his heart would ease.

Bedford Square

❦

Ben's door stood open when Sally mustered the nerve to climb the stairs and look for him. She should have been reassured that he hadn't closed it, but the choice seemed too deliberate.

Nothing to hide here, it said.

Ben was reading on his bed, his back propped on pillows that were stacked against the head rails. A thick automotive manual lay on his lap. As she watched, one battered but graceful hand turned a page. Per usual, he'd been tugging at his hair, and now it stood up in sun-streaked tufts. His long, lean legs were crossed at the ankle, pointing up the fact that his feet were bare. His feet were long, she noted, their arches higher than hers.

Her body heated unexpectedly, causing her to grit her teeth. She *wasn't* growing aroused because of Ben's naked feet. She *couldn't* be.

"You going to stand there all night?" he asked.

When she jerked her eyes up, his were cautious. At least he wasn't hiding his feelings on that score. Sally cleared her throat and tried to force her fingers to uncurl. They remembered too well how silkily his private parts fit their hold.

"Estelle popped in for a visit," she said, a mortifying warmth welling from her sex. "Mrs. Mackie is making toad-in-the-hole, and then we thought we'd see a picture. Graham, too. He got home early tonight."

Ben stared at her, the steadiness of his gaze increasing her nervousness. Was it her imagination, or did his attention stray for just a moment to her breasts?

"You should join us," she said, her words beginning to tumble. "Mrs. Mackie will be insulted if you don't."

"Mrs. Mackie will." He pulled a face and looked away, which somehow freed Sally to shut the door and step closer.

"Ben," she said as his head turned warily back to her. "I know . . . what happened between us makes things awkward, but I don't want us to be at odds."

Ben's snort of laughter was bitter. "Sally, you and I have been 'at odds' almost since you learned to talk."

"We haven't! Or not only that. And, anyway, fighting with you is fun."

"Not for me, it isn't. Not anymore."

He wasn't joking. His face was too serious. Had she been hurting him all this time and not known it? Sally's eyes burned with shame. Estelle and the rest were right. She wasn't a nice person.

"I'm sorry," she said, turning away before her eyes overflowed. She fumbled for the doorknob, which her tears were making hard to see. "I'll leave you alone."

"Sally." Ben made a sound of exasperation and jumped from the bed. He caught her to him, his arms crossing gently over her chest. His cheek pressed against her curls. "Don't, Sally. Don't be sad."

"But I've been mean to you," she choked out. "All these years, I've been mean and unfair and wrong."

"It's all right, Sally. I've been mean to you, too, sometimes."

"Not as mean as I was!"

He laughed and turned her, and she couldn't help hugging him.

"God, Sally," he said over her head. "What am I going to do with you?"

Love me, she thought. *Forgive me*. Since she couldn't say those things, she snuffled into his shirt. His warmth felt wonderful, his gentleness. His hands were stroking down her back over her cashmere sweater, his heartbeat kicking up a bit behind his ribs. That couldn't help but get her attention. She tilted her head back to look at him. His thumb brushed a final tear from her face, his eyes troubled—for both of them, she supposed. Sally swiped a hand beneath her nose.

"You know," she said. "You smell pretty good for a grease monkey."

She'd meant to make him laugh, but a flush swept up his chiseled jaw. Evidently, anger wasn't all that fueled it.

"Sally," he said in warning.

He was going to push her away now. She knew he was. And then she feared they would never be friends again. With more desperation than good sense, she flung her arms around his neck and kissed him.

The kiss was like throwing up the sluice gates on a dam. Ben made a sound, low and throaty, and then he kissed her back, instantly voracious. His tongue was hard but skillful, asserting his right and his ability to do whatever he pleased to her. Sally wasn't inclined to contradict him. His mouth tasted every bit as enticing as she remembered.

"Sally," he moaned, his lips tearing free, his hands tightening under her bottom to lift her up and onto him. She felt him swell and harden between his legs, beneath his worn corduroys. The transformation seemed magical. Surely no woman had ever delighted in her power as much as she. Enchanted, she squirmed against him to feel it more.

Ben slammed her back into his bureau, but all she did was moan in approval. Luckily, her skirt was knit and easy to yank up. Her legs were quickly locked behind his narrow waist, as tight as she could make them. One of the drawer pulls dug into her bottom, and she didn't care, just angled her hips to get a better friction from the urgent rocking of his rigid bulge. They ground themselves into each other, making rough, hungry noises, pushing their hands under whatever clothes they could loosen. When Sally reached Ben's back, it was sweating.

Loving the evidence of his excitement, she shoved his shirt off his muscled shoulder and licked the salt from his skin.

"Sally," he gasped, his hand finding her breast and squeezing. Sally writhed as his calloused palm compressed her nipple, the rough caress far more pleasurable than logic said it ought to be. Ben couldn't miss her reaction—or remain unmoved by it. His next thrust rolled up his whole body. He groaned his need into her ear. "Christ, Sally, you're going to make me come in my pants."

"Come in me," she pleaded, reaching frantically for his trouser fastenings. A second later, she cursed. The metal hooks were stuck, lodged in place by the pressure of his huge erection. Ben's fingers joined hers to help, fumbling almost as badly in his eagerness.

"Yes," he said, low and urgent. "Yes, yes, *yes.*"

"Sally?" Estelle's voice called from the stairs. "Was Ben up there?"

Sally swallowed back a moan of frustration.

Ben dropped her like he'd been burned, the release of his support so precipitous that she staggered for her footing.

"No," he said, pacing a two-step path with his fists yanking at his hair from either side. "We are not doing this again."

Sally knew she couldn't afford to lose her head the way he was.

"He's here," she answered Estelle as normally as she could. "We'll be down in a minute."

Flustered, she shook her clothes straight and looked at him. Ben had stopped pacing to glare at her.

"You stay away from me," he said.

"Me!" She could have given him a hundred reasons why this wasn't all her fault. It required a heroic effort to hold them back—not that Ben gave her any credit for that.

"You're the girl. You're supposed to have more control."

"Well, I don't," she huffed. "Apparently."

Ben's face fought its own war, but after a few seconds he blew out a breath. "Just go downstairs."

"What about you?"

"I need more time to . . . relax."

Sally's gaze fell irresistibly to his groin.

"Jesus," he said as the slightly diminished hump swelled at least an inch. Sally's skin prickled like it was being stroked by electric wires. All she had to do was look at him, and he grew aroused.

"Fine," she said, reluctantly tearing her eyes from the evidence of her power. "I'll go down first. But don't blame me if I have to spend all evening with my arms crossed over my nipples."

"Sally," he groaned and spun away from her.

She shouldn't have said it, and she certainly shouldn't have smiled at his reaction, even to herself. She did, though, and for long enough that she had to wipe her hand down her grin before she entered the dining room.

Estelle wasn't home, which rather panicked Edmund, his heart pumping in his throat like a human's.

Pull yourself together, he ordered himself. *She's probably with a friend.*

That possibility was less frightening, though it did insult his pride. After what he'd faced for her tonight, shouldn't she have been waiting in her flat for him? Wasn't she looking forward to a reprise of the night before?

He felt quite the idiot when he found her eating some horrid sausage concoction with his own family. Her gaze found his the moment he stepped into the dining room, reading both his relief and his ensuing sheepishness with an ease that should have alarmed him. She'd come *here* to reassure Edmund of her interest. Amusement twinkled in her eyes, along with a warmth he thought would cause his heart to swell twice its size. As if to salve his ego, her cheeks colored beautifully when he smiled back.

"Toad-in-the-hole!" Sally exclaimed delightedly. "We knew you had a class, so Mrs. Mackie cooked Ben's favorite."

Bless his youngest. He could count on her being oblivious to the most obvious undercurrent. She looked as soft and innocent as a kitten in her fuzzy light blue sweater. Graham, by contrast, was looking from him to Estelle like a spectator at a tennis match.

"My lecture was canceled," Edmund lied absently. "Leaky roof in the hall."

"Today was dry," Graham said.

"Right. That's why the workmen are in there now."

Graham looked down at his plate. His expression was as stolid as ever, but Edmund could imagine the stew of anger and guilt fighting in his breast. He knew the boy loved him; knew, too, that loyalty meant everything to Graham. He must hate thinking his adoptive father was a monster.

I'm sorry, Graham, he thought, his heart aching. *I'd tell you everything if I could.* The impossibility of doing that was par for the course. Edmund was keeping secrets from everyone in his life, including Aimery. One person who knew something they shouldn't could bring down his whole house of cards.

"Mrs. Mackie fixed you a tray," Estelle said. "Something a bit more to your taste. I think she left it in the cold storage room."

"You should join us at the cinema," Sally said, her fork waving. "It's Busby Berkeley. You know you like him."

Edmund did like the American choreographer's silly musicals, somewhat to his chagrin.

"You should," Estelle seconded, which let him know what he wanted: that she was going.

"Very well," he said. "Finish your meal, and I'll join you before you go. If you like, I'll chauffeur us all in the Minerva."

"Yay!" Sally cried as if she were seven instead of seventeen.

The mention of the motorcar drew Edmund's attention to his middle son. Ben was slumped in his seat opposite Sally, a strange species of sullenness radiating from his form. Come to think of it, wasn't Sally's cheer a tad forced tonight? No doubt the pair had been fighting. Ben wasn't perfect, but he took a lot from his sister, usually with a patience Edmund marveled at. Proud of him, Edmund squeezed his lean shoulder. Ben didn't have an ounce of fat on him, despite eating like a stevedore.

"You all right, Ben?" he asked softly. "You've been quiet."

"I'm peachy," he said, clearly not meaning it. He shook himself and straightened in his chair. "I'm fine, sir. Just busy at the garage."

Edmund ruffled his perpetually messy hair, though the boy was too old for that these days. Sadly, Edmund knew he'd still want to ruffle it when it was gray.

"Good," he said, ignoring the prick behind his eyes. "Enjoy your meal."

He left them to his find his own. With any luck, Mrs. Mackie would have prepared a nice rare roast his wolf could enjoy. If she had, this wouldn't be the first time he'd closed the door and gone beastly in the cold storage.

The Imperial

The Imperial was Sally and Ben's favorite cinema: gaudy but comfortable. Families crowded it in the evening, but that didn't bother them. They liked to whisper comments to each other during the film, and the general noisiness made it less likely that they'd be shushed.

Usually they sat together off on their own, toward the front or back, depending on their mood. Tonight, to Edmund's dismay, they'd chosen to sit bookending him and Estelle, with Graham taking the seat directly in front of him. Edmund adored his family, but their proximity made him itchy now. He'd become too used to hiding the existence of his sexual appetites from his children.

Determined not to let all his hopes for the night be dashed, as soon as the theater darkened, he took Estelle's hand.

He smiled to himself when her fingers curled between his, amused by his own happiness. Such a simple pleasure this was. Human warmth. Human affection. Nothing could match its wonderful innocence.

And then Estelle crossed her legs, the faint rasp of her hosiery striking a match to his libido.

He clenched his jaw and ordered his eyes to stay on the screen, where a horde of women in bathing costumes were, for reasons unknown to him, forming their bodies into giant flowers in a deep blue pool.

Estelle crossed her legs the other way.

Blast, he thought. His touch must be arousing her. He had her right hand in his left, and flashes of her thoughts were shooting up the link. She was asking herself if he was hard (he certainly was then!) and remembering how warm and satiny his cock had felt on her tongue. That was disorienting, to say the least. He squeezed her fingers in the remote hope that this would shift her train of thought onto a safer track. Instead, she wondered if he'd fulfill his threat to kiss her clitoris, and whether she'd be too embarrassed to enjoy it. She hoped she wouldn't. The little organ was pulsing uncomfortably hard, and having his mouth there, suckling it as expertly as he'd sucked her breasts, would probably be a supreme relief.

Then she imagined him kneeling between her legs right in the cinema.

Edmund jolted to his feet as if a flaming pitchfork had prodded him, which—truth be told—wasn't far off the mark.

"So sorry," he mumbled around his fully erect fangs. "Should have used the facilities before we left."

Lord, what an idiot he sounded, but, "Me, too," Estelle said and jumped up with him.

Edmund groaned to himself. His cheeks were hot with what he suspected was a very human blush. More than his family was gawping at them. Too bad he didn't have the strength of character to fob Estelle off.

"Mummy," complained the child in back of them, "make them sit down!"

"Stay," he said to his own children, putting a mental push behind the order. "We'll be back shortly."

Despite his embarrassment, he kept Estelle's hand in his as they squeezed down the row and up the aisle. He could see better in the dark than she could.

"I'm sorry," she whispered as she hurried to keep up with him. "I couldn't sit there a second longer. Not with you next to me. Not when I've been thinking of you all day."

"It's all right," Edmund panted, his various sensual aches now at the stage he could only call unholy. He rolled his lips into a concealing line. He was having difficulty thinking as he scanned the Imperial's lobby, looking for the smallest scrap of privacy. The WCs would have been an option if they hadn't been gender specific. Though he could have cloaked them in his glamour, he doubted Estelle would accept that choice without question, and questions were bad right now. Questions added awful minutes between him and having her.

"Please," Estelle begged, surprising him. "Find someplace we can be alone."

He looked into her lust-flushed face, into her bright, trusting eyes. For a second, all he could think was that her creamy cheekbones had been born to be that color. His brain snapped back a moment later, and he had to wonder at what she'd said. Estelle was no wanton. Had the strength of his needs communicated themselves to her, or was their relationship bringing out some latent earthiness? Either option made him want to groan. Her thighs rubbed together beneath her skirt, her weight bouncing impatiently on her toes.

"A cloakroom," she suggested. "Anywhere. Just hurry."

He grabbed her hand and tugged her down the nearest corridor, striding faster and faster as the urgency that goaded him intensified. Maybe both their lusts were driving each other's. Estelle began to stumble but not complain. He was going to go mad if he couldn't take her. He was going to drag her to the floor and—

"Closet!" Estelle gasped, pointing.

He turned the knob too fast to ascertain if it had been locked, or if his strength had broken it. They tumbled into the dark space kissing.

"I'm sorry," Estelle apologized between his ravenous intrusions. His fangs were daggers. He was going to cut her any second now. "I thought I was going mad."

"I'm already mad," he assured her. The Imperial was indifferently heated, and patrons rarely took off their coats. Now he struggled to remove Estelle's hip-length Cossack-style jacket so he could touch more of her. To his frustration, the closet didn't provide the maneuvering room he needed to drag the suede down her arms. His own heavy chesterfield didn't help matters. The thing was big enough to be its own person. His foot clanged against a mop and bucket when he tried to move.

"Stupid coat," he muttered to himself. "I don't even feel the cold."

"It doesn't matter." Ever practical, Estelle was busy with his buttons. "I'll just open it." Reaching his waistcoat drew a moan from her. At once, she slid her hands around the hard swell of him. The pressure was so welcome, he moaned back. "Oh, God, Edmund, is this why you locked yourself away that night in my flat? Were you so aroused you had to pleasure yourself?"

He couldn't speak. Her fingers were massaging him, all the way under his balls. If that wasn't enough, he thought she might be implying *she* was that aroused, and it rather shorted out his brain. Her hands fell from him, and he blinked at the sudden return of thinking power.

His *upyr* eyes had adjusted to the thin strip of light that came under the door. When he saw what she was doing, he doubted his thinking power would last long.

"Oh, God," she moaned, wriggling her skirt frantically upward. "There's hardly room for me to lift my legs."

There was room, just, but they were going to make a racket bumping into all the cleaning equipment this closet held. Edmund doubted his concentration was up to mounting her *and* covering the sound with his power. At least they weren't kissing anymore. His whole mouth was humming, and he feared he must have nicked her a tiny bit. He closed his eyes at yet another insane-making surge of blood to his groin. As desperate as he felt, no-holds-barred copulation was all this was going to be.

"We could look for somewhere else," he panted even as he ripped down his zip. His cock sprang free without assistance, a thunderous creature too big for its own skin. It wanted badly to be sheathed in her wet softness. *Soon*, he promised it. "Maybe there's a larger place."

"No," Estelle groaned. "I need you to take me now."

Her fingers found the source of his madness, ringing his shaft and pulling the circle upward with sweet intent. Her right hand remembered precisely how he liked his foreskin played over his crown. Having *her* hand do it rather than his own—*her* warm, feminine fingers—caused Edmund's nerves to shoot off rockets. With a flash of necessity-fueled brilliance, he lifted her off the floor and kicked a pallet filled with who-knew-what under her feet.

"Hold your skirt out of the way," he said with the harshness of extreme desire. "And spread your legs. I've got you at the perfect height to slide in."

"I want to climb you."

"You'll kick things down, and someone will come. Trust me. This will work."

He hoped it would at least. He wasn't sure what he'd do if it didn't, or what she would, for that matter. She whimpered when he slid one testing finger inside her sheath, her sex so wet, so hot he could have screamed with frustration for not having his cock inside it that instant.

"Shh," he soothed, manipulating her firmly. "Try not to make noise."

Hoping to take her edge off, if not his own, he brought her to a quick, hard peak with his hand. Her gasps and contractions were almost too much for him. With the sense that he was about to go straight to heaven or hell, he tucked his crazily throbbing penis against her gate.

The orgasm seemed not to have calmed her.

"In me," she demanded. Her fingers dug into his neck as her stance widened. "Put yourself in me now."

There could be no waiting. She was ready, and he was dying. Despite the hardness of his erection, he rammed into her pussy in a single stroke. Ecstasy blinded him, like shoving his cock into liquid fire. Lord bless humans and their heat. Lord bless Estelle and her snugness. The bands of her inner muscles rippled over him. He almost forgot to stop her when she tried to lift her thighs around his waist.

"No," he grunted, pushing them down. His body was shaking, his need immense, but he waited to make certain she would obey. In the pause, her hand slid between them to clutch her mons, squeezing her swollen clit between two fingers. She let out a sound that was like a sob. When he brushed his lips across her cheek, he found tear tracks. She wanted him literally enough to cry.

Everything in him that could soften did.

Everything that could harden set new records.

"I'll do that," he crooned to her. "Let me take care of you."

He took care of her, but not gently. That wouldn't have done the job for either of them. Rather, he braced his feet and drove into her like a berserk machine, his fingers working her clitoris as strongly as he thought her human flesh could take. She was slick and very swollen, twitching inside and out at the circling pressure he was exerting on her pleasure's pearl. Her jerks of reaction were so violent he had to brace the door behind her with his other forearm, to prevent it from rattling in the frame. Keeping himself from thumping her into the wood was a true challenge. He knew she wanted to be shoved against it, to be decimated by every thrust, just as he wanted to be decimating her. At the moment, though, *up* was the only direction it was safe to drive into her.

He did that so forcefully he lifted her off her feet.

All of it—the obstruction of their clothes, the smallness of the space, the constraints on their positions—focused him on that one length of naked connection, where the hardest part of him lived only to pump and pump into the softest part of her. The nerves in his cock were painfully alive. Never had he been so aware of every movement, of every shift of pressure or increase in his partner's lubricity. Estelle's cream was dripping down him, and he could have sworn he counted the drops.

"Edmund," she gasped, panic in the sound. She, too, felt the intensity of this joining and feared just how powerfully she was about to go over.

"Bite my shoulder," he ordered as her pussy tightened warningly. "Otherwise, you'll cry out."

She cried out anyway, but at least it was muffled, her inner muscles clamping with amazing strength on him. Her contractions tugged his climax from him in a searing rush, the relief so overpowering it weakened his knees for a few heartbeats.

Estelle's hips continued to squirm.

"It's all right," he said at her involuntary mournful noise. "I've got more for you tonight."

He had more for her than she could imagine, his pace picking up almost before it had slowed down. He was in a frenzy for release, no readier to settle for a single orgasm than she was. He had to press her head against his shoulder to keep her from seeing what she did to him. He did sink his fangs into her collar a time or two, the tang of sueded leather a poor substitute for his drink of choice.

With his sixth skull-lifting orgasm, sanity returned.

It seemed to do so for her as well.

"Oh. My. Lord." The words gusted from Estelle, the exclamation more than he could manage. "Oh, Edmund. Every inch of me feels *incredible*."

He discovered he could go to his knees, after all, or maybe they just gave out. Their essences mingled strongly below her waist. His kind's emissions evaporated swiftly, but he'd shot so heavily into her that they were still running down the inside of her legs. The wolf in him longed to roll in their blended smells. Offering it a compromise, Edmund placed his kiss exactly where he'd promised to, where her silky, swollen pearl poked out from her nether folds.

The pulse he found there was delectable. He had to pull it into his mouth, had to tug it with a rhythmic suction and coax it harder with his flickering tongue.

"Oh, I can't," she said, but her hips were cocking closer, her fingers tangling in his hair with renewed interest. Edmund dug the tip of his tongue under her little hood, delicately teasing the naked rod.

"Oh, Lord," she murmured a bit higher. "Edmund, how do you *do* that?"

She made him want to show off all five hundred years of his cleverness. He brought her off twice more with his expertise, curling his thumbs inside her when she swore she couldn't come again. Edmund knew better. Edmund knew all a woman's trigger points.

When she came the final time, he had to rise and catch her before she fell.

Close to boneless, she rubbed her face across his chest. Her fingers kneaded his shoulders through his coat like a cat. When she said his name, it came out a purr.

"Better?" he growled back.

"Mmm," was her hummed answer.

"We should return to the others," he said, though he didn't loosen his hold on her. "We've been away at least a quarter hour."

"Is that all it was?" Estelle shook with a breathless laugh. "It felt like a really wonderful lifetime. You're the goods, Professor. I think you made me see stars a couple of times."

What she'd seen was probably his aura blazing out of control at his climaxes. He was fortunate she was inexperienced. Without that to help explain his various eccentricities, he'd have had to erase more of her memories than he wanted to.

Estelle had lost half her hairpins in the broom closet, obliging her to remove the rest and let her silvery brown waves fall free. Edmund smiled at her self-consciousness as she pulled her tobacco brown beret over them. It was a good thing MI5 hadn't wanted to recruit her. If she'd tried, she couldn't have drawn more attention to the fact that she was carnally mussed.

"It's fine," Edmund said softly, patting her arm. "You look lovely."

His assurance didn't help. Estelle's afterglow was well and truly gone. "What you must think of me," she exclaimed under her breath. "What they must!"

By "they" she meant his children. The trio were ahead of them, following the crowd out the lobby door.

"They'd be shocked," Edmund admitted. "If they knew."

"Graham knows. I'm sure of it. You should have seen the way he narrowed his eyes at me."

"They'll all find out eventually." At Estelle's expression of horror, he squeezed her right hand—not as dangerous now that she wore gloves. "This is no game I'm playing with you, Estelle. I mean to keep you, if you'll have me, and I'm only going to hide what I feel for so long."

"Keep me," she murmured faintly, hand to her slim, strong throat.

You mean like a mistress? he heard her think quite clearly.

"Keep you as mine own heart," he corrected, grinning when the flush he was so fond of stained her cheek. Despite—or perhaps because of—her conservative upbringing, the idea of being a kept woman secretly excited her.

"I'd rather the others didn't find out just yet," she said tartly. "I'm not used to the idea myself."

"You're getting used to the pleasure," he teased closer to her ear. "That part hasn't been difficult at all."

She frowned at him, which made him grin harder.

"Beast," she whispered.

"But that's the way you like me."

He was elated, and not half as concerned as she was about his children finding out. Of all his secrets, his adoration for Estelle was the one he could best part with. He didn't deny that his feelings and his behavior had been rash. The truth remained, though, that Estelle Berenger *was* his heart. Let the world know it, if they wished.

The decision seemed to lift his feet off the ground . . . until he spotted the slight, fur-cloaked figure waiting opposite the cinema.

Nim Wei stood alone beneath an omnibus shelter, diminutive as a doll, but not remotely as harmless. Her white face was a beacon within her hood of mink, her beauty like a witch's from a fairy tale. He could not read the black glitter of her eyes: whether curiosity or malice lay behind her watchfulness. All he could tell was that her gaze was centered on Estelle.

Graham was walking ahead with Ben and Sally. Prodded by the instincts Walser had prized in him, his head twisted back to see what had attracted Edmund's attention. His step hitched and then continued determinedly—an odd reaction, Edmund thought.

Did Graham know Nim Wei? Was London's queen playing some sort of game with his eldest son? Did she hate Edmund enough to make his whole family her target? Edmund found that hard to believe. He wasn't convinced she'd loved him in the first place. She hadn't acted heart-broken when they'd parted ways.

But maybe she was here to prove his threats didn't frighten her. Maybe he'd made things worse by confronting her.

Edmund forced himself to emulate Graham's example and resume walking. His neck prickled as Nim Wei's eyes followed. Estelle's hand tightened on his arm.

"Do you know that woman?" she asked.

"I used to," he said. "A long time ago."

Well, she's beautiful, Nim Wei thought, watching the woman Edmund had threatened to kill her over stroll away on his arm.

His Estelle was as regal as humans came, despite the spidery marking around her right eye. The odd stain glowed to Nim Wei's vision like an *upyr*'s bite. She expected humans thought it ugly, an unfortunate blot on the girl's good looks. Nim Wei sensed it didn't bother Edmund's lover. Whatever insecurity the mortal harbored came from other causes. Youth, most likely. Or inexperience. Both of which she suspected would please Edmund. To be loved by an innocent would make him feel he really was worthy.

Nim Wei suppressed a snort. As if Edmund's paltry sins were anything to be concerned about.

His little family disappeared around a corner, leaving London's queen to ponder whether she felt any the wiser for this intelligence-gathering trip.

Tottenham Court Mansions

Estelle barely noticed where Edmund was leading her. A storm was brewing in her heart, due in part to having thoroughly shocked herself. The remaining turmoil was thanks to the strikingly lovely woman in the fur coat. Only when Estelle spied the Minerva's long black bonnet gleaming beneath the streetlamps did she remember they'd parked around the corner from the cinema.

Sally had already bagged the front seat by the time the rest of them arrived.

Edmund opened the passenger door and tutted at her. "Back," he said. "The front is for guests."

"It's just Estelle!"

"Back," he repeated more firmly.

Sally pouted and looked at Estelle, probably waiting for her to insist she stay where she was. Normally she would have, but tonight she didn't have the energy. After a moment, Sally flounced out.

As if Estelle cares where she sits, Estelle's funny ear heard her say.

"Fine," Sally said almost at the same time. "But Graham can sit in the middle. Ben's always poking me with his sharp elbows."

"Whatever keeps you quiet," Graham said, his unaccustomed bluntness causing Sally to jerk her head toward him. Ben restrained himself to a quiet snort.

"Oh, just try to deny you're skinny," Sally snapped.

It was too late for Estelle to say anything to improve the mood. Silence seemed the wisest choice as she let Edmund help her into the seat and shut the door behind her. He'd done such courtesies for her a thousand times, though his hand didn't usually linger gently around her arm.

Inside, the Minerva was as impressive as it was out: rich, dark leather that never lost its aroma, fancy custom wood on the wheel and dash. Built solid as a tank, the car was nothing like the rickety Model T she'd first seen him in. Sally's father had a knack for investing, and his books did well for scholarly tomes. People who could plow through them liked his theories of history.

All of which observations were Estelle's sanity attempting to preserve itself. If she kept her mind on facts she could accept, she wouldn't have to face the ones she could not.

None of this is real, she thought. *My funny eye went haywire or something. I didn't just have sex with Sally's father, repeatedly, in a broom closet. He didn't just tell me I was his heart.*

Most of all, she hadn't laid eyes on his ex-lover.

She knew that's who the petite woman was. No man said he *used to* know a woman in quite that tone unless they shared a romantic past. Logic said Edmund had to have had lovers, even if he'd been circumspect for his family's sake. He was a man, and not in his dotage, and certainly blessed with good looks. Female students didn't occasionally follow him home because they admired his brains. Estelle had to accept she wasn't the only woman he'd been intimate with.

The problem was, how did she know the gorgeous creature she'd seen tonight was strictly from Edmund's past? She'd been so lovely she'd almost glowed, and the way she'd stared at Estelle! Cold as ice her dark eyes had been, as if she wanted Estelle to freeze and break into a million shards. How "ex" could you be if you stared at your lover's current paramour like that?

Oh, stop it, Estelle scolded as Edmund shifted into bottom gear and pulled the long saloon car into the line of traffic leaving the cinema. He shot a glance at her that made her think her expression must have betrayed her thoughts. With an effort, she schooled her features to smoothness.

She was being ridiculous. Edmund was no cad. And even if he had been, what right would she have had to complain? She wasn't sure *what* was happening between them: temporary derangement, chances were. Whatever it was, it couldn't be permanent. It couldn't even be public, no matter what Edmund said. Why, look how Sally had reacted to Estelle taking "her" seat! Estelle shuddered to think what Sally'd do if she became her father's mistress, or—God help them all—his wife. Graham was only four months younger than Estelle, hardly a candidate for a stepson. Edmund would turn himself into a laughingstock.

She nearly jumped out of her skin when he reached over to squeeze her glove.

"You're mumbling to yourself," he said.

She was mumbling to herself. That's how unhinged this whatever-it-was was making her.

"Sorry," she said, and turned her face determinedly to the view outside the car window.

The atmosphere did not lighten when they reached Estelle's flat on Tottenham Court Road. Graham exited the car as Edmund did, pushing past Ben's legs so he could reach the pavement at the same time as his father. Graham was red-faced and angry, though Estelle could see he was trying to control himself.

His efforts were undercut by the ham-sized fists he was making.

"I'll see Estelle up," he said with an unconcealed hint of pugnaciousness.

Edmund went as still as a statue. Estelle couldn't see him blink, he was so shocked by Graham's interference. She was feeling shocked herself. Graham was usually respectful of his father.

Of course, knowing Edmund was sleeping with his little sister's oldest friend might throw a spanner in those works.

"Your escort won't be necessary," Edmund said.

He stood beside Estelle, close enough that their shoulders brushed. His hands hung by his sides, fingers relaxed, his gaze supremely steady as it met Graham's. Despite his serene demeanor, Estelle couldn't help but think of two gunslingers from a Western readying to draw.

The mere idea made her blood run cold.

"No one has to see me up," she said, her heart thudding too quickly inside her chest. "I know how to work the lift myself."

"You should have an escort, and Graham can leave that to me."

Edmund's voice was eerily calm, and yet beneath that calm an even eerier growl seemed to trickle out—not a human growl, but an animal's. His eyes were as icy as the woman in the mink's had been. They narrowed on Graham's, actually driving him back a step.

Estelle had the queer impression that Edmund was *willing* his eldest to concede to him.

And then Graham shook himself like a dog, squaring off again with an effort that was painful for Estelle to watch. "Estelle is my friend," he said stubbornly. "And she's Sally's. It makes more sense for us to keep her company."

This time Estelle did not imagine Edmund's growl, low though it was. She couldn't fathom how his throat was making that sound. The primitive warning stood all the hairs on her nape on end. Oddly enough, it also set a pulse ticking hard and wet between her legs.

"Let me sleep over!" Sally cried, breaking the peculiar tension by leaping out and skipping around the car. "Oh, say I can, Estelle! It's Friday. We can stay up talking and drink cocoa. Graham, you can walk us up."

Graham and Edmund both gaped at her, but Graham found his tongue first. "Estelle needs someone . . . male to stay with her, after what happened at Harrods."

"What happened at Harrods?" Sally asked.

"Nothing," Estelle said, giving Graham a repressive look. She'd refrained from telling Sally the story because she hadn't wanted to frighten the younger girl, but Edmund must have filled Graham in. "Just a scuffle with someone who shouldn't have been in the store."

"Oh," Sally said, accepting this explanation. "Well, that's jolly awful, but Graham can't stay with you *alone*, no matter if you are friends. That wouldn't be proper. I think you have to have both of us."

"Maybe Estelle doesn't want company," Ben put in from the car.

"I don't," Estelle said. "I'm sure I'm perfectly safe."

"You're not," Graham and Edmund said at the same time.

Their expressions were identically mutinous. If the idea hadn't been ridiculous, she'd have said they were jealous of each other, that they were locking horns over her. Sally was looking between them, saucer-eyed. Edmund's daughter might be self-engrossed, but she wasn't blind. In half a tick, she was going to jump to the same conclusion.

"Sally," Estelle said, hoping to distract her. "Graham. Would either of you like to stay in my flat tonight?"

"Yes," said Graham.

"Yes?" said Sally less surely.

Edmund could only shut his mouth. Estelle bit her lip and wished she could think of something soothing to say that wouldn't give too much away. The set of Edmund's face told her he was very angry, his cool blue eyes hiding simmering flames.

"I suppose this leaves Ben and me to entertain ourselves."

His mild observation worsened Estelle's discomfort. Didn't he see she *couldn't* invite him up instead?

"Fine with me," Ben said. "No offense, Estelle."

"Oh, you'll have a lovely time," Sally assured him too chirpily. "You know someone has to look after the old dear."

Edmund's temper truly must have been short, because the glare he turned on Sally had her jaw dropping.

"I'll run and get the lift," his daughter said nervously. "Estelle, could I have your key?"

Estelle gave it to her, and she flitted off before she could be scolded. Edmund's attention shifted back to Estelle. To her relief, his gaze had softened.

"I'm glad you were able to come tonight," he said, his voice like velvet stroking her. "Please don't hesitate to call if you or Graham need anything."

She wanted to touch him, but she couldn't. Graham's arm was slung protectively around her back, heavy and restraining.

"I will," she said, her tone as gentle as Edmund's. "Thank you for your concern."

He smiled, then nodded a trifle sternly toward his eldest son. The knot in Estelle's chest eased. His manner was cool but not angry. As strange as the contretemps between them had been, it appeared to be over now.

"Take care of her," Edmund said and got into the car with Ben.

My," Sally said languidly a short while later. "The car was stuffy tonight."

Estelle watched her flutter the neck of her cashmere

sweater in and out. She was wandering Estelle's living room, running her dainty fingers over the furniture, bemoaning the absence of a phonograph or wireless. Music was what they needed, according to her, or a good radio play. She seemed to have forgotten she'd begged an invitation into this prison of boredom.

Though less vocal, Graham didn't appear any more content. He sprawled across her low streamlined couch, much too big for it and probably unaware he'd be sleeping there. The upholstery's tiny brown chevron pattern matched his hair exactly. What it didn't match was his brooding expression.

How did I end up with these two? Estelle wondered. All she'd wanted was some time to think on her own, *thinking* being something she hadn't done enough of since changing her relationship with Edmund.

"I haven't unpacked my books yet," she said aloud to Sally. "Maybe you could help me arrange the shelves."

Sally wrinkled her nose, but came with Estelle to drag the neatly labeled cartons from her back closet. Graham grunted and bestirred himself. Bad mood notwithstanding, no woman could lift anything while he was about.

"The professor would buy you a wireless," Sally said, watching with absentminded admiration as Graham hefted four big cartons all at one go. "I know the licenses are dear, but he has pots of money."

"Christ Jesus," was Graham's unusual response to that.

"Well, he does," Sally said. "Being rich is nothing to be ashamed of."

"The professor has already been generous," Estelle said. "I can save up for a wireless myself."

"Oh, you and Ben," Sally poohed. "Always saving up."

"Did you and he have another row?"

"No!" Sally said. "Why does everyone keep asking that?"

"You were awfully sharp with him tonight, and you

didn't sit together at the cinema, even after Edm—the professor and I left the seats empty."

"We're not rowing," Sally insisted, her cheeks gone pink. "Ben and I don't always fight."

They had trailed their pack mule, Graham, back into the living room.

"Sally," he said, dropping the cartons in front of the fireplace's built-in shelves. "The only time you and Ben don't fight is when *he* decides he's tired of it."

"Fine," Sally huffed, her arms flapping. "I'm a horrid, ghastly person who can't be nice to anyone."

Her theatrics tugged up the corners of Graham's lips. "No need to lay it on that thick. I'm sure you've been nice to people once or twice."

Sally spun away from him and pressed her fist to her mouth, at which point Estelle noticed tears glittering in her eyes.

"Oh, sweetheart," she said, pulling the girl to her. "Graham was only joking. We know you're nice most of the time."

"Most of the time!" Sally began to weep in earnest.

"What did I say?" Graham asked, clearly at a loss.

"No one's nice *all* the time," Estelle assured her, which—while honest—was not the comfort Sally desired.

"You hate me," Sally sniffled against her breast.

"No one hates you. We love you, Sally. All of us. Including Ben."

"Especially Ben," Graham added, trying to help. "Look what he tolerates."

Estelle knew this wasn't the right thing to say, but fortunately Sally laughed. She pushed back from Estelle and swiped her nose. "Look at me! What a silly watering pot. I'd better go make tea."

"Hot cocoa," Estelle urged, wondering how convinced she ought to pretend to be by Sally's instant recovery. "The milkman delivered this morning. Here, I'll help you find everything."

"I can manage," Sally said, waving her off even though she didn't usually like to be in the kitchen alone—some childhood bogey, Estelle thought.

"Do you think she's all right?" Graham asked, looking toward the hall where she'd disappeared. He was himself again, his knowledge that his baby sister was upset having blown away his sullenness.

"I expect so," Estelle said. "You know Sally. She's full of storms, but they always pass."

"Right," said Graham. One big hand scrubbed at his temple as if it hurt. "Estelle . . ."

Estelle's shoulders tensed. She had a feeling she knew what was coming.

". . . as long as Sally's in the kitchen, maybe you and I could have a private word."

Estelle looked into Graham's brown eyes. They weren't angry, just determined and concerned.

"Very well," she said. "Why don't we sit in the dining room?"

A wry expression flickered across his face. He, too, realized this was the farthest possible spot from Sally's long ears.

N ot knowing how to start, Graham reached across the corner of the dining table to take Estelle's hand. Though she didn't resist his hold, she looked wary. Graham was acting on instinct rather than a plan. He didn't think he could wait for MI5 to answer his request for help, not when he'd witnessed how far Estelle and the professor's relationship had progressed. It had been clear, at least to him, that they hadn't left in the middle of the film to wash their hands. Estelle had come back starry-eyed and tousled, while the professor had been as loose-limbed as a cat.

Graham shifted in his chair, not wanting to think about how they'd gotten in that state but unable to help himself.

His cock thickened warningly. Ever since he'd allowed his new handler to work her oral magic on him, he'd been seeing sex everywhere he looked, even in places it couldn't be—as if the topic were a splinter that had gotten lodged in his brain.

To his chagrin, his awkwardness was apparent. Estelle patted one of his hands.

"We're friends," she said. "You can tell me whatever you feel you need to."

Except he couldn't, not truly. *You're being rogered by a vampire, and I know this because I'm a spy.* That ought to fill Estelle with confidence, assuming it didn't outright earn him a slap.

Knowing he had to begin, he drew a breath. "Estelle, I hope you know I respect you. Any family would be lucky to have you in it. You're the absolute best."

This assurance appeared to be presumptuous. Estelle's brows arched up on her forehead, and she'd leaned back against the slats of her chair. Sweat broke out beneath Graham's arms. Facing superhuman creatures was easier than this.

He scooted forward to try again. At least he knew she was listening. Estelle wasn't the sort of person to dismiss anyone out of hand. "You don't know the professor. I know you think you do, but he's . . . he's a lot older than you. He has a history. He has secrets."

"Everyone has secrets."

"Not like this. I don't think it's safe for you to be serious about him."

This caused her brows to draw together.

"Graham," she said after she'd taken a pause to think. "Forgive me for asking, but are you upset about me and the professor because you're interested in me yourself?"

"No!" Embarrassment heated his cheeks. "I mean, I care about you, of course. You're a lovely woman and—" Maybe he *had* thought about her once or twice, but that had nothing to do with this—something Estelle would never believe, given how hard his hands were clutching hers. Cursing himself, he forced his fingers to relax. "My affection for you has nothing to do with my concerns."

"Cocoa!" Sally announced, rolling Estelle's tea trolley into the living room. "I put out a few biscuits, too."

Sally must have caught the tail end of what he'd said. When she turned her face to Estelle, Graham saw her mouth and eyes *O* dramatically.

Bugger, he thought. That was all this evening needed: for Sally to decide there was the smallest chance Estelle might become her sister-in-law. Estelle as a mother she'd hate; she wasn't about to share her "old dear" with any woman, but as a sister— She'd dropped a hint or two to Graham before, hints he'd studiously ignored. Even if he did think Estelle was a damned nice girl, he'd never let the likes of Sally help him along that way.

"Biscuit?" his infuriating sister asked, sweetly offering him the plate. "*Estelle* picked them out herself."

Resigned to probable months of just such heavy-handed comments, Graham took a chocolate iced and shoved it into his mouth.

Estelle's books proved to be the unexpected savior of her hostessing duties. In the course of unpacking them, they discovered Sally's favorite as a girl: J. M. Barrie's *Peter Pan*. Offering to read a chapter to her guests was a good deal easier than floundering about for safe conversation.

The Fitz Clares were a family of easy physical affection, with Sally the most demonstrative of them all. Estelle wasn't surprised when she crawled onto the couch and curled up against her brother's side. What did surprise her was how the simple entertainment seemed to soothe Graham.

Estelle had always envied the warmth he and his family shared. Only now did it occur to her they might have missed having a mother read to them. And maybe Edmund had missed it, too. Looking back, it had been bold of him to adopt a family on his own. His children had turned out as wonderful as they could be, but the wisp of a wish blew through Estelle's heart: that she could travel back in time to be a mother to the three of them, that she could have helped the professor in the brilliant job he'd done.

She turned the final page with her vision blurred.

"Oh, that was wonderful," Sally sighed, her blonde curls resting on Graham's broad chest. She was the picture of a child-woman, if a bit more devious. "Doesn't Estelle have a lovely voice?"

Graham rolled his eyes but answered in the affirmative.

"You tell a story," Sally said, craning her face to him. "I'm not ready to go to bed."

"You want *me* to tell a story?" Graham appeared dubious.

"Oh, yes," Estelle said. "Why should I do all the work?"

"As you wish. But I'm not sure Sally will like this one."

"Why wouldn't I like it?"

"Because it's about Ben, and how I found you two at the orphanage."

"Oh, I know that story." Sally snuggled back down and closed her eyes. "Everyone at the orphanage picked on Ben, and you saved him from being thrashed."

"Not exactly." Graham's eyes were also closed, but he was smiling with rare mischief. "You see, there was a reason Ben was being picked on. This orphanage wasn't the place it should have been. Too many children. Too few supervisors and supplies. Sometimes their charges slipped through the cracks. There was a girl, no more than four. Wouldn't speak. Wouldn't smile. Wouldn't even eat unless she was coaxed, and since there was barely enough to go around, who was going to make her? Ben spotted this girl and took her under his wing. Literally. Carried her everywhere on his hip. It was because he wouldn't let her go that the others teased him and beat him up."

Sally pushed herself up to look into Graham's face.

"Yes," Graham said to her unspoken question. "That little girl was you. Ben gave up half his meals so you wouldn't starve. Remember that the next time you accuse him of having sharp elbows."

"He was a boy," Sally said. "They probably gave him more."

"Perhaps, but as I recall, when I got to the orphanage, he didn't have much more meat on him than a scarecrow. I remember I could hardly believe he had the strength to carry you. I think he must have gone hungry so you could eat."

Sally stared at him and then swallowed. "Why haven't you told me this before?"

"I didn't think Ben would want me to. And it was a long time ago. What I remember most from that period is how grateful I was to find you both."

"Because you'd lost your parents, and you were lonely."

"Yes." Graham stroked her baby-soft hair as she subsided against him again. "Having you two to take care of made me less afraid."

"*You* were never afraid."

"Everyone is sometimes." His eyes lifted to Estelle's, his expression haunted.

She wanted to ask what was frightening him now but suspected she wouldn't like the answer.

"Why don't I run a bath for you?" she said to Sally, who always bathed at night. "Before you drift completely off."

"I can do it," Sally said. She didn't look at Estelle as she wriggled up, but Estelle thought her eyes were red.

Her own eyes were burning more than a bit. She'd always considered the Fitz Clares an extraordinary family, but that little tale was something else. She was having trouble clearing the lump it put in her throat.

"I upset her," Graham said once Sally was gone.

"I wouldn't worry," Estelle said a little huskily. "I expect it did her good to hear that. She's old enough to stop treating Ben like her personal plague."

"Those two . . ." Graham wagged his head and looked at her. He was leaning over his knees, a healthy bear of a man with the most decent face in the world. "Estelle, about what I was speaking of earlier . . ."

"Graham, I appreciate your concern. I really do. But Edmund has never been anything but good to me. Nor to you, if it comes to that. Or have you forgotten the part of the story that comes after you saving Sally and Ben?"

"Sometimes I wish I could."

His voice was so strange, so troubled, and it wasn't like Graham to be that way. Graham was solid and reliable—a dull dog, he sometimes said himself. Estelle went to him, kneeling on the floor so she could place her hands lightly on his knees. "I *will* be careful with the professor. And with your family. Believe me, I know the potential awfulness that could come from this. Sally's such a daddy's girl."

"It isn't that, Estelle. It's that he isn't *safe*."

Estelle could only squint at him in confusion.

He let out a long, raw sigh. "I know. You don't believe me, and I can't explain. Estelle, just try, please, try to stay away from him."

Estelle stared into the trunk of extra blankets and pillows that sat open at the foot of her bed. She barely saw them; she was too busy struggling not to be spooked.

What did Graham mean, Edmund wasn't safe? Why not say *he'll break your heart* or *you know you're too young for him*? Why use that word? Why say *safe*?

Estelle shivered long and hard.

The professor was eccentric. She'd always known that. But unsafe? That suggested something worse than criminal. The sound of his growl came back to her mind, the way he'd faced his own son down. And then there were her fuzzy memories of him rescuing her from the attack at Harrods. There had been a hint of the uncanny about that night, a hint that slipped away from her even as she tried to get a grip on it. She remembered a window exploding, didn't she? A man flying back when she punched him. She clutched her right elbow with her left hand. That had been *her* strangeness, but wasn't Edmund—somehow—tied up in it?

Hating her own thoughts, she grabbed the topmost blanket and pillow and hugged them to her breast. She was in no position to judge anyone's oddities. She had plenty herself. Edmund was a good man, with a true and caring heart. Determined to keep that truth firmly in her mind, she carried the bedding out to Graham in the living room.

"Damn," she said even as his mouth opened to thank her. "Forgot the sheets. I'll be straight back."

She left the blanket and hurried to her bedroom, where she realized she had a problem. She only had one extra set of sheets. The ones on the bed, which she'd been planning to share with Sally, had been used by her and Edmund.

"Blast," she muttered under her breath. She might not be the worldliest woman on the planet, but she knew the carnal act left signs. She'd heard the married women she worked with complain about "wet spots."

She stripped the bed as quickly as she could. Graham would have to make do with two blankets. She simply couldn't leave those linens on. Given how fast Sally's crowd sometimes was, she might actually know what the stains were evidence of.

"Estelle, I—" With her usual impeccable timing, Sally stuck her head around the bedroom door. Estelle spun guiltily, the heap of bedding clutched to her chest. Sally was wearing her bath wrap. "Estelle, what are you doing?"

"Changing the sheets. You're a guest."

Sally laughed. "That's nice of you, but you can't have

slept on them but a couple times. I swear I don't think you're dirty."

Estelle willed her cheeks not to flush. "Did you need something for your bath?"

"Oh, no, everything's smashing. I just wondered if you wanted me to take a *long* bath." Her brows wagged up and down. "Give you and Graham a chance for a tête-à-tête."

"Sally, you're barking up the wrong tree there."

"Am I?" Humming to herself, Sally pranced off to have her soak.

Estelle wanted to curse, but decided it was more important to shake out the crumpled sheets.

To her amazement, they were perfect. Not only weren't they stained, they'd wrinkled less than if she'd slept on them alone. Perplexed, she held them to the light and turned them back and forth, but the picture didn't change. These sheets looked fresher than the ones she'd stored in her chest.

"That's impossible," she murmured, a chill sweeping up her spine. She remembered Edmund spilling himself in her, remembered, too, how much of his seed there had been.

Then she realized she wasn't sticky, either.

She'd lost count of how many times he'd climaxed in that broom closet. Her legs should have been streaked with his emissions, her clothing stiff. Instead, she bore no more signs of a sexual encounter than if she'd stayed in her seat holding his hand.

That can't be right, she thought, her mind slowing to a crawl in confusion. She stuffed the sheets into her hamper distractedly.

She was misremembering, that was all it was. Edmund must have used a French letter without her noticing—as indeed he should have done. Estelle was no stranger to her mind playing tricks on her.

Despite her efforts, she couldn't squelch the feeling that the oddness of her and Edmund's relationship must run even deeper than she'd thought.

* * *

Estelle had the best hot water—better than they had at home. Sally sat in the steaming bath and hugged her shins. Lavender clouds rose around her from Estelle's scented salts. She should have been soothed; she loved bathing, loved the health and prettiness of her young body. Ben was forever yelling through the door for her to hurry up.

And she was forever ignoring him.

Sally pressed her cheek to her knee, the tears she'd been fighting beginning to flow silently.

He'd starved himself for her. He'd saved her life as surely as Graham or the professor. She didn't remember it, but she knew Graham wouldn't lie.

Her body knew it, too. Her body wanted to make it up to Ben in the most primal way. She wanted to take him into her, to shelter him, to pleasure him with all she was. Graham's attraction to Estelle finally coming out into the open could not take her mind from her desire. Instead, she found herself wondering what Graham might want to do to Estelle, and if Estelle would like it.

I'm bad, she thought. *Bad and selfish and probably a nymphomaniac.* If the others had known what was inside her, none of them would love her.

When Estelle opened her eyes, Sally slept quietly beside her, her body curled into a girlish ball. Dawn was breaking outside Estelle's bay window, another gray November day. She couldn't hear Graham or the other tenants, but something had woken her.

Then she saw it, a spot of rich, dark crimson on her windowsill.

She was slipping out of bed before she knew it. A single rose lay on the painted wood, beads of mist sparkling like diamonds on its velvety red petals. Its thorns were stripped. It must have come from a greenhouse.

From Edmund, she thought, heating from her center out at the thought of him. A tiny shiver followed the rolling wave of warmth. She was on the fifth floor here, and the outer door was latched.

If this rose was from Edmund, how the devil had he delivered it?

The City of London Nest

***

"Why didn't Fitz Clare kill her?" Li-Hua demanded. "Doesn't he truly love that mortal? We left him all the evidence he needed to blame Nim Wei. Those were *her* men we set on his lover. The queen's supposed to be dead."

She knew her voice was wild, but she didn't care. One of the few benefits of living in the central London nest was that the walls were thick. Frank's walls were, at any rate. Thanks to his position as Nim Wei's chief of security, his apartment comprised ten rooms. Li-Hua had a meager two, yet another slap to her immortal face. Frank had done his best to console her over the years. He was older than she and had money; most *upyr* learned to accumulate riches. For her sake, he'd turned his quarters into a Victorian treasure house, crammed with the prizes she had coveted when she was alive. He'd even enslaved a painter to decorate his faux windows with Mayfair scenes. Though the human had been skilled, the effect couldn't measure up to the real thing.

Nothing would measure up to being her own mistress.

"Maybe Fitz Clare wasn't powerful enough to kill her," Frank said.

While she paced, he lay on the bench to her baby grand, one foot planted on the cushion and one on the patterned Turkey red carpet. He wore fancy dress black trousers, but his big chest was bare. His hands were folded calmly on his flat belly. Their queen had left bruises there when she'd fucked him. They'd healed, of course, just not in Li-Hua's mind. She knew Frank had enjoyed the sex. Couldn't help it, truth be told. Their queen knew every trick there was to pleasuring a man.

Tonight, she'd used them on Frank for at least an hour.

Li-Hua looked away from him. "Fitz Clare is nearly an elder. He should be one already. His brother reached that level ages ago: his *younger* brother."

"His half brother," Frank corrected. "Perhaps their slightly different bloodlines affected the results."

"Lucius White changed Edmund. He's the most powerful *upyr* the shapechangers have."

"The most powerful *upyr* any of us have," Frank agreed. "But, unfortunately for our purposes, a wholehearted pacifist."

Li-Hua dug her nails into the dark-stained wood of Frank's mantelpiece, leaving deep half-moon marks. "I know Nim Wei found a method to prevent her get from absorbing her power when they're changed. It's no accident that her nests have so few elders. She doesn't want us making our own children."

"Perhaps, but it's pointless to be upset about what can't be altered yet. We knew we might have to wait for Fitz Clare to involve his brother. Together, they're more than strong enough to defeat our queen."

"And if she discovers what we're up to in the meantime?"

"She won't," Frank said, an assurance Li-Hua didn't put any more stock in than he did. Nim Wei hadn't gotten where she was by failing to sniff out her enemies.

"We have to push harder," she said. "Get Fitz Clare off the mark. You and I both know the longer this takes, the greater danger we'll be in."

The piano bench creaked as Frank sat up. "Our queen followed Fitz Clare and his family to the cinema tonight."

"You didn't tell me that!"

Li-Hua had spun to him in surprise. Frank smiled devilishly, his noble, golden beauty squeezing her heart. The tips of his fangs pushed over his lower lip, this evidence of his excitement exciting her. "Graham Fitz Clare caught a glimpse of her. I think for a moment he thought she was you. Edmund saw the whole thing."

"Did he?" Li-Hua's blood began to move. "Maybe we can use that."

"Maybe we can." Frank's hands were on his trousers, slipping the metal fastenings free, pulling the dark cloth open as his erection rose. Li-Hua licked her own lengthening teeth as his many inches began to stretch. His veins were swelling, blue as ink beneath his pale skin. "Why don't you play for me? You know Rachmaninoff helps you think."

Feigning innocence, Li-Hua stuck one fingertip in her mouth. "Where will I sit? You're taking up all the room."

"I have a spot, my love. A special spot. If you rub it just a little, I think it will grow big enough."

"I think your 'spot' might distract me from my playing."

"Then I'll have to punish you, won't I?"

He caught her wrist, tugging her into the space between the bench and the piano, twirling her to face the instrument with a knowing smile. Her thin silk robe was no barrier to his hands, no barrier to anything. She moaned as he pulled her slowly onto his lap, facing away from him. The slightest shift of her hips allowed his immense erection to spear into her. He didn't need rubbing, after all. Sinking down on him took a good, long time.

A faint tremor shook him once he was in, his desire rising faster than his control. Li-Hua's response to that was smug. For all their ruler's erotic talents, she wagered Nim Wei didn't make Frank shake.

"Don't jostle me," she cautioned, squirming just a little as her fingers settled on the keys.

"Never, my pear blossom," Frank promised.

He would, though. Frank was a man whose lusts rode him hard, a trait their queen had never been shy of exploiting. Even now he was dragging his fangs in longing up and down her neck. The muscles of his thighs bunched beneath the smooth cloth of his trousers.

"Shall I pretend I'm performing for my old audience?"

"I'd like that," Frank said, his cock pulsing thickly inside her. "I like remembering how we met. You were the loveliest human I'd ever seen. Up on that concert stage, an entire orchestra waiting on you. You reminded me of a flame burning in the dark."

"You'd have to stay very still," she cautioned him throatily. "Otherwise, the audience will see you're giving me more than a place to sit. They'll see your trousers are open. We can't have that whole crowd of people knowing your big, hard cock is shoved into me."

She'd always drawn crowds when she was alive. They'd come for the novelty of a pretty Oriental woman playing Tchaikovsky. They'd come back because her talent was much more than a parlor trick. Ironically, one of Nim Wei's first acts after changing her was to bar Li-Hua from public performance. The queen said she hadn't the skill to pass as human. Li-Hua suspected Nim Wei was jealous of the adoration she'd inspired. In fifty years, she hadn't lifted the ban.

But that was neither here nor there. Frank growled

into her ear, every bit as titillated by this scenario as she'd hoped.

"I'll try not to give myself away, love. And if I fail . . ." He tightened his buttocks so that his hardness pressed deeper. "If I fail, you have my permission to punish me."

Café de Paris

All weekend, Graham and Sally stuck as close as shadows to Estelle, refusing to return home for so much as a change of clothes. They rung Ben up instead and had him deliver them.

"What flea got in their ears?" he asked from Estelle's threshold.

Estelle was only free to shrug. Graham and Sally were in the kitchenette heating soup. Estelle was certain the attack at Harrods had been a freak occurrence, the result of being in the wrong place at the wrong time. Edmund's old girlfriend aside, there wasn't a reason in the world for anyone to wish her harm.

"You know—" Ben lowered his voice as he handed over the satchel. "I wouldn't mind if the professor was sweet on you, assuming that's what's behind my siblings' sudden desire to imitate guard dogs. I think you'd make a darling mum."

Estelle was startled into snorting, which inspired Ben to wink and start whistling "Love Is the Sweetest Thing" as he soft-shoed back to the lift. Nice as his endorsement was, Estelle wasn't comfortable with it.

Given the company she was keeping, she'd never been so happy to return to work as that Monday. For one thing, Graham and Sally had run through her entire supply of tinned meals. For another, she was ready to be alone. Suspecting Graham would be lying in wait outside the Underground after work, she took a taxi home. Once she arrived, her flat surrounded her in silence. The relief was so great she simply dropped her coat onto a chair and closed her eyes where she stood.

This peace was what she'd gotten her own place for.

"Hm," said a voice that couldn't have shocked her more if it had materialized out of thin air. She hadn't had any sense someone was there. "You don't appear to be in the mood for company."

"Edmund," she breathed, all heat and vibrato.

He leaned, smiling and arms crossed, against the entrance to the hall that ran to her bedroom. Edmund probably didn't want people to know, but Estelle thought he harbored a touch of vanity about his wardrobe. His clothes always seemed a bit more tailored than others' did, a bit more costly. Tonight he'd outdone himself. He was dressed in elegant evening attire she hadn't known he owned: boiled white shirt, bow tie, dinner jacket with a long white scarf draped around its black lapels. He looked tall and lean and absurdly dashing, his artist-long hair gleaming like a golden pelt where it brushed the wide, straight line of his shoulders.

Her body took exactly two seconds to decide solitude was not the prize it wanted most.

"Well, that's better." Edmund's eyes seemed to glow as he read the change in her expression. He pushed off from the wall and prowled toward her. "Perhaps I *can* persuade you to go out with me tonight."

He stood before her, his scent as dark and cool as a forest. Drawn like magnets, Estelle's hands slipped up the hardness of his chest. He wet his lips and looked down at her. As easy as that, Estelle melted.

"I wanted to call you," she said.

"I understand why you felt you couldn't."

"I thought all weekend about what we did."

"So did I," he whispered.

It was that whisper, that simple suggestion that he was as weak with desire as she, that had her knees giving way. He caught her elbows and smiled.

"Careful. If you end up on the floor, we'll never make it to dinner."

"I don't need dinner," she declared huskily.

"You do." His eyes had gone midnight dark. "And I have a need to take you there. I don't want to be anyone's father tonight. Not anyone's teacher, or anyone's 'old dear.' Tonight I want to be a man out on the town with a beautiful woman I adore. I've done that fewer times than you can imagine."

His arms were wrapped behind her waist, supporting her. Where their hips met, the ridge of his erection was large and noticeable. Estelle bit her lip against an urge to squirm closer. She'd played the sex fiend quite sufficiently at the cinema.

"I don't think I have anything nice enough to wear."

Edmund dipped her as if they were dancing.

"That's where you're wrong," he murmured against the helpless arch of her throat. "Assuming you'll permit me to present you with a small token."

He'd made her too dizzy to protest as he led her back to her room. A Harrods box sat on her bed, its presence more suggestive than it should have been. Estelle meant to ask him how he'd gotten in, now and before, but it seemed unimportant with her blood thick and simmering in her veins. With Edmund there, she couldn't hold on to the fears Graham had put into her head. She was simpler with him:

more body and less mind. As she touched the coverlet near the box, the folds of her sex felt plump and sensitive.

She wanted his long, hot length between them. She wanted him loving her.

"Open it," Edmund coaxed.

With shaking fingers, Estelle did.

Beneath the tissue paper lay the beautiful backless frock she'd been admiring before the trouble started at Harrods: the bias-cut satin she'd thought Sally would like dancing in. This version was silver instead of pink—to match *her* coloring, she realized.

"Oh," she sighed, lifting it up by its cool shoulders. The sleeves were mere fluttering triangles of cloth, but Edmund had included long white gloves to supply the lack. "It's my size. Oh, Edmund, how did you know? It's quite the loveliest thing I've ever seen."

"I'd offer to help you put it on, but I suspect we'd miss our reservation."

He made it impossible to do what she ought. Estelle dropped the dress and flung her arms around him, reveling in his pleased laugh of surprise. "I know I shouldn't accept it, but I can't resist."

"Good." He chuckled, giving her earlobe a playful nip. "I never want you to resist anything I offer you."

The light pressure of his teeth sent champagne tingles streaking to the base of her spine, where they pooled and tickled between her legs. She moved her head to brush his lips, to encourage him to kiss her. His breath rushed out at the invitation, suddenly hot. For a heartbeat he molded his mouth to hers, its firm, curving surfaces as smooth as the satin gown. Then he took her shoulders and held her slightly away from him.

"Wait," he said, his voice hoarse but gentle. "Let this wait for later."

"I'm not sure I can."

Light flared behind his eyes at her confession. "Wait for now, and I'll make love to you all night when we get home. I want to enjoy your company, Estelle. I want to dance with you and laugh with you and hold your hand where people can see. I want to woo you, love, like an ordinary man. Please don't deny me that pleasure."

When he put it that way, how could she refuse? She shook her finger at him nonetheless.

"I'll wait," she warned, "but don't think I won't hold you to your promise."

Estelle wasn't the only one who was going to have trouble waiting. Never mind this had been his idea, Edmund wanted her nearly to insanity. His cock was heated steel inside his evening clothes, his fangs run out until he dared not smile with anything but his eyes. The distance driving the car put between them only helped a bit. Estelle was turned to him in the passenger seat, her gaze admiring every move he made. Her arousal was preventing her from sitting still, and the recurrent hiss of satin shifting against her body might as well have been brandy poured onto a fire.

"Where are we going?" she asked.

"It's a surprise," he said.

She pulled her velvet wrap around her shoulders, its black a perfect foil to her glowing skin. "Like the rose you left on my windowsill? Someday you're going to have to tell me how you managed that."

How he'd managed that was by climbing her building's wall before the crack of dawn, a rather childish instance of showing off—though he'd been quick enough to avoid being seen. He'd wanted her to know he was with her, even if Graham and Sally stood in his way.

"A man should be allowed his secrets," he said mildly.

"I thought it was women who needed secrets."

"Not you. You've enchanted me exactly as you are."

She laughed, a mix of flattered amusement and disbelief. "Really, Edmund, I never would have guessed you'd kissed the Blarney stone."

"If I did, it was only to give me the power to compliment you as you deserve."

She laughed again, then tipped her head to the side to consider him. "I think I like you this way: relaxed and happy and a bit silly."

"Silly!"

"Silly," she confirmed, her eyes twinkling.

He turned the car onto Coventry, his heart light enough to float. "Good," he said. "I think I like me this way as well."

She sat up straighter when she saw where in Piccadilly they were.

"Oh, we aren't," she cooed. "We can't be going to the Café de Paris."

They could, of course, and by happy coincidence he found a spot to leave the car in across the street. He thought it would be safe there. On the sides of the neighboring buildings, huge electric signs touted Gordon's London Gin and Schweppes, keeping the area bright. A number of the ritzy locale's club and theater marquees also bore strings of fairy lights, the swags of evergreen beneath reminding him what season of the year it was.

"It's December first," she murmured, her mind following his. "Lord, where does time go?"

He tried not to think of that, preferring the pleasures of the moment to the worries of the calendar. When she slid her hand into his, forgetting them became easier. Her fingers squeezed his excitedly.

"I'm glad I let you give me that gown. This place is so fancy."

He was glad as well, though for different reasons. He saw none of the other well-heeled patrons as the maître d' led them to their table. Estelle had a tendency toward starchiness in her work clothes, but her curves slinked beneath the silver satin like a born siren's, her paucity of underthings delightfully obvious.

The plunge back might have been invented to torture men like him.

They were seated on the first of the café's two levels, adjacent to the dance floor. Two sweeping stairways led up to the balcony where the bar held sway. Between the steps' graceful curves, the orchestra had their stage. The musicians hadn't yet set up, but Edmund was looking forward to guiding Estelle around to their playing.

That pleasure delayed, he ordered wine, she oysters and filet mignon.

"I've never had oysters," she confessed, thankfully not pressing him about eating. The fewer fictions he needed to maintain with her, the happier he'd be.

"Do you know," he said, "not so long ago, mainly poor people ate oysters. They could dig them up for free and, consequently, rich folk wanted nothing to do with them. It was only when natural oyster beds were depleted that they began to seem more elite."

Estelle smiled at him as she tore a roll in half. "You like teaching, don't you?"

"Oh, Lord. So much for leaving 'the professor' home."

Estelle shook her head. "I like listening to you. Your students are lucky to have a teacher with your passion."

She blushed a little at the word, which made him feel better for having forgotten himself.

"What about you?" he asked. "Do you have a passion for typing?"

"Sometimes." Her face split into a grin, the expression wonderfully gleeful. "I'm really, really good at it. None of the other girls are as fast as me. Plus, I love working at Harrods. That motto 'everything for everybody, everywhere' isn't empty words. The store is a museum of shopping."

"I'm sure Sally would agree. Alas, the other kind of museum never interested her much."

"You've done a good job with them. You let them all be just who they are."

For a moment, Edmund's throat was too tight to speak. "Well," he said, after clearing it. "One hopes, of course, to live up to one's responsibilities as a parent."

"You're embarrassed." She laughed softly. "Don't you know how wonderful you are?"

He really couldn't speak then. She had no idea how sweet her judgment was to him. He knew he hadn't been the perfect father; no one could, and certainly not a man with the limitations on him that Edmund had. But he'd so wanted to raise his humans well, so wanted to redeem himself for all the times he'd let loved ones down. Temporarily overcome, he swallowed hard and stared at the trembling surface of his wine. He was gripping the stem of the glass dangerously tight.

"I worry," he confessed. "I know my behavior must seem strange to them sometimes. My sun allergy. My peculiar hours. They must have wanted a more typical father once or twice."

"If they did, they never mentioned it to me."

"Well," he said. "Thank you for telling me that."

She stretched her legs beneath the table to give his ankles a stealthy hug. "You surprise me. I wouldn't have expected you to have doubts. Here you are: handsome, brilliant, at the top of your field. You make me wonder what you're doing with me."

"Estelle." He reached between the glasses to take her hand. The scar around her right eye darkened with emotion. "I think you see me as others don't."

"I think I see you as you are."

"Then, perhaps, you'll allow the possibility that I see you as you are as well."

She held his gaze, her lovely gray eyes stormy. "The day you met me, you thought me kind."

He smiled, slow and warm, recalling the moment with a precision that likely would have shocked her. "The day I met you, in Sally's schoolyard, apart from the others with your nose buried in a book, I thought you had kindness in you. I *called* you kind to bring it out. Believe me, Estelle, I also knew you harbored plenty of resentment, jealousy, and sulkiness. I think I rather liked you for it. Those are traits I once—and maybe still—knew extremely well."

Estelle blinked at him. "If that's what you thought of me, why on earth did you ask me to look out for your daughter?"

"Because, as I said, I knew you had kindness in you. I expected you would enjoy being inspired to express it. It's been my experience that it's pleasanter to be kind than cruel."

"You trusted me."

"I trusted you, and you never once let me down. To the contrary, you've exceeded every hope I could have had for you. Can you deny there's very little of that prickly girl in you now?"

Her mouth was gaping. "That wouldn't be true if your family hadn't welcomed me as a friend, if you hadn't all made me feel valued."

"That's a two-way street, Estelle. We wouldn't be what we are without you."

"I haven't done anything to change you."

"You have. Your steadiness. Your patience. Your sense of right and wrong. They set an example without you saying a word."

She sagged back in her chair, her hand pressed to the pulse beating in her throat, inadvertently reminding him of other reasons he wanted her. "You think that highly of me?"

"I do. I also think you're a tiger and a half in bed."

She snorted out a wonderful laugh. The blush that rose up her cheeks caused her already shining eyes to gleam like stars. "A tiger and a half . . ."

"At the least. We have, after all, only begun exploring that side of your nature."

She smiled over that through her whole dinner, savoring the food all the more because she was happy. He pretended to eat a bite of steak to please her, but was content to enjoy her enjoyment. Even the wolf in him was satisfied. Oh, his body was still warmer than normal, his heart beating steadily, but her simple presence was a comfort he hadn't known he needed. He had her all to himself at last.

The only moment that could have been unpleasant was when the young male waiter came to clear her plates. With a French accent as false as Edmund's humanity, he expressed a hope that *monsieur* and his daughter had enjoyed the meal.

Edmund laughed, but Estelle's umbrage burst out as soon as the man walked off.

"For heaven's sake," she said, sotto voce. "Surely I don't look that young!"

"Love, I don't believe it was *your* age the young man was commenting on."

He knew what the boy had seen when he looked at him: a distinguished, silver-haired gentleman whose too pale face was creased with laugh lines. Though he couldn't be certain what Estelle perceived through her "funny" eye, he suspected it was closer to his real appearance.

"Even so," she muttered. "They should train waiters better here."

"Perhaps he meant to insult me. He may have been jealous of my cadging such a beautiful companion."

There was no maybe about it. The waiter had been broadcasting his resentment as clearly as the BBC. Estelle, per usual, was underestimating her effect on the males of her species. He knew she wasn't precisely insecure, but she did not by any stretch of the imagination comprehend her own gorgeousness.

Graham's attention to it had not escaped Edmund, the yearning looks he sometimes sent Estelle—looks his quiet son might not have been aware of. The looks weren't love, Edmund didn't think. Sex attraction, maybe, but even more, he thought Estelle's warm and caring side was what drew Graham. As the eldest of the siblings, he'd always taken care of the others. It wouldn't be a wonder if he wanted a woman who would mother him just a bit.

Edmund had stayed out of his way all these years, but Graham never made a move. Nor had Estelle encouraged him to. That would have posed a moral conundrum, but the pair were simply friends, as much as men and women were able to be. Now that Edmund and Estelle were together, Edmund wasn't going to step aside for anyone—not even to avoid accusations of robbing the cradle. He *was* robbing it, after all, and far more than these humans supposed.

Estelle opened her mouth to protest the waiter's rudeness, then let out her breath and relaxed. "You don't want me to be angry on your behalf."

"I don't," he agreed, loving her for how quickly she understood. "I want you to enjoy yourself all night long."

She was enjoying herself, more than she could ever remember doing. Being with Edmund relaxed her. She hadn't expected that. The excitement he stirred in her was still there, fizzing just beneath the surface, but he was easy to talk to—or not talk to, if she wished. If there were an awkward moment, it didn't seem important.

His eyes approved of her, no matter what.

With the handful of men she'd dated in the past, Estelle had always felt she was putting her feet slightly wrong. She was too bold or not bold enough, too smart or not smart in the right areas. She'd never just plain liked other men the way she liked Edmund. To be fair, her lack of enthusiasm had probably discouraged her dates' ability to shine at their best, but not a one of them had struck so many different sparks in her.

It was funny, because Edmund certainly had his quirks, but he was her ideal of what a man should be.

Once the café's orchestra began playing, he even danced like an ideal. One couldn't put one's feet wrong with a partner as assured as he was. The waiter's opinion notwithstanding, there were advantages to life experience. Edmund knew how to sweep a woman around—and never mind he was as handsome as sin in his evening clothes.

He had Estelle's gloved right hand in his left, while his right pressed with perfect, flat propriety against the skin bared by the plunging back of her dress. One long, warm finger was all he needed to steer her between the other well-dressed couples. To top it off, their surroundings were too posh for words, all gilding and velvet and diamonds sparkling in the light from the chandelier. The aristocracy came to the café to see and be seen. Estelle never would have guessed she could feel at home in a place like this.

Of course, it didn't hurt that every woman in the club was sneaking looks at Edmund. His female students would have swooned to see him now. The movements of his hips were rife with sexual implications, the princely way he held himself. Here was a man in complete command of his body—and he only had eyes for her.

"You're smiling," Edmund said as the rhythm of the music swept them into a turn.

"I'm happy. I believe this is the most . . . romantic night I've ever experienced."

He grinned, a flash of white almost too quick to see. Something about it sent a delicious shiver racing down her vertebrae. "You don't have to hesitate when you say that. I am trying to romance you."

She squeezed his shoulder for the pleasure of testing his hard muscles. "I have to confess you don't really have to. Romance me, that is."

"Oh, I could win you without it then? For as long as we both shall live?" He smiled at her gasp of shock, no teeth this time. "Yes, I have high ambitions for the two of us. I believe achieving them is going to require a bit of effort on my part."

He'd struck her speechless. *As long as we both shall live* was serious, and he wasn't the sort of man to choose words irresponsibly. She closed her mouth and swallowed. Edmund's eyes were sleepy and amused. He hadn't missed a step through any of this discussion.

"Something to think about," he drawled. "While you're deciding if I deserve you."

"If you . . ."

She couldn't repeat his words. She didn't have the ego. He laughed, low and male, and jerked her closer—too close to qualify as polite. His right hand slid smoothly up her back to cup her neck, the touch abruptly as hot as fire. His legs were moving between hers, their actions now resembling a different sort of dance. The ridge that swelled from his groin was quite apparent. Estelle felt her skin blaze with self-consciousness. Her sex blazed with something else, with cream and quivers and the pumping of her too eager blood.

Edmund whispered smokily into her ear. "Put your head on my shoulder, love. Pretend we're invisible."

"But I can feel your . . . excitement," she murmured back.

"My *excitement* is rather obvious," he conceded in an even lower tone. "And likely to grow more so with every brush of your gorgeous legs. I think you had better continue to hold me close, so as not to expose me to ridicule."

"Ridicule!" Her exclamation was a breathless laugh. "More like amazement."

Edmund licked a sensitive stretch of skin beneath her ear, his tongue sharp and flickering. "Are you amazed, my love? More importantly, are you wet? Are you perhaps wishing we could be dancing like this without our clothes?"

She saw the image before she could prevent it: them, naked, grappling to lock their sexes together in front of the gaping crowd. Desire sluiced through her in a sultry rush. Edmund's hand glided to the small of her back, which she knew was dewed with arousal. One of his fingers drew a tiny circle on her skin.

"I wish we were home," she said, meaning it to her bones. "I wish I had you to myself."

She turned her head toward his neck, her cheek rubbing the smoothness of his dinner coat. Some unsuspected instinct guided her to press her teeth to his skin. Edmund sucked in a breath, his pulse leaping suddenly. She bit down harder, tasting his sweat.

He stumbled and stepped on her toe.

"*Jesu*," he muttered, recovering his balance.

When she smiled at him, his fingers tightened on her hand. She'd shaken him, enough that a flush swept up his normally ivory skin.

"Very well," he said. "Let's see how quickly we can make your wish come true."

The car ride was touch and go. How she'd known to bite him as foreplay, Edmund couldn't say, but why her hand kept sliding up his nearer thigh was no mystery. His erection was a shuddering mountain in his lap—a mountain of temptation, apparently.

"Estelle," he gasped as her right hand gripped his shaft through his trousers and gave it a tight, slow pump. She hadn't taken off her long white gloves, and the image that presented was distracting, to say the least. "It's difficult to drive when you're doing that."

"It's difficult to see the state you're in and refrain." She'd kicked off her shoes already. Now she tucked her feet beneath her on the seat and leaned closer. "I want to take you out, Edmund. I want to put your cock in my mouth and lick it all over."

He was shifting gears to take a turn and could only groan when she reached for his waist closure. "Please, Estelle, we're almost there."

But her hands were quick, and in moments her head was on him, bobbing gently up and down, her tongue running in circles around his crest while her lips squeezed the flaring rim. Estelle was a woman with a powerful focus. Even in this situation, she was paying attention to what he liked. His thighs were soon knotted at the waves of pleasure, gears grinding as he fought not to beg her to suck harder and finish him. Nighttime or not, they were lucky the car was closed. The people sitting on the upper deck of the buses in the adjoining lanes would have gotten an eyeful.

"Estelle—"

"Oh, God, Edmund," she moaned. "I can't even describe how smooth your skin feels here. It's like it isn't even human flesh."

It wasn't human flesh; it was a hell of a lot more sensitive. His kind experienced every aspect of living more intensely than humans. Not quite sensible enough to stop her, he groaned as she sank again. She'd decided to dig her hand into his trousers, and was now cupping his drawn-up balls. The pressure she exerted verged on the lovely edge of too much. Streetlights wavered in his vision.

"Please," he begged, feeling his orgasm begin to swell. Lord, it was going to be a big one. "I want to save my first release for your pretty cunt."

He couldn't deny being sorry when she rose from him

and sat on her heels. She was running her tongue around her lips as if he'd tasted good, her eyes molten silver in her rosy face. That flush of hers was going to be the death of him.

"I think I like that word," she said with a small but seductive smile. "You have my permission to use it again."

The wave of lust that swept through him nearly stole his breath. "I have nicer ones," he panted. "I'd be happy to try them all."

For all he knew, he parked the car sideways at her flat—though he was smart enough not to touch her in the lift this time. She smoldered at him from the corner he'd ordered her to, her body restless, the scent of her arousal as potent as a drug.

"I'll unlock my door tonight," she said. "You look like you'd drop the key."

He probably did. He was trembling with need for her, beyond out of control. He should have let her finish him in the car. At least his chances of biting her would have been reduced. He didn't stop her, though. He didn't walk away. He wasn't sure he had the strength for it, and he definitely didn't have the desire.

"I love you," he growled when her door swung shut behind them. "More than you could possibly believe."

She smiled, slow and creamy. What little restraint he had snapped like a twig before she had a chance to put any sort of response in words.

He fell on her like the Vikings he'd sprung from, spinning her around and pushing her shoulders so that she had to grab the front of her couch or fall. The rational corner of his mind knew it would be better if she couldn't see his face when what was left of his glamour inevitably fell. Little of his human pretense remained right then. Her white-gloved hands were spread for balance, the sight of them undoing him. She was elegance incarnate, femininity consumed by lust—not to mention completely vulnerable to him.

Too impatient to use the zip, he tore his trousers open, cloth ripping like he had claws. He shoved the slippery silver dress up to her waist and kicked her legs wider. Her thighs were glistening with arousal, her sex ripe and flushed. Edmund grabbed his cock and steered.

The sound he made as he plunged into her hot, tight heat was dangerously close to a scream.

He'd forgotten the wolf in him liked this position more than a bit.

Estelle seemed fond of it herself.

"Oh, yes," she moaned, her hips writhing over him like a dream. She had muscles he wouldn't have expected in a typist, and her undulating bottom was a vision he couldn't tear his eyes from. "Oh, Edmund, *yes*."

He gripped the back of the couch, planting one knee on the cushion between her legs so he could keep the thing from tipping over while at the same time he spread her more. That done, he wrapped his right hand around her pubis. Her clit was a bursting berry slipping under his fingers. Feeling a bit too aroused by that, he gritted his teeth, squeezed her clit in its hood, and tugged it a dozen times. That was all it took for her. She came with a suddenness and a violence that astonished him.

She felt so good clamping around him that his lips peeled back from his throbbing fangs, though all they had to snap at was air.

"Oh, God," she said. "Oh, please, make me do that again."

Happy to oblige, Edmund set his feet and began to drive himself more solidly into her. He kept pumping her little rod, grateful for the delicacy his fingers were capable of. Her cries urged him faster, the rippling of her pussy, the welling rise of his immanence. *Big* didn't adequately describe his coming orgasm. They hadn't been at this two minutes, and he already hung on the teeth-grinding edge. With another woman, the force he used might have been too much, but Estelle seemed to revel in the strength of his thrusts. She came again, and he didn't have the self-control to hold back. The climax exploded from him in a spear of bliss so hot, so strong, he half expected to burst into flame.

He was lucky his wolf had its own instincts. It would grip a mate but not draw blood. Edmund had his lips tight to the back of her neck, his fangs pressed to it but not piercing. He was sucking the fragile skin between them, pulling her blood close to the surface. The flavor of her sweat changed as that blood drew nearer, his tongue helpless not to curl out and sample. As he furiously ordered himself to release her, Estelle squirmed around his still hard cock. His shaft twitched inside her.

He'd faded but not enough.

"Mm," she said, a lovely throatiness to the sound. "What you're doing to my neck feels good."

Oh, she had a gift for tempting him to do the very thing he had to resist. He didn't know where he found the strength to simply kiss her nape and draw back.

He drew his cock from her, too, then discovered he couldn't live without more contact. Her folds parted for his crest as he rubbed his burgeoning thickness between them, running it back and forth, back and forth, massaging the bump of her clitoris while wallowing in her warm, wet cream.

Estelle shivered and squirmed again.

He caught a flash of her thoughts: that she'd been wishing he'd run his long, hot length between her labia. Coincidence maybe, but it startled him. He wasn't certain how he could know what she wanted without reading it from her mind.

Her rather imaginative mind, truth be told. For a woman who'd come to him a virgin, she certainly knew how to dream things up.

"Tired?" he asked, his arms hugging her securely.

"Oh, no," she assured him, as he'd hoped she would. "I think my 'tiger' could stand another round or two."

Clearly, the world was mistaken about older men, though perhaps the women who enjoyed them were deliberately keeping mum. Estelle should probably follow their example. After that first desperate act of coupling—which she'd found embarrassingly exciting—Edmund had been as tender as he was untiring. He'd left her exhausted come Tuesday morning but very satisfied.

She only wished he'd stayed long enough to enjoy breakfast. He'd been gone by the time she woke, propping another perfect rose on her pillow as a parting gift. That was sweet, but his presence would have been sweeter. She could have assured him she didn't mind if sunshine turned him blotchy.

"He minds," she told the steaming surface of her tea, a pick-me-up she sorely needed this ack emma. "So you just let him have his vanity."

She smiled, fox in the henhouse, to remember how many reasons for vanity he had. They'd christened her shower and her bed . . . and her kitchen . . . and the polished floorboards in her bedroom hall. Her heels were still a little bruised from her efforts to dig in there. No question, Edmund had been wise to insist they go out for dinner. They'd enjoyed precious little conversation once they'd returned here.

You should tell him the truth, she thought. *About your funny eye and all that.*

She'd never had an urge to do this before. Mind, she wasn't sure Edmund ought to be thinking along the lines of "till death do us part," but considering that he was, he had a right to know her secrets.

St. Paul's Cathedral

❦

Graham swam up to consciousness in the foulest of foul moods. He lay in his bed in Bedford Square, with an erection the size of the Eiffel Tower between his legs. Its intensity accounted for why he'd roused. Unable to ignore the thing, he fisted it grumpily and began to pull. That felt good enough to bring him close to moaning. It did not, however, brighten his outlook.

What the devil was wrong with him anyway? He'd always had what he thought of as normal drives for a man his age, but lately he couldn't turn around without getting hard. There must be something in the water—or maybe his elusive handler had unknowingly flipped a switch inside him that couldn't be flipped off. Now, apparently, he didn't need a woman to excite him. Being alive and breathing was cause enough. He was certain things like this weren't supposed to happen to British agents, not without a pretty foreign operative nearby. Graham hadn't even had a sexy dream to account for this morning's prodigy. No, he'd been dreaming about the Underground all night, about searching for Estelle among the dark and twisty tunnels, while she ran stubbornly away from him.

No doubt Dr. Freud would have a theory about that.

Grunting, he rolled onto his left side and let his right hand work faster on his throbbing shaft. The hard, dry friction suited him perfectly. The sheets began to rustle, and he didn't care. He was still angry about Estelle ditching him, though she hadn't actually agreed to let him pick her up after work. Her resistance stymied him. How was he supposed to protect her if she wouldn't cooperate?

He'd tried to find her at her flat, but she hadn't been there, either. Reluctant to do nothing, he'd looked up an old school chum, one with connections at Scotland Yard. Cecil had been quite chatty with a few G&Ts in him, revealing that the Yard remained mystified by Martin Walser's death. As far as Cecil knew, they didn't have a suspect in the civil servant's murder. Cecil had heard nothing at all about a recent break-in at Harrods, or of two bodies being found on the grounds. Either the thugs who'd attacked Estelle had regained consciousness and walked away, or Graham's guardian had gotten rid of them.

From what he'd seen of Edmund's strength, that wouldn't have been difficult.

Graham's buttocks tightened with a combination of tensions, his left hand reaching unthinkingly to tug his beaded right nipple. He'd always liked the feel of that, but didn't usually indulge himself, because the habit didn't seem masculine. At the moment, though, he wasn't really concerned with what his hands were doing and—as a result—his body jumped at the chance to get what it preferred. Caught up in his train of thought, he hardly noticed his legs were shifting on the sheets, their muscles clenching and releasing hungrily.

He'd parted from his old friend Cecil slightly tight himself, which probably explained why he'd returned to

Estelle's flat to peer into her big front window with his spyglasses. He'd discovered her and the professor casting rather unmistakable silhouettes. Jesus, they'd been going at it like there was no tomorrow, a ruddy pair of minks who couldn't fuck fast enough—despite a perfectly good bedroom mere steps away. And, of course, Edmund *would* take Estelle that way, ramming into her from behind like the dog he was.

Graham's prick thudded in his fist, the fingers of his other hand giving his nipple a particularly brutish twist. He would have stopped then if he could; he didn't want the image of the two of them in his mind. Unfortunately, his body had raced past the point of turning back, demanding in no uncertain terms that he tighten his grip and wrench faster at himself. Two furious strokes were sufficient to slam him over the brink. Sensation powered through him: surging up his legs, coiling in his balls, pushing out his cock like a sledgehammer. He ejaculated in a great hot gush, the climax overwhelming him too swiftly to grab a handkerchief and come into that.

Christ, it was a good, hard come—pure, fiery sweetness shooting down the length of him, thick and strong to the very last contraction.

Graham gasped hard in the aftermath, trying to get the air to fill his lungs again. He felt far too good for comfort. His muscles hummed with relief, not only in his groin but all over. The sheets in front of him were soaked. Just what Mrs. Mackie needed for her next wash day.

Cursing himself, Graham flopped onto his back. He knew he didn't want to think too hard about what had just happened.

When his ears stopped ringing, he could hear Ben moving around the room next to his, getting dressed for work at the garage.

Work. Graham stifled another groan. He'd almost forgotten, but now it rushed back to him. His American boss was due in town today, which meant long hours trotting after him and little chance to watch over Estelle.

Damn, but he wished Nim Wei had responded to the message he'd left in the kiosk outside St. Paul's. He had to do something to protect Estelle, and he couldn't handle it on his own.

With thoughts like these, the physical relief that had flooded him faded fast. Sighing, he pushed into a sitting position on the side of his bed. He'd have to try to reach his handler another way—maybe through the newsagent she'd used to contact him. The strategy might or might not work, but it was better than sitting on his thumbs while Edmund drew his net ever tighter around Estelle.

The newsagent's was a small shop on the corner, down the street from Bedford Square. In addition to papers, it sold postcards, sweets, and common toiletries—the sort of items one might run out of and want to buy right away. A flower seller had set up a stand in front. Graham stepped past her big, fragrant baskets and into the shop's dark confines. The door creaked and jingled shut behind him.

The usual man sat on the stool behind the counter, fiftyish and stocky with a grease-stained cap. Per usual, he looked as ordinary as Graham himself. Graham fingered a packet of crisps on one of the shelves and decided on his approach. He'd come here on his lunch break. He didn't have time to be elaborate.

He waited for another customer to finish being rung up, then carried a copy of *The Spectator* to the register. According to its front page, Germany had plans to sign a nonaggression pact with Poland. Graham supposed that would please his boss. Arnold Anderson said he sometimes wished his own country handled its riffraff with as firm a hand as *der Führer*.

"Excuse me," Graham said to the man he presumed was the shop owner.

The man looked up, his rheumy eyes impassive. He wore a scarf wrapped high on his neck.

Graham was taller than most people. He leaned his elbow on the counter to bring their heads level. "Last week, you sold me a special copy of the *London Times*. I really enjoyed it, and I'm wondering if you have any more like it."

The man's face didn't move except for a rise of his shaggy brows. "I got the papers you see out there, Guv. You can buy any one as looks good to you."

"Then maybe I could give *you* a special copy," Graham suggested.

He slid the folded *Spectator* across the counter with a crisp ten-pound note flattened beneath his hand.

The man eyed the money, then took the paper and opened it. The message Graham had hastily scribbled and tucked inside fell out.

"C. Wren's tomb," it said in bold black letters. "11:45 tonight."

"That don't belong there," said the newsagent, handing it back to Graham.

Graham accepted it reluctantly. He'd have felt better if the man had kept it, but at least he'd taken time to read what it said.

"You need change for this?" the newsagent asked, indicating the overly large banknote.

Graham shook his head.

The man grunted, made the money disappear, and returned his attention to the racing form he'd been reading. Graham concluded his best course of action was leaving.

"Oy," called the man as he gathered up his purchase. He nodded at *The Spectator*. "Can't guarantee you'll enjoy that as much as the other, but good luck."

"Thanks," Graham said, his heart sagging to his boots in relief.

He had made contact, after all. Now all he had to do was hope his handler would accept the meet.

Graham was not religiously observant, but he'd always thought of St. Paul's as a place where a calm deity lived. To him, the interior's soaring cream white marble and rich gold leaf epitomized all that was graceful and orderly. Mathematical precision ruled the march of pillars and arches. The dome was dizzying, of course, due to the volume of space that rose up to it, but that, too, he approved of. This was God's house and not a man's. Awe was exactly the emotion that should be inspired.

Nervousness was more what Graham felt as he ran up the west porch steps. Thankfully, the main doors were open, and he didn't have to employ his lock-picking skills.

He wondered if this meant his handler had arrived ahead of him.

Hoping it did, he tugged open one heavy door and stepped into an unfamiliar world. St. Paul's after dark was a different creature from what he was used to. Eerie shadows stretched back from the light of the great bronze torchieres, turning the most saintly statues into grotesques. Above him, a Stygian gloom filled the normally sunlit vaults, hiding who knew what within its cloak and casting highly unwelcome doubts on hallowed ground meaning anything.

Rolling his eyes at himself, Graham hurried up the nave's south aisle toward the dome. He had enough trouble on his plate without letting his fancies run away with him. The entrance to the crypt was on the dome's south side. He wanted to get there before some wandering padre spotted him.

Despite his wish to be quiet, his footfalls echoed in the stairwell as he descended. He came out near Nelson's tomb. The admiral's resting place was, as always, grand, but too exposed for his purposes. He continued to the southeast corner of the crypt, where the impression of being enclosed—and even oppressed—by the columned arches increased. Here, beneath the plainest of marble markers, lay the earthly remains of the cathedral's architect, Christopher Wren.

Lector, si monumentum requiris, circumspice, declared the tablet on the wall above the nook. *Reader, if you seek his memorial, look around you.* Graham had admired this inscription since he'd read it as a schoolboy. "Judge me for what I have accomplished," was how he interpreted it. "Anything else is meaningless."

Tonight, one stubby candle burned above the plaque, lending a soft gold glow to the secluded space. A festoon of melted wax said it had been sitting there a while.

"Interesting choice of meeting spots," Nim Wei observed.

She stepped out of the shadows and robbed Graham of the power to speak. She was dressed like an Englishwoman, or at least a well-paid English working girl. Her long black hair was tucked into the female version of a fedora, and her double-breasted navy suit could have been seen in any office in the city—the only difference being that Graham's handler wore the garment unusually tight. His mouth went dry to see the fine wool skirt stretch across her hips, her mound a gentle hummock between them. The height of her heels would have felled a lesser woman, but Nim Wei strode toward him as if she were barefoot. The delicacy of her ankles momentarily flummoxed him.

"Er," he said, yanking his gaze to her face. "I've been reading up on vampires. Folklore suggests they can't enter sacred ground. I thought it would be best if none of them could spy on our meeting."

Nim Wei smiled and stopped in front of him. She slid her fingers beneath his greatcoat's open lapels, causing him to shiver. "That was clever of you, Graham."

"Thank you for coming," he added, awkward at her nearness. "I know I should have waited for you to contact me."

"Nonsense." She leaned close enough to let him know she wore no brassiere beneath that snug blue suit. "How could I resist when you picked my favorite hour? You've no idea how fond I am of midnight."

She had him backed against the golden stone of the wall. Her strength should have been negligible compared to his, but the pressure she commanded was mysteriously compelling. Graham knew she didn't think much of him. He'd twigged onto that five minutes after meeting her. Consequently, neither respect nor affection was driving her current behavior. He cleared his unavoidably husky throat.

"Look here," he said. "I'm flattered, but maybe we should keep this professional."

"Is that truly what you want?"

Her touch drifted down his waistcoat to the nascent bulge swelling at his groin. The first cupping, rubbing squeeze of her fingers brought him to full hardness.

"Oh, God," Graham gasped as she rubbed some more, adding his balls to the firm massage. His knees were already wobbling, his thighs on fire. It might have been months since his last release, instead of only this morning. The itchy need that had plagued him then was back in full force.

"I think you should lean down," his handler murmured. "You really are too tall for me to kiss."

She was too quick for him to evade. Her hand was inside his trousers before he'd felt her undo the clasp, her smooth, cool fingers wrapping his shaft strongly. She pumped him with a lack of care that should have been insulting, but it didn't matter a damn. All that mattered was that she had her bare, silky hand on his burning skin. Graham groaned and bent to her.

"I want you to kiss me," he confessed.

She went up on the toes of her teetering shoes. "Do you like a little pain, Graham? Because I'm seeing signs that you do."

He couldn't answer. In truth, he could barely think. She was licking the side of his neck with her pointy tongue, her hand gone warm as it fisted his aching shaft. Her roughness felt better now, more necessary. His hips were moving with her strokes, encouraging the pressure. She latched her lips on him, forming a circle against which she sucked his skin. The sting of that had him shuddering with anticipation. He wanted something he couldn't put a name to . . . until two points of icy fire punched into his skin.

The pleasured shock of it made him come—no more buildup, just an instantaneous discharge of fluid and nerves firing. She drew on him, moaning softly, and the glorious bliss deepened. He remembered this, didn't he? Hadn't she drunk his blood in the train? From his cock that time. He couldn't decide if the answer mattered, and a second later he couldn't recall what the question was. His head was whirling, his hand lifting to cradle the back of hers. Every one of his responsibilities seemed to drift away. The wall behind him was all that prevented him from falling.

All too soon his handler drew back from him. Her snow-white skin appeared to be glowing from the inside, hypnotizing golden glints swimming in her eyes. Graham felt drunk with pleasure, his thoughts moving as thickly as if his brain had turned to treacle. He groaned, helpless not to, when she ran her tongue around her lips.

She'd painted them the oddest shade tonight, so red it resembled blood.

Graham shook his head in hopes of making room for more rational thoughts. What had she done to him? His limbs were shaking, his undershorts sticky with semen. He remembered her hand on him, but it was gone, and when he glanced down, his trousers were zipped. He hoped he hadn't come just from her kissing him. That would be embarrassing.

"There," she said, her voice vibrating with triumph. "Now we're ready for business."

"Business," Graham repeated, trying to seize on something that made sense. "Right. I know you said Edmund wasn't likely to harm Estelle, but I'm concerned about how close they've become. She hasn't been acting like herself lately."

"How has she been acting?"

"Like . . . like a woman of easy virtue," he burst out unwillingly.

"I see." Nim Wei turned away and tapped her lips. Her manner was sober, but Graham had the odd impression that she was smothering a laugh. "Your guardian's kind are seductive creatures. Perhaps the danger is greater than I thought."

"So you'll help me protect her? My boss has returned to town, and I won't have the time to watch over her the way I'd like."

Nim Wei looked at him over her shoulder, her eyes glimmering slits of gold. He thought she was the feyest person he'd ever seen. "I have a better idea, if you've got the courage to carry it off."

"Anything," Graham swore, ignoring the implied insult.

"I think it's time you confronted Edmund with what you know."

"Confront him?"

Nim Wei stepped back to him, her slender hands flattening on his chest. "Aren't you angry enough to do it? Don't you care about your friend?"

Her questions seemed to echo inside his mind. It

occurred to him that he *was* angry enough, that his rage was a beast longing to tear free. The fury strengthened him, filling him with a satisfaction as deep as his recent orgasm. In that moment, he could have killed Edmund cheerfully. That would end this. That would save Estelle once and for all.

"Er," he said as rationality returned a heartbeat later. "Not that I doubt your judgment, but if I push him, won't he just swat me like a fly?"

"He's too committed to denying what he is and too attached to his invented identity. He won't want to expose his powers in front of you, at least not the obvious ones."

"The obvious ones."

"His strength. His ability to change form." Nim Wei waved her hand. "What he is likely to do is try to thrall you."

"To thrall me," Graham repeated.

"His kind can capture unsuspecting humans with their gaze and force them to do their bidding."

"Like he's done with Estelle."

"Exactly." Nim Wei's approval, or possibly her closeness, caused his heart to beat faster. "If we don't save her soon enough, his influence over her may be permanent."

"I want to save her," Graham said. "But . . ." He hesitated. Questioning his handler required an effort of will, but he knew he had to ask this. "Exactly how will confronting him help Estelle?"

"You're thinking too much," Nim Wei scolded, her eyes narrow. "You should leave the thinking to me."

"Yes, but—"

"Confronting Edmund will oblige him to put more effort into deceiving everyone, to prove your accusations are untrue. He might even decide to leave your friend alone."

For a while, maybe, Graham thought but could not bring himself to say aloud.

Nim Wei continued. "Heed me well, Graham. I know more about these creatures than you do. You need to be extremely careful not to look into his eyes, no matter how much *you want to.* I'm sure as soon as you try not to meet his gaze, *it will seem impossible to avoid.*"

Something pushed at him from her eyes, so powerful, so palpable, that he could have sworn it shimmered in the air. The candle guttered on the ledge above the tomb. Her emphasis was confusing him, as if she both wanted and didn't want him to resist Edmund's thrall. The effect on his thoughts was like taffy being pulled in two directions. When she gripped his jaw in her hand, directing his eyes to hers, he couldn't restrain a gasp.

It felt like a fist was squeezing his heart.

"You mustn't let him know about me, Graham. That's the most important thing of all. He could read my image straight out of your mind. In fact, he might suspect someone put you up to confronting him. He might think I was trying to turn his family against him. Whatever you do, you mustn't *let him know what I look like.*"

As she said this, the strangest event of all tonight's strange events occurred. His handler's face changed before his eyes. It grew harder, cleaner, the angle and cut of it subtly changed. It became the face of the woman he'd glimpsed across the street from the cinema, the one he'd briefly mistaken for Nim Wei. The image seemed to burn itself into his brain. Unforgettable. Unconcealable. No matter how he tried to keep it to himself. Sweat broke out across his skin at the thought of what failing meant. His handler dead . . . Estelle a slave to Edmund's will . . . his family at risk . . .

"How can I stop him from seeing?" Graham pleaded desperately.

"As you've discovered from your research, vampires don't like Christian symbols. You'll put our secrets in a box in your imagination, a gleaming silver strongbox, with crucifixes laid over it."

The instant his handler finished speaking, Graham could picture it vividly. His success relaxed him, at least a bit.

"You're sure that will keep him out of my head?"

Nim Wei's smile was slow and catlike.

"We'll have to hope so," she said.

Bedford Square

Naturally, Edmund wasn't home when Graham returned. He'd be at Estelle's until dawn, working his infernal wiles on her between the sheets. Despite the delay, Graham suspected his absence was for the best. Nim Wei hadn't warned him to wait, but in the stories he'd studied, vampire hunters always faced their foe at sunup, the better to catch them when their powers had ebbed.

Christ, Graham thought disgustedly. *My life is turning into a pulp novel.*

He forced himself to lie down in his room, though he knew he'd never sleep. The sun rose late in winter, plus he'd have to delay until Sally left for school and Ben for work. He didn't want his siblings interfering and possibly getting hurt.

He snorted out a bitter laugh. Truth was, he didn't want Ben and Sally discovering what he was up to. They'd think their brother had gone mad.

His life might have been easier if he had, but he'd seen the reality of Edmund's nature with his own eyes. Come to think of it, he'd felt Edmund's thrall pushing at him the night they argued over who should stay with Estelle. Graham's fury swelled at the memory of how brief that victory had been. As it had before, the emotion steadied him. Graham ought to be angry. Edmund had been deceiving them since the day they'd met.

Knowing he needed to be steady, he fed that anger as the hours drew out. After a while, it wasn't work at all. He didn't feel like two separate Grahams anymore: one tormented by guilt at what he had to do, the other straining at the bit to smite his enemy. Rage clarified his indecision. Rage strengthened his purpose. Loyalty belonged to those who had earned it.

His heart scarcely sped up when the attic window creaked at the break of dawn. Edmund had come home.

Determined to stick to his plan, Graham joined Sally and Ben for breakfast, after which he instructed Mrs. Mackie to take the day off. None of them seemed to notice anything was wrong, but why would they? Graham was no quieter this morning than he'd been a hundred times before.

After they'd left, he climbed the stairs to Edmund's third-floor bedroom.

The door was locked, but that didn't stop him. Martin Walser himself had trained Graham in the art of bypassing locks, his old hands magic with the picking tools. Graham's own kit had been a gift from the murdered man, handed over with a soft, "You'll do more with it than I will."

But that was just one more loss to lay at Edmund's feet. Grim now, Graham picked the mechanism quickly and stepped into Edmund's room, a fine, clear fire burning in his veins. The room was dark, the heaviness of its draperies taking on a new, more sinister meaning. If that weren't ominous enough, Edmund slept in a heavy, curtained four-poster bed. Its rich brocade hangings were better suited to a medieval castle than the modern day. Then again, maybe the age of castles was when he'd come from. Graham had no idea how old his guardian was.

Everything about him is a lie, Graham thought, his jaw tightening. And no wonder he'd been brilliant as a professor of history.

Graham pulled the hangings back and tied them. True to Graham's research, Edmund didn't stir. He lay like a dead man in the center of the big, soft bed, his soul—if he had one—gone who knew where for the day. He was on his side, knees slightly bent, covers pulled to his chin with his hands tucked under the pillow. Graham couldn't remember if he'd ever watched his father sleep. Though he didn't breathe, his pose was a human's and not a fiend's. He seemed smaller asleep, far smaller than his oldest son. For a moment, Graham's resolve faltered.

Then he began to notice how different Edmund looked from his everyday self.

The hair that flowed across his pillow should have been a distinguished silver. Instead, it gleamed like new-minted gold. As if the clock of the years had been turned back, the lines that normally creased his face were gone. Seeing his guardian's true form from a distance on Hampstead Heath hadn't been like this. Not only did Edmund appear as youthful as Graham himself, he was more beautiful than any natural being could be. His skin was the white of marble, its pores too fine to be seen. His lips glowed like rubies a poet might write about. He resembled a precious object, carved and painted by a jeweler's hand. Even the faint tracery of veins beneath his skin struck Graham as artistic. No pulse beat through them that Graham could see.

This beauty is part of his power, he warned himself. *This is how he seduces the unwary.*

In a single, determined motion, he grabbed Edmund's wrist and tugged him out of the bed.

Edmund's naked body thunked to the carpet as if he were made of something harder—and heavier—than flesh and bone. Even then, his eyes didn't open. He moaned a little, as if troubled by a dream, but didn't struggle as Graham dragged him across the floor. Only when Graham hefted him onto the window seat did he seem to rouse.

"Graham?" he asked in a thick, rough voice. "What are you doing?"

Graham ripped the draperies open and flipped up the shade. Light poured through the glass in a silvery square, not bright but bright enough. Edmund cried out and tried to scramble away. His limbs weren't working well enough to succeed. Graham caught his shoulders and pinned him in place.

"I know what you are," he said.

"Jesus, Graham. What I am is half asleep."

He was more than half asleep. His head was lolling, and he was struggling to keep his lids lifted—this despite the instant flush of a sunburn blooming on his skin.

Ordering his heart to stay hard, Graham shook him impatiently. Mercy had no place in this. "No more lies. You've been shoving them down our throats since the day you adopted us. All that rot about saving us. About how lucky you were to have us to love. All the time you were a damned monster. I saw you and your friend, Robin, turn into wolves. I saw you rip a hare apart and eat it whole. Some 'delicate stomach' you turned out to have! Tell me, *Dad*, what have you been doing to us all these years while *we* slept? Drinking our blood to sate your foul appetites? Christ, were we ever more to you than a handy meal?"

Edmund's pupils had shrunk to pinpricks, but his clouded eyes managed to widen at Graham's question. "Never," he said, the declaration slurred but ringing with sincerity. "Never that, Graham. Never a single drop."

His hands were clamped around Graham's forearms,

seemingly as much to keep himself from falling over as to prevent Graham from harming him. Graham's heart pounded like a drum. He hadn't missed the implication behind Edmund's words. He wasn't denying what he was. He wasn't doing what Nim Wei said he would.

"You're admitting you're a vampire," he rasped.

Edmund swallowed. "I'm admitting it."

Graham's throat tightened at the plea in his guardian's gaze. He tore his own away, remembering almost too late that he wasn't supposed to look in his eyes. Edmund could trick him if he did that.

"I never bit you," Edmund said. "Not you and not Estelle."

"You can't deny you used your thrall on us. On Ben and on Sally, too." A memory rolled back to him, shoring up his stubbornness. "Remember when you ordered her to stay away from the stove? For a month, she couldn't go near the kitchen without shaking."

Edmund choked out a sound of disbelief. "I used my thrall on Sally because she was five years old, and she'd just set her hair on fire to see if it would look pretty. I didn't know the methods other parents used. I had to do the best I could."

"The best you could." Graham sneered at him. He was clear now, so clear he felt like a fresh-honed sword—one some knight of old would have named. "Were you doing the best you could when you hired those men to attack Estelle so you could 'rescue' her? Were you doing your best when you killed Martin Walser? I wonder how Estelle would feel if she knew she had a murderer in her bed?"

"Don't make this about her, Graham. Whatever you think I did, don't bring her into it."

"You brought her into it when you used your vampire tricks to make her fall in love with you."

"Maybe it's easier for you to believe that's what happened, but—"

"Easier! *Easier!*" Graham was shouting and couldn't make himself stop. He'd rocketed from clear to out of control in a single second. His heart was beating so hard he feared he'd throw up, words spurting from him like they were blood. "I liked Martin Walser, and I love Estelle. Which part of you being a vampire and a murderer and a . . . a fucking wolf do you think is *easy* for me?"

"Son—"

Graham's vision disappeared in a haze of red. Before he knew it, the crystal vase that sat on Edmund's bureau was in his hand and flying across the room. The long-stemmed roses it had held scattered out.

"Don't," he screamed, absolutely hysterical. "Don't bloody call me *son*!"

The demand struck Edmund like an iron fist, rocking him backward with an almost physical pain. He thought he'd been braced for Graham's accusations, but nothing could have prepared him for this eruption of vitriol. He barely heard the vase explode as it hit the wall. His head was ringing with Graham's words. It took a moment for him to find his breath again.

"Graham," he said in the gentlest tone he had. "Estelle's free will is precious to me. Love that's forced doesn't mean a damn."

"What do monsters know about love?"

Graham had released him when he threw the vase. Now Edmund reached for his son's shoulder, gripping it even as Graham attempted to shake him off. At least this fight had woken him up. He wouldn't have been able to hold on to a kitten if it had not. Since hiring Mrs. Mackie, he'd gotten out of practice at forcing himself to function during the day. Graham's head was lowered, refusing to look at him, maybe because he'd begun to cry silently. Even now the tears were dripping off that truculent jaw of his. Graham might look like a man, might be one by human standards, but in many ways this son of his remained a boy.

Hurt though he was, Edmund knew his heart had never ached more for him.

"Think," he said. "If I'd forced Estelle to love me, wouldn't I have forced you?"

"Maybe you did."

"You know better than that. You know you love me, even with the truth staring you in the face. If you didn't, this wouldn't be hard for you."

The tears came faster, a little rain on Graham's clean white shirt. "I ought to kill you. I ought to want to. You've betrayed our trust in every possible way."

"You *could* kill me," Edmund said. "If you held me in the sun long enough."

Graham's gaze flashed to his for a startled second, long enough to take in the tiny blisters forming on Edmund's skin.

"You'd fight me," he said unsurely.

"Only if I could do it without hurting you."

"It's another trick."

"Given my age and power, I've got about fifteen minutes before my hair starts to smoke, and maybe as many more before a flame gets going. If I had clothes on, I'd last longer—as you may recall from the days when I'd take you children to school. You should also know my kind get sundrunk from exposure. My head is spinning from it now, as if *you'd* tossed back a couple glasses of straight whiskey. I expect burning to death would hurt despite that, but I might not scream too loudly. If you wanted to kill me quickly, you'd be better off with an iron stake. Slam it straight through my heart, and I'd disappear in a flash of light. You wouldn't even have a body to worry about."

"Why are you telling me this?"

"Because I want you to understand I trust you with my

life. Because I never want you to doubt I love you. Whatever else I've lied about, the last thing I could ever be is your enemy."

A single sob tore from his son. He was hunched over himself as if his belly hurt. He swiped his nose impatiently on his sleeve. "You are my enemy. And you killed Martin Walser. You *drained his blood*. That makes you the enemy of the whole country."

Well, that was a piece of irony, considering Edmund had defied his own brother's noninterference edicts to ally himself with Walser. It was precisely because he loved England, because he didn't want *upyr* kind playing power games with humans, that he and the director had established X Section.

Somehow, he didn't think Graham was going to believe that.

"I didn't kill Martin Walser," he said. "Yes, it probably was a vampire who did it, but that vampire wasn't me."

"As if you'd tell me the truth!"

This was, at least in part, the cry of a child, one who secretly wanted to be lied to. *Convince me*, it pleaded. *Restore my faith in you*. Edmund touched the side of Graham's face, but he shrank away. The redness of his own hand shocked him. He had better settle this before he really burned. "Graham, I swear to you I'm not lying. Look into my eyes, and you'll see."

"I can't look at you. You'll put me under your thrall."

Despite Graham's near panicked claim, his eyes lifted. "I can't help it," he whispered, clearly horrified at himself. "The harder I try not to do it, the more impossible avoiding it becomes."

Edmund wasn't understanding this. Why would Graham be unable to avoid his gaze, especially if he knew the danger? He looked into Graham's deep brown irises, glittering now with tears. And then he sensed it: someone else's mark

on him, someone else's influence. Another vampire had
bitten him. Dismayed he hadn't seen it sooner, Edmund
clasped Graham's head between his hands.

"Who did this to you? Who put you under their compulsion?"

"No one did! No one at all!"

He was lying badly, and Graham was a good liar.
Edmund peered into him harder. "Someone put you up to
this. For both our sakes, tell me who."

Graham's barriers to reading had always been stronger
than most mortals'. Lately, they'd been virtually impregna-
ble. Edmund expected to have to push, but to his surprise,
Graham's resistance toppled at the first good shove. He
found Graham holding a thought form inside his head, a
heavy silver box with Christian crosses laid over it. Graham must have been reading too much folklore. Vampires'
supposed aversion to silver and crosses was mere disinformation, put out by their own kind.

"No," Graham moaned, sensing his incursion. "People
will die if you open that."

He seemed so convinced Edmund hesitated.

"Please," Graham begged. His pupils were as big as
pence, as big if he were drugged. In a way, he had been.
Whoever had laid this compulsion on him had set it to
intensify if it were threatened. "Please, you're not allowed
to see her face."

That was enough to decide Edmund.

"I'll be careful," he promised, his voice grimmer than
he intended.

He was careful, in case the thought form was booby-
trapped to injure Graham. It wasn't, as it happened. When
he gingerly lifted the imaginary lid, nothing slipped out
but Graham's memories.

The very first thing they revealed was Nim Wei's face.

Graham whimpered as Edmund's anger flooded his

unshielded mind. With an effort of will greater than he'd
ever exerted, Edmund forced himself to watch the rest with
an icy calm.

Apparently, his old lover was behind this. She'd told Graham where to find him and Robin hunting. She'd told him
Edmund was a vampire and played on his human fear of the
unknown. Hell, she seemed to have killed Walser, or how
else could she get away with posing as Graham's handler?
She meant to turn Edmund's family against him. She meant
to make him hurt as he'd hurt her all those years ago.

"Stop," Graham whispered with what sounded like his
last breath. "Your hands are burning me."

Edmund practically threw himself back into the room's
shadows. He'd left two red palm prints on Graham's face,
burning his son as the sun burned him.

"Oh, God," he breathed. "Graham, I'm sorry. I didn't
mean to do that. I didn't know I could."

Graham pushed to his feet, shaking. His face was
twisted with self-disgust, despite which he held himself
with dignity. "You got what you wanted," he said. "You
don't need any more from me."

Edmund's heart ached for him. He remembered what
else he'd glimpsed in the silver strongbox, a secret Graham
might not know himself. Edmund wasn't the only person
he was angry at. Part of him felt his parents had betrayed
him, too, by dying when he was a boy. Part of him feared
no one would ever love him and stay true.

"Graham," he croaked. He wanted so much to tell
his son that his fears were lies, to force him to believe it.
Unfortunately, his burst of strength was fading now that he
wasn't in direct danger. Adrenaline, humans called it, and
evidently the *upyr* version had run out on him. Edmund
cursed as his knees gave way and banged to the floor. Damn
it, he couldn't sleep; he had to make his son understand.
"Gra—" His head was so heavy it seemed to be dragging
him off balance. The room was spinning drunkenly from

the sun he'd taken. "Gr—" And then the carpet rose up to smack his face. He couldn't see. Couldn't. Think. A blackness shot with gold cloaked him.

"I won't let you burn," someone said sadly. "Maybe I should, but I don't know how to make myself."

With the very last of his awareness, Edmund felt a thick wool blanket being pulled over him.

Sally was in the kitchen assembling a sandwich when the doorbell rang. For some unknown reason, Mrs. Mackie had taken the day off—without so much as leaving a stew to heat up for dinner. Sally could cook, a little, but ever since an incident when she was a girl, she'd been uneasy near the stove alone. Alone was what she was tonight. Ben was pub-crawling with a mate, Graham was who knew where, and the professor was closeted in his study with orders not to be disturbed.

Sighing, Sally set down the cheese knife and went to answer the door. It would serve her family right if she let in a crazed killer.

It wasn't a killer, though the professor's friend, Robin, did appear somewhat crazed. Sally wasn't clear what the connection between the two men was, but he'd been to their house a few times before—always to speak to her father privately. Despite the wildness of his hair and eyes, he was far too handsome not to recognize.

"Mister—" she said and then had to stop. Did she know his last name? Maybe he was a distant relative of the professor. They did look a bit alike.

Robin didn't seem to notice her lapse. "Is my—Is your father at home?"

"Yes," she said. "He's up in his attic study, but—"

Robin was taking the stairs two at a time, so light on his feet he barely made a sound.

"He asked not to be disturbed," she called after him.

"He won't mind me," Robin called back.

He disappeared too quickly for Sally to ask what the matter was or to offer to bring up a pot of tea. She wanted to, for curiosity's sake, but the professor tended to see through such strategems.

"I hope nothing's wrong," she murmured to herself.

With a sick clenching of her stomach, she prayed her father hadn't found out about her and Ben.

Over the years, the best of the house's worn-out furniture had migrated to Edmund's study. Here, the history of his little family lived on in mended chairs and nicked tables. Framed photographs decorated the slanting walls: Sally clutching her favorite doll, Ben on his bicycle, Graham after his first growth spurt with a skinny sibling slung over each shoulder. Graham was grinning in that one, the expression as rare as it was beautiful. At the bottom of the picture, Sally had printed "The Fitz Clare Strongman!" in crooked block letters.

It was this photo that Edmund had lifted off its hook tonight. He touched the glass above the caption as he held it in his lap, his eyes burning with a love too big to contain. Though he heard Robin coming, he didn't set the picture aside until the other man burst into the room.

"Jesus, Dad," Robin said, breathless with emotion. "Are you all right? Something woke me this morning. I knew you were in trouble. It was all I could do to wait until nightfall."

They were lucky they were alone, because Robin crossed the cluttered room with a speed and agility no human could have called upon. When he reached Edmund, he looked like he wanted to yank him out of the chair and pull him into an embrace, to reassure himself in the simplest manner that he was all right. Feeling too weary for that, Edmund patted the faded cushion on the rocking chair next to him.

"I'm fine," he said as Robin sank into the seat. "I took a little sun, but the damage healed while I slept."

Robin gave him a look. "From what I sensed through our connection, you more than 'took a little sun.'"

Edmund gripped the arms of his chair. He wasn't looking forward to explaining this. "There is good news. I don't have to wonder what Graham has figured out anymore."

"Oh, blast," said Robin.

"Quite."

"Is he—" Robin hesitated and rubbed his chin. "Is he the one who pulled you into the sun this morning?"

"Yes," Edmund said, then told him what had happened. "I burned him, Robin. With these two hands, I burned my own son. I can't say I'm surprised he's run off. You should have seen his expression. He thought I'd betrayed him. He thought I'd never loved him at all. Hell, he called me an enemy to England."

"Why not tell him you work for MI5 as well?"

Edmund's jaw dropped as he turned to stare at Robin. "You know about that?"

"Well, of course I do. I haven't told anyone. I know how Uncle Aimery gets about us taking sides in human affairs. Not that I think founding this X Section counts as taking sides. You're simply keeping an eye on what other *upyr* are up to—and what humans know about us. It shows foresight, if you ask me."

Edmund let out a sigh. "Is there anything you don't know? Like what Mrs. Mackie cooked for dinner last night?"

"I keep track of you," Robin said, struggling visibly not to squirm. "Exactly like you do for me. Or did you think you were the only one with a protective streak?"

"But I'm your father."

"And I'm glad of it. Practically speaking, though, once one hits the five-century mark, how much difference can a few decades mean? Unless you want to claim you're inherently more adult than I am."

Edmund laughed ruefully. "No. More adult is not what I'm feeling now. What I'm feeling now is that I'd like to rip Nim Wei's head off with my bare hands. And I'm pissed as hell to be uncertain that I'm strong enough."

Tired of running over and over the same mental ground, he rose and went to the window. He needed air—or possibly more brain cells. Robin turned the rocking chair to watch him.

"Do you want to take this up with Uncle Aimery?"

Edmund snorted. "That would bloody well make his year."

"He'd stick by you, Dad. I'm not sure he'd help you kill her, but he'd impose some consequence. London's queen has crossed the line by involving Graham."

Edmund pressed the heels of his hands into his forehead. "There's the rub. I can't figure out what she's playing at. I'm not even sure . . . Robin, I read the pictures out of Graham's mind, and I'm still not convinced she's pulling the strings. I've been thinking since I woke up, and I can't make the pieces fit. I'm not saying she's not a killer; I know she is. She's also devious enough to pull off a complicated revenge. The thing is, Nim Wei is one of the three most powerful *upyr* alive. Auriclus, Lucius the White, and her: They're the triumvirate. If she wanted me dead, I would be. If she'd thralled Graham, he'd have stayed that way. Humans simply don't shake off her influence. And he did shake it. In the end, Graham *couldn't* see me as a monster."

"You and I both know Graham isn't the average human, no more than you're the queen's average opponent."

"Maybe. But if I'm to go up against her, I need to be certain she's guilty."

Robin came up behind him and laid his hand on his back. "If you're going up against her, I want to help."

"No." Edmund shook his head firmly. "I don't want you in danger."

"Dad, if you're close to being an elder, chances are I am, too. We don't just share the Fitz Clare blood, we share a sire. Lucius made us both, and you know he's no weakling. If Auriclus walks into the sun and pushes you over the brink . . ."

"If you become an elder, I want you looking after my family."

"Dad!"

"Promise me."

"I damn well won't!"

Robin's color was high for one of their kind. Needing his agreement, Edmund took him gently by the shoulders. "What if I promise not to move against Nim Wei without telling you first?"

"That's dirty pool!"

"They're only humans, Robin. Without me, they'll have no one to protect them. I don't think I could bear knowing that." His voice choked up without warning, and he had to blink hard.

"Oh, Christ," Robin swore. "Don't you go crying in front of me. I wouldn't just abandon them if . . . if something happened to you. I'm not that hard-hearted."

Edmund looked away and swiped at his cheeks. "Sorry. Didn't mean to do that."

"Like that makes it better," Robin muttered.

"I won't do anything reckless," he promised.

"You'd better not. I'm not as keen on playing nanny as you are."

In spite of everything, Edmund smiled. "You're a good son. Better than I deserve."

"Don't I know it!" Robin said feelingly.

Tottenham Court Mansions

❧❧❧

Estelle had fallen asleep on the sofa, waiting for Edmund to show up. She woke when he eased *The Maltese Falcon* out of her limp hands.

"Edmund," she said, his name distorted by a yawn.

He scooped her up into his arms, his lips pressing a tender kiss to her temple. "Why don't I carry you to bed and tuck you in? From the looks of things, I haven't been giving you the rest you need."

"Not complaining," Estelle mumbled against his broad shoulder. "I like the way you keep me up. 'Sides, don't want my pretty nightgown to go to waste."

Despite the assertion, she let him lay her down and cover her. The sensation of being cared for improved distinctly when he removed his clothes, slid under the sheets, and spooned her from behind. Though Edmund's muscles were hard and lean, the texture of his skin was smoother than her sleeping gown.

She hummed with pleasure as he wrapped one strong arm around her, her fingers playing with the silky hair on his forearm. "Stay for breakfast tomorrow. I'll close my new window shades."

Edmund made a sound that mingled pain and humor. That alone would have alerted her something was wrong, but when his hold on her also tightened, she had to twist around. "What is it, Edmund? What happened?"

He kissed the palm she'd laid against his cheek. "Graham and I . . . argued."

"About me?"

He hesitated. "In part. But not because of you." His eyes searched hers in the moonlit darkness, their hair mingling in waves on her pillow. A single furrow cut between his brows. "I thought perhaps I ought to stay away from you. Not rub that particular wound rawer."

"I don't want you to stay away," she protested.

He smiled and kissed her softly, those satiny lips of his like a dream. Estelle sighed and pressed back at him. As close as they were, she felt his sex begin to lift even before his tongue slipped into her mouth to explore.

"Estelle," he murmured, pulling the front of her tight to the front of him. "I couldn't stay away from you. Not even to spare Graham's feelings."

To Estelle's delight, he deepened the kiss. He was making love to her mouth, a slow, intimate claiming she could hardly have liked better. His hand made one long pass down her spine, skated over her bottom, then dragged the hem of her nightgown up. She lifted her hips to help him, which caused him to rumble out a groan.

"I need you tonight, Estelle. I need to love you."

She parted her legs for him and rolled onto her back. His intensity squeezed her heart; the idea that a man she loved so much could need her. His eyes were smoldering as he shifted over her, his breath quickening. His knees moved into the space she'd made, that simple act exciting her. Her heart beat faster as his hand dropped to his groin. He was holding himself, positioning the broad, warm crest of his penis against her entrance.

"Slow tonight," he said, the promise smoky. "We've never done it slow."

He seemed determined to make up for that. He pressed into her inch by inch, growing hotter and swelling thicker with each small moan of bliss she couldn't keep inside. The skin of his prick was velvet, the core within hard as steel. His expressions of pleasure as he gradually pushed inside her were a drug she'd never tire of.

It occurred to her that she ought to ask him about prophylactics, as she'd never quite brought herself to do before. The words were swallowed this time, too. Letting him love her seemed more important. That long, hard part of him stretched her deliciously, pulling silky liquid from her walls to ease his way. His golden lashes dipped as he looked down their bodies to watch his progress. He shuddered with excitement at the halfway point.

Seeing how the sight affected him, she had to watch as well. It was something: to witness him taking her. The veins that wound up his shaft seemed to strain darkly against his skin. He swallowed, his Adam's apple bobbing, and pulled his gaze upward to her breasts. What he wanted couldn't have been clearer. With a feeling of incredible power and freedom, she peeled the bodice of her gown away.

"Kiss me here," she said, and Edmund's gaze went dark.

He bent to suck her, his lips parting in anticipation before he got there. He was near to panting, simply at the thought of tasting her. Surrounding the sharpness of her nipple drew a small, pained sound from deep in his throat. He tugged her deeper into his mouth, her insides clenching when he made the soft noise again.

His greed was equaled only by his care. The flesh of his cheeks enveloped her, his tongue flattening around the peak as he sucked her more strongly yet. Something hard began to squeeze her areola, something smooth and curving. She moaned at the sensation, her back arching. As if the pleasure points of her breasts and sex were wired to each other, her pussy quivered and flooded him.

"Ah, God," he rasped, pulling free. "You're too sweet, love. I don't want to hurt you."

"You're not hurting me," she assured him.

He'd planted his hands outside her shoulders so he could prop his upper body on his arms. She gripped his corded forearms, borrowing his rather amazing strength to increase her leverage for rolling her hips up the length of him. Oh, that was good, especially when he ground his pelvis down into her, increasing the penetration until his balls were squashed. Loving the sensation of him so deep inside her, she wriggled blissfully.

"I won't hurt you," he promised on a pleasured gasp. Groaning, he drew out to his rim and speared her slowly again. "I wouldn't hurt you for anything."

"Good," she said, craning up so she could nip the impressively bulging muscle of his shoulder. She didn't know why, but she had an almost uncontrollable craving to bite him. Fortunately, he seemed to like it.

"Neck," he pleaded, twisting his head almost violently to the side to give her access. His lips were rolled over his teeth in a tortured line. "*Hard.*"

He increased his thrusting as she complied, writhing like an eel each time he reached the deepest point inside of her. As much as she loved the pressure, he must have loved exerting it. He repeated the grinding motion again and again. Coupled with her nipping him, he was soon beside himself.

"Yes," he moaned when she sucked his flesh more strongly against her teeth. His body rolled helplessly—quicker, harder, shoving his erection into that sweet spot in short, rough jerks. "Oh, yes. Yes. *God.*"

And then he shuddered and spurted forcefully into her.

Estelle laughed at his expression of surprised dismay. They'd barely gotten started, after all.

"Well, I would be annoyed," she said, hugging his lightly sweating back, "except I know from experience that you can do that again."

He growled and gave her a kiss so wet and deep and explicit it swiftly had her blood racing. "I can do that again, and this time it's all for you."

It was all for her, and the next time as well. When she'd finished shaking from her third lengthy orgasm, he insisted she sleep—despite certain signs that he was capable of more bed play.

"Rest," he said, low and sexy beside her ear. "Tomorrow is another night."

"I love you, Edmund," she murmured contentedly.

He stilled behind her, and she realized she hadn't said this aloud before.

"I love you, too," he said huskily, after a pause. "Now sleep and store up your strength."

From the feel of what was nestled against her bottom, she was going to need it.

Edmund's body didn't start shaking until he felt her slip into sleep. He couldn't deny his tremors were a fear reaction. He should have stayed away from her, but not because of Graham. Tonight he'd come closer to biting her than ever. She'd offered herself to him so trustingly, her wish to comfort him as obvious as it was touching. Long though it was, his life had not been filled with people who wanted that. He suspected the only thing that had stopped him from taking everything Estelle had to offer was her biting him. His emotions *had* been running high, but he didn't think he could blame his loss of control on that. The closer he and Estelle grew, the more he wanted a true union, the more he wanted all of her: body and blood and soul. Even now, his fangs throbbed with hunger. He rubbed their bases through his upper lip, trying to encourage them to retract.

That was no help at all. If anything, the kneading made them surge longer.

He eased out of bed with a silent curse. He didn't want to leave altogether, her company was too sweet, but lying next to her wasn't safe right now, not with the scent of her recent pleasure filling the room. He padded naked to her kitchen, hoping ordinary food would help. Her refrigerator held a roasted chicken he thought his wolf would like, though she'd probably wonder how he'd managed to eat the entire thing. Then again, being a thoughtful guest was not his priority.

He changed as quickly as he could, wincing at the awkward scrabbling of his nails on the linoleum. These "mansion" kitchens weren't designed for giant wolves. He had to tuck his tail between his legs to keep from accidentally sweeping her counters clear. Cramped quarters aside, the chicken was tasty, probably thanks to the Harrods food hall chefs. He ate it in short order, then ordered himself to change back before the restless beast inside him could convince him to have a trot around Estelle's flat. A midnight snack was one thing. Stretching his legs the way he wanted would have to wait until he was alone.

He felt calmer with his belly full, which told him he needed to take extra care to feed his wolf from now on. Though this would help, he knew it wouldn't solve his deeper dilemma: that of safeguarding his beloved's independence of heart and will. More than ever, he was determined to do that. No matter what, he wasn't going to become the monster Graham feared he was.

He tucked himself back around Estelle with a sigh that was part worry and part pleasure. He had tonight, and he had her love. For the time being, he'd have to be content with that.

Bedford Square

The next day, while eating a somewhat irritating breakfast alone, Estelle made up her mind to talk to Graham.
Edmund's happiness mattered to her, and she didn't want
to be a source of tension between him and his eldest son.
Maybe if she was very clear about her feelings, it would
help. At the least, she'd prove she wasn't a coward.

Debating with herself over how plainspoken she ought
to be distracted her most of the day. She was fortunate her
work didn't require much intellectual power, though she
felt less fortunate when she reached the sooty entrance to
her usual Underground stop. Graham wasn't waiting there.

Had he given up his fixation with protecting her? She
looked up and down Brompton Road, but didn't see his big
silhouette in either direction. Maybe the fight between him
and his father had been worse than Edmund let on. Maybe
he wasn't in the mood to have anything to do with her.

Shrugging to herself, she trotted down the stairs into the
Tube station. She'd try him at home, she decided—anything

to get what was sure to be an uncomfortable conversation out of the way.

Her luck didn't seem to be improving when she arrived at the Fitz Clares'. The night was dry but chilly, with dead brown leaves blowing in biting swirls out of the empty park. Lights were on behind the ground-floor windows, but she rang the bell three times before someone let her in.

Sally and Ben had been too caught up in rowing to interrupt themselves.

"Leave him alone," Ben was saying as Sally opened the door and rolled her eyes. "He's a grown man. He doesn't need you coaxing him to eat like a five-year-old."

"Is Graham in?" Estelle asked, preferring not to know the reason for the fight.

"Graham is missing," Sally huffed. "Not that Ben cares about that."

"Missing?" Estelle asked.

Ben's retort to Sally prevented her from answering. "He's probably on assignment for his boss. Or, hell, out shagging a girl. Men do that, you know. If you're that averse to spending five minutes alone in my company, I can go out and do it, too."

Estelle's eyebrows rose at his language, but Sally seemed not to notice.

"This is nothing to do with you," she said, her cheeks pink with anger. "I'm *worried* about the professor." She turned to Estelle and grabbed her brown suede coat sleeve. "You go up and check on him. Mrs. Mackie took a tray to his study, but I don't think he's eating it."

Estelle looked instinctively toward Ben. He was as red-faced as Sally, his frustration sparking palpably in the air. When she caught his gaze, he had to force himself to breathe his anger out.

"You may as well," he said, civilly enough. "At least your company won't drive him up the wall."

Sally folded her arms beneath her heaving breasts.

"I'll come down later," Estelle said, squeezing Sally's arm on the way past her. "Maybe there will be something good on the wireless."

Sally grimaced but nodded, leaving Estelle to hope her and Ben's fight was winding down. She shook her head as she climbed the stairs. One would think those two were married, the way they went at it like cats and dogs.

The attic landing was narrow, Edmund's hideaway from his family remote in more ways than one. The study door was closed, so Estelle knocked.

"Professor? Are you in there? It's Estelle."

She received no answer, but heard a strange, hurried scrabbling noise. Something about it made her scalp prickle. Too many odd events had been happening. Rather than knock again, she gripped the knob in her strong right hand and turned.

Metal snapped as the lock gave way. Too worried to be surprised, she opened the door. Edmund was nowhere to be seen.

"Edmund?" She didn't let the piles of books and student essays on the floor slow her down, but strode between them toward the scratching sound. It was coming from behind his battered antique desk. As she got closer, she heard panting noises there as well.

If Edmund had fallen . . . If he were hurt . . .

She rounded the desk and stared straight into a pair of glowing blue canine eyes. Her heart stopped, as she'd thought it only did in novels. The wolf—for it could not in a million years be taken for a dog—was crouching down on all fours, clearly trying to hide behind the barrier. Edmund's dinner tray sat between its huge forelegs, nothing left of its contents but a few lick marks. Seeming as surprised to see her as she was to see it, the wolf let out a whining growl.

Estelle's heart lurched into action with a great, hard thump. The creature's tongue was lolling, its fangs drip-

ping saliva. It wagged its tail unsurely, but that did not
soothe her. Staggering back as her knees threatened to
buckle, Estelle sucked in a breath and screamed.

Stop, Edmund pleaded with his thoughts, not knowing
what else to do. In her panic, Estelle was shrieking like a
banshee. *You're going to bring the whole house up here.*

He knew his mind voice had gotten through, because
Estelle slapped her hand over her funny ear and screamed
louder.

Lord help him. She wasn't only going to call the others;
she was going to shatter glass. Too distracted by the noise
to change, he vaulted in his wolf form over the desk. The
door stood open, its lock broken. He landed on a tattered
rug and skidded like a genie on a flying carpet. By luck as
much as intent, he knocked the door shut again.

Estelle stopped screaming to catch her breath.

"Nice wolf," she said. The hand she held out in front of
her trembled as badly as her voice. "Please don't eat me."

She was edging toward the garret window, probably
planning to climb out. Edmund couldn't hold the door
closed and move to stop her at the same time—which he
needed to do if he didn't want her to break her neck. She
had no idea how steep and slippery those roof tiles were.

Bugger it to flaming hell, he thought, hearing Ben and
Sally clattering up the stairs.

With more desperation than technique, he closed his
eyes and returned himself to human form.

Estelle's gasp of shock was louder than a pistol shot.

"Don't scream," he said as quietly and firmly as he
could. "You saw a mouse, and you were frightened."

Estelle's eyes were as wide as saucers, her skin nearly
as white as his. She took another step back from him, her
heel landing on an old croquet mallet that sent her crashing
down on her bum.

"Oh, my God," she breathed, barely seeming to notice she had fallen. "You're glowing like a firefly."

It didn't surprise Edmund that his glamour was out of commission, though the sight of him in his natural glory must have seemed quite bizarre to her.

"You saw a mouse," he repeated just as Ben reached the door and tried to open it. Edmund didn't have time to thrall Estelle into cooperation, even if he'd thought the power would work on her.

Please, love. Don't frighten my children.

"Estelle!" Ben called, followed by a shout from Sally. "Is everything all right in there?"

Edmund knew Ben couldn't break the door down with him blocking it. He also knew that wouldn't matter if Estelle chose to give his secret away. Apart from Graham, she was the most believable witness he'd ever met.

Please, he said, putting his soul in it. *I know you can hear me. I'll explain everything as soon as I can. Just don't destroy the love my children feel for me.*

Her hand was on her throat, her fingers slim and lovely and pale. Her pulse fluttered beneath them like an aspen leaf. His own didn't feel much calmer as the length of time her eyes held his stretched out. The surface of her pupils jittered with shock. Ben and Sally both called again.

The doorknob rattled behind his back. Estelle inhaled. Edmund braced for another scream.

"I'm fine," she said huskily. "I . . . saw a mouse. The professor is shooing it out the window."

"Ben can help," Sally volunteered. "In case there are any more. Good Lord, Estelle, you were squealing like a stuck pig."

"I've taken care of it," Edmund said, not about to open the door in his current unclothed and unglamoured state. He knew he wasn't capable of reconstructing his disguise, not even to spare his family seeing him like this. "I think Estelle needs more time to calm before she comes out."

Ben—bless him—seemed to realize more than a mouse had caused the trouble, though who knew what he thought had actually occurred.

"Come on, Sally," he said. "We'll go downstairs and make cocoa for when Estelle feels better."

Estelle should have known Edmund wasn't a normal man. Certainly she should have guessed before she slept with him. Graham had warned her he was dangerous, and Edmund's own behavior over the years had been nothing if not peculiar. Now, because she hadn't wanted to face the truth, because she'd wanted to be happy and in love, she'd trapped herself in this attic with a nightmare.

She tried to scramble farther back, but there was too much Fitz Clare clutter in her way. Apparently, the monster she knew as Edmund didn't like discarding his children's things. She was finding it impossible to look away from him, though his present appearance was nearly as disturbing as his furry one. Human skin didn't come in that shade of white. Human skin didn't glow like its owner had swallowed a thousand stars.

"You're a werewolf," she said.

Edmund broke into a nervous laugh.

"Sorry," he said a second later. "I know this isn't funny to you."

"You're not a werewolf?"

"I'm an *upyr*." He took a careful step toward her, stopping when an involuntary keening came from her throat. "An *upyr* is what you'd call a vampire. Some of us can change shape into animals. As far as I know, werewolves don't exist."

"You're a vampire." Estelle had to swallow as soon as she repeated it.

"It's not as bad as it sounds, at least not in my case. I

don't know who Mister Stoker's source was, but he got a number of the details wrong."

"You're a vampire," Estelle said and pushed shakily to her feet. She told herself this was still Edmund, and he wasn't looking like he wanted to bite her neck. Truth be told, he looked more afraid she would run away. Since standing wasn't working out too well, she lowered herself onto a sagging twenty-year-old couch.

"*Upyr* sounds nicer," he offered hopefully.

"You drink people's blood," she said, the words thoroughly surreal.

"I don't have to. I can eat in my wolf form. That's what you caught me doing. I wanted to— That is, I was hoping—"

In a single unearthly flash, she saw what he was trying to find an inoffensive explanation for.

"You were hoping you wouldn't be too hungry when you made love to me tonight. You've been trying to hide your fangs from me."

Evidently, merely alluding to him drinking her blood was enough to make his teeth lengthen. His incisors jerked over his lower lip in a short, hard spurt.

"Blast," he said, sounding embarrassed as he spun away.

His naked rear view, both shining and muscular, temporarily distracted her. The conformation of his back was lovely—a hypnotizing interplay of grace and strength that narrowed to a pair of marble hindquarters Michelangelo's David would have been jealous of. Even now Estelle wanted to touch him. Even now she wanted to run her tongue all over that glistening skin.

She hugged herself in a futile attempt to stop shaking.

"Why *didn't* you bite me?" she asked, her eyes welling with tears she didn't understand. "It's not as if I could have stopped you. It's not as if I even wanted to."

He was by her side literally before she could blink. That

was startling, but he was *her* Edmund again. It was in his eyes, if not his supernaturally white skin. He wrapped his arm around her shoulder. Though he looked like ice, he was warm. She peered at his mouth, but his teeth were normal again.

She wouldn't admit even to herself that this disappointed her.

"Sweetheart, I didn't bite you because I love you. Taking blood gives my kind an extra hold over our . . . over humans. I wanted you to love me of your own free will."

"*Extra* hold?"

He flinched at her emphasis. "The more powerful among us can influence humans with our gaze alone."

"You can do that. I saw you try to do it to Graham."

"He's resistant," Edmund said. "As are you."

She looked at him, hoping to discern if he were lying. His eyes were the same bright blue as his wolf's. Something tugged at her mind, almost emerging into awareness, but Edmund was still speaking.

"You have more gifts than Graham does," he continued gently. "You can hear what people are thinking with your funny ear. You can see through my glamour with your funny eye. You can punch grown men halfway across a room. I've never been able to deceive you as completely as I do others."

Then she realized he was telling her the same thing her subconscious was.

"Your wolf," she said, barely breathing it. "Your wolf leapt between me and that lightning bolt. You saved my life eleven years ago."

He'd gathered her hands in his. "I wanted to, Estelle. And so did my wolf. You owe me no debt for it."

"You . . . you gave me part of your powers."

"I didn't plan to, but, yes, I think that's what happened. I think when the lightning passed through my animal form, the energy changed into something else. I think it carried a bit of me."

"So . . . I'm not human, either? Or maybe just my funny ear and my funny hand are immortal? I'll be dead, and they'll be crawling out of my coffin?"

He laughed. She wished she could as well, but these ideas were all a shock to her. "I doubt it," he said once he'd recovered. "Certainly not your funny ear. If you like, though, you can put a codicil in your will that all your parts should be burned."

"Oh, my God." She fell back against the cushions, her head spinning. "Graham knows about this, doesn't he? That's why you and he were fighting."

"Yes," he said, "though I think he also has a crush on you."

"Is he all right? Sally said he went missing."

"I think he's brooding. At least I don't sense that he's in trouble. I think he needs time to come to grips with what he found out."

"Oh, my God," she said, feeling like a broken gramophone. Edmund could "sense" how his children were. He could probably sense how she was, too. That's how he'd known to rescue her at Harrods. Dimly, she remembered the sound of glass breaking. He'd dived through a plate glass window like it was a pool. And he'd ended up without a scratch on him. Cold sweat began to trickle down her back.

"Are you all right?" he asked, giving her hands a squeeze. "Would you rather I left you alone for a while?"

"I don't know," she said slowly. "I don't—I mean, I *think* you're still you. A very strange you, but you. You're the man I fell in love with. In fact, maybe you're even more amazing than I knew. You adopted a human family, and you love them. I know that isn't pretend. You used to take Sally to school. In the daytime. And you had more than a sun allergy. I thought being their only parent was a challenge for you. I can't imagine how hard raising them as a vampire must have been."

He shook his head. "It wasn't hard. It was a privilege."

Estelle pressed her hands over a breathy laugh. "I have a million questions. Maybe a million and a half. But I know I couldn't take the answers in. Would you . . . would you walk me home tonight? Would you just stay with me until morning?"

His eyes took on the glow she'd always interpreted as her funny eye acting up. "You'd trust me to do that now?"

"There's no one I'd trust more," she said sincerely. Whatever else she had doubts about, that was the unvarnished truth.

Edmund's vampire gifts came in handy for sneaking out of the house without being caught. He and Estelle crept straight past Ben and Sally in the library—and they weren't even providing cover by bickering.

Edmund drove them to Estelle's flat, where they talked late into the night. Edmund answered every question Estelle asked, with an honesty that surprised her.

"Auriclus's line aren't killers," he was saying, after some hours had passed. "Or not generally. Auriclus has always been fond of humans, and he tried to instill the same respect in his children. Which is not to say killings don't happen now and then. People with power occasionally forget they're not really better than those without."

Estelle sat sideways on her modern couch, one foot tucked beneath her with her head propped in the cup of her hand. Edmund had been standing, and sometimes pacing, in front of her tiled gas fireplace. She could sense his nervousness as strongly as she sensed his determination to tell her whatever she wanted to know. Now he ran his hands through his golden hair—as his youngest son often did. Unlike Ben, Edmund's hair immediately settled back into its gleaming, perfect place. She began to understand that more than good tailoring lay behind his clothes never rumpling.

"Have you killed anyone?" she asked, knowing she had to have this answer.

He let his gaze rise from the hearth to her. "When I was human, I did. I fought to defend my country and my family's estates." Because he was looking straight at her, she couldn't miss the ghosts that shadowed his eyes. "That was a long time ago. I didn't kill as many as I might have. My brother, Aimery, was the warrior of the family."

Estelle thought she heard more than he said in that last statement, and she didn't need her funny ear to help. She shifted on the couch to face him more directly. "How long ago were you human?"

"I was born in 1337 and made immortal at seventy, so 1407 was my last mortal year. Our line encourages people to live out their human lives before they're changed. In part to formulate such rules, Aimery founded the *upyr* Council. They enforce the laws for shapechangers. My brother is a good man. We don't always see eye to eye, but he's done a bang-up job of bringing order to our kind."

"And the other kind of vampire? The ones who stick to big cities and only drink blood?"

"Their queen, Nim Wei, keeps the nests in line, more ruthlessly than my brother, but it seems to work. No *upyr* with sense wants humans to know we exist. There's simply too many of them and too few of us. That alone keeps the punishment for wanton killing severe."

Estelle shivered. Edmund had told her that Nim Wei— the beautiful vampire who'd locked Estelle in her sights outside the cinema—might be behind the assault on her. Estelle couldn't like the reminder, or his mention of "wanton" killing. It suggested *non*-wanton killing might be okay. She'd been happier thinking of the attack on her as a coincidence. She was relatively certain one didn't get to be queen unless one was powerful.

Seeing her response, Edmund came to sit beside her. His long, cool hands gently stroked her face. "I don't want you worrying about her, love. I'll get to the bottom of what happened, and I'll protect you in the meantime. If I'm not around, you can go to my son, Robin."

"Your son!" Estelle had thought she was beyond surprise, but this news stole her breath. "Did you adopt someone else?"

For the first time, Edmund seemed reluctant to answer. His hold dropped from her face. "Robin was my mortal son. It was easier not to let my new family know. Fewer stories to concoct. I wasn't much of a father to Robin, I'm afraid. Ironically, it took becoming a vampire for me to learn how to be a decent human being—not that I haven't made a mistake or two since then."

"But you chose to become a vampire?"

"I chose," he confirmed. "It's against Council law to change a human unwillingly."

The darkness hadn't yet lifted from his face. With her thumb and fingers, Estelle caressed the back of the hand he had let fall onto her knee. "Everyone makes mistakes, Edmund."

His smile was a subtle lifting of his mouth's corners. "I believe I've heard that before."

"I think you adopted Graham and Ben and Sally to make up for yours."

"Probably. But that isn't why I feel lucky to have them."

She slid onto his lap and held him, pressing her ear to the steady pulse beating in his neck. The sound was comforting; deceptive, perhaps, but comforting. Even more comforting was the way his arms gently circled her.

"Emotion," he said, catching her thoughts and not hiding it. "It makes my heart rate kick up. I suppose I'm anxious about your reactions. I've never told anyone so many of my secrets. My pulse will slow to nothing for my daytime sleep."

As if this were a signal, Estelle yawned.

"Bedtime," he said with a laugh. "Tomorrow's another night for questions."

But she had a few more before she slept. Edmund spooned her, as he had the night before. His length fit hers perfectly, every part of him tucked neatly into or around every part of her. Despite her fatigue, her body stirred with interest. His stirred, too, which sent little waves of heat lapping from her center to warm her skin.

"Edmund?" she said, because he seemed prepared to ignore what was happening between them. "Are you certain that if you bit me, it would be bad? You did say I was resistant to your power, and when you didn't bite me, I could tell it bothered you. As if, maybe, your—" She searched for the proper words. "As if maybe your climax wasn't as good as it could have been."

Silence greeted her query, but she knew he'd heard. His cock had been half hard before, and it had risen, jolt by jolt, as she spoke. Now it throbbed stiff as iron along the cleft between her bottom cheeks. If she'd needed confirmation for her theory, she had it. She fought an almost uncontrollable urge to squirm. His groin wasn't the only part of him that had tautened. His chest was hard as a board.

"Edmund?" she had to ask.

Edmund let out a tight, quick sigh. "I'm not sure what the effect of biting you would be. I don't think I want to risk it."

"But you *do* fancy doing it? I, er, seem like I'd be tasty? As tasty as anyone you've bitten before? Have there been a lot? Maybe I shouldn't ask, but I find it's preying on my mind."

"*Jesu.*" Edmund laughed, but tensely. "Yes, I fancy biting you, and, yes, I'm certain you'd be delicious. I can tell that from how good you smell. I have . . . bitten a number of women, but I assure you, on my mother's soul, none of them tormented me the way you do."

That pleased her to an embarrassing extent—and aroused her as well. Pushed past controlling herself, she gave in to her urge to wriggle, which caused Edmund to grab her hips to keep her still. She wasn't certain, but she thought he might be grinding his teeth.

"Edmund." Her voice had sunk an octave lower than normal. "You're thinking about biting me now, aren't you? Your fangs have shot out again."

Edmund groaned and rolled away from her. She should have left him alone; he was only trying to protect her, but she simply couldn't make herself.

She turned after him and crooked her chin over his shoulder. It required an effort, but she didn't rub her puckered nipples against his back. "Couldn't I look at your teeth for a moment? I'm curious to know how sharp they are."

"Estelle," he growled, resisting her attempts to see. "You don't want to be my puppet. Not even if you love me."

"I just can't help wondering what it would be like to have you bite me. I know I enjoyed it when I bit you."

"You probably enjoyed that because my desires were communicating themselves to you. Thoughts aren't all that can travel across our connection."

The heat that surged through her then was truly sweltering. She had to press her thighs together to contain it. "Really? You mean, I could find out what you want without you telling me?"

"That isn't supposed to excite you!"

Estelle could only laugh at that. "Edmund, if you don't make love to me right now, neither of us is going to sleep a wink."

He did as she asked, with a speed and energy that left her head spinning. As soon as he came the first time, he flipped her over and began again, arranging her so that she was braced on her hands and knees. She quite liked being taken from behind; it seemed to free the animal in him, maybe because she couldn't see his face with his fangs run out. His hands traveled greedily over her—her bottom, her breasts, her spine—then settled in to grip her hips.

She could tell he planned for them to stay there while he pounded into her. His strength was amazing, his passion seemingly inexhaustible. Estelle thought she'd never been on the receiving end of anything so marvelous as his powerful lovemaking. He drove her to climax after shuddering climax and joined her three times himself, grunting with each thrust as his peaks approached. When his orgasms broke, his seed shot from him in long, wild spurts—which she now knew were as different in nature as the rest of him. Somehow, this made his ejaculations all the more exciting, sending hot tingles streaking through her as he gushed. When he finally groaned and sagged on top of her, Estelle felt both thoroughly pleasured and pleasantly sleepy.

Apparently reluctant to withdraw from her, he eased her onto the mattress on her side, with him still seated long and solid inside of her. She didn't think he was unsatisfied, just hankering—if only a little—for that final intimacy.

"You feel so good," he murmured, turning his face back and forth in her tousled hair. "I could sleep like this every night."

"I love you," she said, and his cock twitched just a tiny bit.

The reaction made her smile to herself. He hadn't bitten her, but she decided she could wait for that.

Happily, she didn't think he'd be able to resist his instincts much longer.

Tottenham Court Mansions

◆━━━━━◆

For once, Estelle didn't object to Edmund leaving before dawn. She understood he wanted to check on his children, though maybe not that he needed a period of distance from her. His hungers grew too sharp if he enjoyed too much time with her. He thought it best that he spend the day in his own bed.

That day over, his heart raced at the thought of her the instant his eyes snapped open at sunset. What could have been the worst moment of his life—being discovered by her in his wolf form—had turned out to be the best. He probably broke a land speed record closing the distance between his house and hers. Ignoring the lift, he bounded up her stairs with the eagerness of a boy he hadn't been in five hundred years. Opening himself to her, without reservation, was an unexpected delight. After all she'd heard, Estelle still loved him. She wasn't running away.

Not only wasn't she running away, she was waiting behind the door for him. They started tearing off their clothes as soon as he kicked it shut behind him, falling on each other like they were starved. Neither of them could stand delays tonight.

When they'd sated the worst of their greed, Estelle had a gift for him. After closing her new front drapes, she carried a platter out from her kitchen. Unless his nose deceived him, it held a very rare beef roast. She set the platter in the center of the carpet in her living room.

"I hope the spices are all right," she said. "The cook shop didn't have any unseasoned."

Edmund stared at her in amazement.

She smiled with only a hint of nervousness. "I wanted to see you change. I thought you might need an incentive."

Edmund strode to her, took her face between his hands, and kissed her hard. "I love you, Estelle. More than I think you understand. I don't believe I've ever admired a woman more."

She blushed beautifully beneath his hold, the color warming his palms. "So the way to a vampire's heart is through his stomach, too."

He laughed and stepped back from her. Already naked, all he had to do was close his eyes and think of the sensory memories his wolf most loved: the scent of the woods, the feel of moss and bracken beneath his paws, the pulse-pounding excitement of chasing game. The familiar magic rose easily. Cool blue light rippled through his body, dissolving it like water infused with stars. For a moment he was nothing and everything. Then he was the beast who had, centuries ago, agreed to bind its soul with Edmund's.

Estelle gasped and fell back a step, her instinctive reaction to the hugeness of the creature now inhabiting her flat. She didn't realize she had less to fear from him than a natural wolf. Edmund ruled his beast, though it had its own preferences. It took its own pleasure in padding over to Estelle to nose her hand.

She was not food to it. Humans rarely were to wolves, and almost never to the kind of hybrid Edmund was. In his wolf's experience, humans were interesting fellow predators, sources of both curiosity and danger, who might—on very special occasions—serve as playmates. His wolf whined at her in the hope that she might put her clever hands to its favorite use.

"Oh, my," Estelle breathed, her eyes filling with wonder as she went slowly to her knees in front of it.

The wolf licked her face with more enthusiasm than Edmund might have recommended, but she just laughed and hugged him around the ruff.

"I say, Edmund, he's . . . *you're* beautiful."

The wolf understood the tone if not the words, taking her admiration as his due but also warming with a satisfaction more complicated beings were strangers to. Estelle was his, and Estelle loved him. All was right with the world.

When she plunged her hands into his thick winter fur and gave his flanks a thorough scratching, he became her wholehearted slave, uttering little canine whimpers and wriggling on the floor.

She laughed at that, too, obviously enchanted by her power over this other side of him. Edmund decided her amusement was worth the cost to his dignity.

He ate the roast before he changed again, quickly and with his back to her. He was a tidy enough eater; his kind of wolf left nothing of their kills behind. All the same, having progressed so famously thus far, he didn't want to do anything to disgust her.

He was wondrously relaxed by the time he resumed human form. Perhaps because his blood was flowing so freely, he developed an almost instantaneous erection.

He grinned at the lift of Estelle's eyebrows. "Want to know the other way to a vampire's heart?"

She knew already, tugging him to her bedroom where she pushed him down on her bed and gave his human shape an even more thorough petting than she'd given his wolf. Each time he tried to rise, or at least return the favor, she pressed him back. Her warm, sweet hands stroked every inch of him, until he tingled from head to toe and fisted the sheets in wads. She touched him everywhere but his sex, despite which his cock soon grew painfully erect.

His groans earned him no pity.

"Don't you move," she ordered when he tried to lift his hips suggestively. "I haven't had my fill of the feel of you."

"This part of me feels good, too."

"Too good," she said tartly. "One rub of that, and I'll be climbing on top of you."

Her reasoning hardly made it easier to wait. When she finally consented to him taking her, it was quick and fierce and ended explosively for both of them. Because he had her wrists trapped above her head by the finish, he took her again more slowly—mostly to prove he could, though he gloried in every sigh and spasm he pulled from her. He tired her more than he meant to, but hardly minded when she lay snuggled in his arms afterward.

Edmund's heart was so peaceful with her cheek resting above it that he felt like a different man. Thinking he might sleep in spite of the hour, he drew his hand with sensual enjoyment down the silky waves of her hair. He wasn't sure why he said what he did next, only that he doubted he'd find the strength of conscience to mention it again.

"Your life is never going to be normal if you stay with me."

Estelle's smile tickled his chest hair. "That had occurred to me."

"Someone else would love you. Lots of someone elses."

He knew this was true, his own son being a case in point. Estelle propped her chin on her forearm to meet his eyes.

"Lots of someone elses would love you," she retorted. "And you don't see me volunteering to give you up."

"I simply thought— It isn't that I want you to find some-one else—"

"Don't be a dope," she said. "Being with you is not a sacrifice. In any case, I thought you were eccentric when I fell for you. Why should discovering you're a vampire change how I feel?"

"This isn't a joke," he said, abruptly more earnest than he'd been before. She owed it to herself to take his cautions seriously.

Estelle laid her head back down and closed her eyes. "I'm not joking. You're the man I love. The man who fits me. I can be myself with you, and you still love me. That's pretty marvelous, I think."

It was pretty marvelous. Moreover, it was exactly what he would have said of her.

She was curled against him with her right side up. Tem-porarily stunned to silence by his luck, he feathered a circle around her right eye's scar with his fingertip. He thought it was an idle gesture, but a definite *mine* feeling rose from the wolfish half of his soul.

"Reminding yourself how you marked me?" she asked archly. "That scar does rather say I'm yours, doesn't it?"

"Estelle!" he exclaimed. "You were fifteen when that lightning bolt almost killed you."

"Fine," she said, a smile in it. "I suppose you just like touching the brand your *wolf* put on me when I was fifteen."

Edmund shifted uncomfortably. "Estelle . . ."

She came up on her elbow. "You can't mean to say you're ashamed of that. Do you think you shouldn't have saved my life?"

"Of course I don't, but—damn it, Estelle—that scar reminds me I was attracted to you back then, from the instant I laid eyes on you, and I bloody well shouldn't have been. You were a child!"

"Are you saying you wouldn't have saved me if you

hadn't been attracted? That you'd have let the lightning kill someone else?"

"I don't know. It wasn't the sort of decision one thinks through. I had an instant to act, and my wolf simply took over."

Estelle's hand stroked softly across his chest, following the contour of bone and muscle. "What if I had been a baby in a carriage? Would your wolf have saved an infant? Or, say, a trio of orphans?"

"That's different," Edmund said grumpily.

"Is it?" She held up her right hand, palm out, as if taking an oath on his behalf. "Remember, I can feel the truth in you. Your children weren't food to you, or future bedmates, and you still rescued them."

"I was lonely," he protested. "And no one with a heart the size of a pea would have separated the three of them. Don't make me out to be a hero. You've no idea how many adoption officials I thralled without compunction to cut through the paperwork."

"Well, now I really think you're dastardly! Your children would have been so much better off if they'd been adopted by caring human parents like mine!"

She was genuinely angry. He could feel it in the hot vibration thrumming off of her. He'd known her parents had been appallingly indifferent to her, but not how resentful she remained because of it. God knew why they'd had a child in the first place. Probably because, to them, having offspring was what married people did. "Estelle—"

"No, Edmund. You need to hear what I have to say. I may not have your power, but I sense something else inside you, something that troubles me. When you think of yourself and your brother as young men, when you remember Aimery was the hero, that everyone loved him and not you, *you believe they were justified to feel that way!*"

A tear of fury rolled from her eye. She was biting her lower lip to keep more from coming, the pressure of her teeth whitening the full, rosy flesh. Edmund's eyes burned in reaction to her sharp defense of him, a brief film of pink blurring his vision.

"Estelle," he said, gently wiping her tear away. "If I do think that, I have reasons to. My own wife fell in love with Aimery. She tried to poison me so she could be with him and ended up nearly killing him by mistake. That's how Aimery became *upyr*, because the flaws in my character put his life at risk."

"It sounds like the flaws in your wife's character did that."

He had to smile at her stubbornness. "I've had half a millennium to figure out who I am. I shall never be as good and brave as my brother. I shall never have his integrity. There were times when seeing Aimery rise to authority nearly ate me up with jealousy, but even then there was a part of me that knew—that *knew*, Estelle—that I would have been a curse to our kind had I been given the kind of power he has. I don't have half his evenhanded nature. I don't have his evenhanded anything."

Estelle frowned at him. "You don't have to be the same as your brother to be a good man."

Edmund could see he wasn't getting anywhere with this.

"As you wish," he surrendered, giving her a tiny smile. He suspected he didn't truly want to convince her. He enjoyed her high opinion of him.

It was enough that *he* knew what he knew about himself.

Estelle slept like a baby, her body and heart content. Fear could find no home within her. She relaxed into Edmund's comforting embrace and let her doubts drift away.

She woke sometime later but before dawn. She knew this because the sky beyond her shades was dark. Edmund was gone—or he had been. He stood beside her bed taking off his shoes and clothes. Though he didn't give the impression of rushing, he moved so swiftly the garments seemed to melt away. She wondered how long it would take to grow accustomed to these glimpses of him not pretending to be human. She was glad he felt free to be himself, but they still sent her heart skipping.

He stilled when he saw she'd lifted her head. His quick grin was as bright as an electric bulb. "Had to run an errand."

Naked again and shining with his natural glow, he slipped under the sheets with her. As soon as he did, the linens felt softer. *Well*, she thought. *There's a mystery solved.* Edmund's energy was leaving her belongings in an enhanced state.

She settled into what she'd come to think of as "her" spot against his side, her head in the cup of his shoulder, her hand smoothing the curve of his strong rib cage. He gave a pleasurable shiver as she slung her right leg on top of his. His skin was cool again, but it warmed as he lay by her.

"I went to see a friend of mine," he explained. "A businessman who's used to my hours. Roth and I have whiled away many a predawn hour over a game of chess. He likes to argue with my theories of history." He laughed softly. "Even when he agrees with them, he likes to argue."

"That's nice," she said sleepily.

"You have no questions? Not even if my friend is human or *upyr*?"

"Well, you can tell me if you want to, but I'm all out of questions now. I like lying this way with you. It feels like the best dream I ever had has come true."

His arm squeezed her closer, a quick, warm tightening as emotion hit. "If you have no questions, perhaps you'll answer one of mine."

His glow was lighting up the space around them in the

bed, throwing the folds of the sheets into high relief. Even the golden hairs on his chest were casting shadows. Estelle pushed up a little, her palm flattened across his breastbone. Beneath it, she felt his heart galloping. Considering it didn't actually have to beat, that was a trifle alarming.

"Oh, your face," he said with a nervous laugh. "It's nothing bad. I'm just not sure if it's too soon for this. It doesn't feel too soon for me, but—"

Giving up on explaining, he drew a small red velvet box from beneath his side.

For the second time in a week, Estelle's heart temporarily stopped.

"Open it," he said.

She sat up, and he sat with her, the covers falling to their waists. She took the box with trembling hands. Edmund's glow flared even higher, so she supposed this was a sign of nerves. The box's hinge was tight, but she lifted it. The second she did, a faceted diamond as big as her thumbnail exploded with rainbows. The stone was set in a mounting of buttery gold, the design elaborate enough for a czarina. Smaller rubies and sapphires gleamed on the sides, reminding her of the colors blood came in.

"Roth is Russian," he said before she could speak— something she wasn't going to be able to do until she caught her breath. "A jeweler. An émigré."

"Oh, Edmund," she managed to gasp. "It's too much!"

Her hands were shaking too badly to take out the ring. Edmund did it for her, though his fingers weren't completely steady, either.

"It's not too much. Not for you." He slid the ring down her third finger, then pulled her hand to his heart. "Estelle Berenger, would you do me the honor of marrying me?"

She looked into his luminous blue eyes and saw a man who adored her beyond reason. The strength of his love warmed her to her soul. She knew there would be obstacles for them to overcome, but in that moment none mattered.

"You don't have to answer now," he said a little raggedly.

"I want to," she said. "I want to marry you."

His breath rushed out as he embraced her. "Estelle." He kissed her, claimed her, his tongue pushing deliciously between her lips. He groaned as her clinging urged him deeper. "My star." And then he simply sat back and laughed. "You're daft to say yes, of course."

She couldn't help but grin at his happiness. "Perhaps I am, but that doesn't mean I'm letting you change your mind."

"I won't," he promised, hugging her again. "I'm surer than I've ever been about anything."

"Oh, Edmund." She squeezed him as tightly as she could with her strong right arm. Her left was occupied in displaying her engagement ring behind his back. It was utterly ridiculous, absolutely over the top, and she loved every twinkling karat of it. "I wish I could wear this thing in public."

"Why can't you?" he asked, kissing the hand that held the huge diamond.

"Because no one knows we're together yet."

He smoothed her hair behind her shoulders. " 'No one' isn't strictly true. The rest, or the rest who matter, I have a few ideas about working on . . ."

Bedford Square

❧

Estelle really, truly wasn't convinced this announcement was a good idea, despite Edmund's claim that there wasn't any point in putting it off. According to him, the only thing that might have shaken what she felt for him had already happened. Since they'd both admitted they were decided, he wanted—no, *needed*—to claim her in this traditional way.

"We could at least wait until Graham comes back," she muttered as he led her by the elbow to the cozy Bedford Square dining room. The walls were paneled with glowing wood, and the heavy silver candelabra had been polished until they gleamed. Edmund's hold tightened on her arm as if he knew she'd run, given half a chance.

"Graham will keep his own schedule. I think you know this isn't going to get easier as time goes by."

"Procrastination isn't always our enemy," she retorted.

He smiled and held out her chair for her. It was the "guest" chair, which also happened to be at the end of the table opposite his, exactly where his wife would have sat if he'd had one. When she'd been staying under this roof, she'd taken a guilty pleasure in this seat being reserved for her. Now the privilege had her heart sinking to her toes. Her skin was all over chills with nerves.

"Do you want to borrow my coat?" Edmund offered in a heavy-lidded tease. The smolder of his eyes warmed her handily. He knew loaning her this garment would merely be another way of making his claim public.

Sally walked in as Estelle frowned.

"Hullo, Estelle," she said. "Ooh, good china! What's the occasion?"

"No occasion," Estelle answered hastily.

Edmund chuckled to himself and lit the tall white tapers.

Ben entered as he was lighting the final one. Edmund's son had washed up since coming home from work. His streaky blond hair was combed, his face clean-shaven. Estelle was so used to him she sometimes forgot how handsome he was: troublemaker handsome, with his crooked grin and the dare-me glint in his eye. The candlelight brought out the green in his eyes, or maybe the faint flush on his chiseled cheekbones did that.

He took his usual seat without glancing at his sister.

"You look nice," Estelle said.

His troublemaker's glint was nowhere in sight tonight. His gaze seemed startled as it jumped to hers. He dropped it almost at once back onto his plate.

"Going out after dinner. A mate and I have a double date."

Sally's fork clattered to the floor.

"I'll get that," Edmund said, bending to retrieve it. He wiped the utensil with his napkin and handed it back to her. "Mrs. Mackie made Welsh rarebit tonight."

"On the good china?" Sally's jaw had dropped. "Is it my birthday and I forgot?"

Welsh rarebit was Sally's favorite comfort food. Edmund

smiled at her, his expression so warm and understanding Estelle thought maybe he did know how hard this was going to be on his youngest child. "I see no reason why we can't have toast and cheese sauce on nice plates. Ben, would you pour the wine?"

"Wine, too!" Sally exclaimed as Mrs. Mackie bustled in to serve. She was as round and cheerful as a storybook housekeeper—and justly proud of her kitchen skills.

"Here you are, dears," she said, ladling out their dishes. "There's lovely veggies under the covers. Hope you enjoy."

She was gone too soon for Estelle's preference. Likable or not, Edmund wouldn't discuss family business in front of the housekeeper. He rose as the serving door swung shut. Ruby liquid gleamed in his wineglass as he lifted it formally toward her. His eyes shone so brightly with love they should have lit the room. Estelle's heart beat like a rabbit's in her chest, ebullience warring with anxiety. This would be real once he spoke out loud. This would be happening.

Always quick on his feet, Ben looked from his father to her.

"Oh, boy," he said quietly.

"I have an announcement," Edmund said, his face creasing widely with his smile. "One I'm very proud and happy to share with you. I've asked Estelle to marry me, and she said yes."

Estelle's heart beat twice in the abrupt silence.

"Well, that's not right," Sally said, recovering first. "What about Graham?"

Ben coughed into his napkin, then pushed back his chair and stood.

"Congratulations, sir," he said, shaking his father's hand. "I know you'll make her happy."

"But Graham likes her," Sally said. "*You* can't marry Estelle. She's—You're—" She flapped her hands helplessly.

"We love each other," Edmund told her. "That's been true for a while."

Sally's big blue eyes filled with tears. "Is she going to move in here?" *Is she going to take my place?*

Edmund seemed to hear the unspoken plea as clearly as Estelle. He pulled Sally out of her chair and into his embrace. "You'll always be my baby. Nothing can change that. And think how much you'll like having your friend around all the time."

"She lived here before without marrying you. Oh, Lord! Am I going to have to let her boss me around?"

Edmund laughed into her short flaxen curls. No one could deny Sally spoke her mind. "I expect Estelle will want to leave the bossing around to me, you being such a handful."

"But you'll take her side when I'm bad. I know you will!"

Edmund pushed her gently back by the shoulders, his manner both grave and kind. "I've always expected you to treat Estelle with respect, and you've always managed well enough. She makes me happy, Sunshine, more than I ever thought I deserved to be. Please do me the favor of not making her regret she accepted me."

Sally pulled a little face. "I do want you to be happy. I just—"

Ben cleared his throat. Miraculously, Sally glanced at him, looked abashed, and shut her mouth.

"We both congratulate you, sir," he said. "I'm sure we'll get used to the idea in no time. And Sally and I won't be underfoot much longer now that we're grown up."

Edmund's reaction to this was an almost comical alarm. If either of his children needed reassurance that they were wanted, they had it then.

"I thought, perhaps, we'd look for a larger house," he said. "Maybe with a bit of grounds in the country. Room to run, and all that."

"In the country!" Sally moaned, distraught again.

Edmund shot a silent plea down the table to Estelle.

"The country is a wonderful place for throwing parties," Estelle soothed. "Your friends will love coming to visit. Plus, I doubt we'd be very far from London. Edmund will need to come back to teach."

"Exactly," Edmund said. "And if you really hate the country, I suppose you could stay in this house with Ben. I don't mind keeping it, and I expect he'd be willing to provide what looking out for you still need."

Ben and Sally exchanged a look of mutual horror.

"No!" they said in near unison.

Sally finished for both of them. "I'm sure that isn't necessary. I'm sure I . . . we could get used to living in the country." With an air of determination, she came around the table to stand before Estelle. She held out her hands, the tip of her nose red from the tears she was restraining. "I think it's swell you and the professor have found each other. I want you to be happy, Estelle, no matter who it's with."

Looking up at Sally's pink-cheeked face, being clasped by her warm, small hands, Estelle believed Sally sincerely wanted to mean her good wishes.

Estelle had never been in Edmund's bedroom. This floor of the tall, narrow house was his alone. She'd felt quite conspicuous letting him lead her up to it after their inevitably awkward dinner. Neither Sally nor Ben were unworldly enough not to guess the reason Edmund wanted her alone.

She stared, astonished, at his heavy curtained bed. It was so big, so old . . . so immovable. An image slid through her mind: herself tied naked to one of the thick, turned posts. She jumped when Edmund's hands squeezed her shoulders. She hadn't heard him come up behind her. When he nuzzled beneath the hair she'd rolled and pinned at her neck, her sex quivered. His pelvis brushing her bottom didn't help matters. He was hardening as he stood there.

"Maybe we should go to my flat," she said nervously.

His hands slid down the length of her arms, making them tingle even through her sleeves. "This is part of letting my family get used to my intentions—having you here, in our home."

"Yes, but you don't have to *have* me here, not before we're married."

He hugged her closer, his hot mouth pressing her temple. "I want you here. I want to take you in my bed, to watch you struggle not to cry out while I shove my aching prick up inside you, over and over again. You're so strong here, Estelle." He curved one elegant hand over her mound, his fingers squeezing her softness possessively. "I think the lightning must have changed this, too. I can take you almost as forcefully as I could one of my own kind."

Supposed strength notwithstanding, Estelle's knees gave an embarrassing wobble.

He felt it, naturally, and laughed low and masculine. He was pleased with his effect on her. Before she realized what he was doing, he'd slipped his feet beneath hers and had walked her forward across the carpet to his bed. Then his hands were on her wrists, cuffing them and lifting them above her head. Her body reacted just as strongly as the last time he'd done this. Something about him taking charge of her heated her blood. Shifting both her hands into one of his, he trapped them high against the carved mahogany post. As he did, their breathing sped up in synchrony.

His lips skated down the side of her neck, lingering over her pulse and making her shiver violently.

"Shall I tie you here?" he asked in a seductive whisper. "The way you were just thinking? It might be dangerous, but I think I could keep my instincts in check."

"Dangerous?" Estelle's response was close to a moan.

"It would be dangerous because I'd like it so much.

Because I'd be very, very excited to have you at my mercy."

"Would your wolf be excited, too?"

His body jerked—involuntarily, she thought.

"Yes," he said, the admission going through her like a lick of fire.

His hand had fallen from her wrists, so she turned and began unbuttoning his waistcoat with all the human speed she could command. He said her name, his hips rocking into hers, forcing her to feel his growing erection. As soon as his waistcoat was open, she undid his trousers and worked her hand inside the heated pocket of flesh and cloth. His head fell back as her fingers curled around his infinitely silky skin. She loved how thick he was, how hard and responsive. She tugged his shaft out from his body, wrapping its center in her fist and pulling. The sound of pleasure that broke in his throat elated her. This part of him truly was a fine plaything.

"I'd love for you to tie me up," she confessed. "I'd love to give you and your wolf anything you desire. I do have one condition, though."

"What?" Edmund rasped, his lips tightening painfully. Now that she knew what to look for, she could tell what he was hiding. His body writhed as she tugged his cock again. "What's your condition?"

"I want to look at your fangs first. I want to touch them, to know what I'm supposed to be fearful of."

He lost his hold on his glamour with a rumbling groan. He was bright before her, shaking with need, a candle of bone and muscle lit by his lust. Waves of energy filled the room, like heat washing over her, like sex in electric form. He'd stopped clamping his lips together, maybe to help him breathe. She could see his eyeteeth had run out full length in longing. Their tips were white and shining and sharp, mesmerizing her as if she were a mouse frozen by a cat.

"No," he said, his eyes troubled. "Don't ask that."

"It's what I want, Edmund. It's what's been preying on my mind. I trust you not to lose control."

She wasn't certain the last was true; he looked very close to the edge tonight. Then again, given how her sex was liquefying, she couldn't swear that wasn't why she was asking.

Ben didn't want to leave Bedford Square. He knew he ought to, but in the last ten minutes of arguing with himself he hadn't managed it. Instead, he leaned straight-armed over his bureau, his hands gripping either side of its worn oak top. His head was bent as if he were exhausted, his heart racing unnaturally.

Per usual, Sally was being silly. Yes, she'd have to listen to Estelle if she and Edmund married, but that was probably a good thing; Sally could be too willful for her own good. Her only fear that mattered—that the professor would love her less—was sheer nonsense. Never mind the difference in the couple's ages, Ben could see how happy their father was with Estelle, how much warmer and easier with himself. He'd probably be better at expressing his affection now, and he'd never been stingy on that front.

Ben had been amazed by that from the start: how willing Edmund had been to let them see he cared. Ben's memories of his natural parents had faded over the years, but he knew they'd been too tangled in their own worries to pay him mind. They'd been achingly young and just as achingly poor. When Ben's father had been called up to fight in the last Great War, keeping food on the table was more than his frightened mother could handle. Ben had been obliged to turn thief for both of them. She'd died younger than he was now, throwing herself off Southwark Bridge a week to the day after she'd got the news her husband had been killed. As far as Ben could tell, his existence hadn't so much as slowed her rush into death's arms.

Given this, he had reason to know how lucky he and Sally were.

"Sod it," he muttered to the brush and comb that lay between his straining arms. Liam would be waiting at the pub right now, probably with a plump bird or two picked out. They'd take them back to Liam's place and give his lumpy double beds a good workout. Ben could practically hear the springs creaking. He wanted to hear them creaking, that was for sure. His cock had been knocking up at him for attention since he'd sat down at dinner, growing thicker and more uncomfortable as the minutes passed. It was a steel spike now, refusing to relax no matter how many cricket statistics he recited in his head. The last thing he needed was to stay here soothing Sally's fears. Ben wanted a partner he didn't have to be ashamed of desiring.

It was just too bloody bad he couldn't forget the stricken look on Sally's face when she'd heard their father's announcement.

His knuckles whitened as he clenched his teeth. This whole blasted house stank of sex, with the irresistible essence of bodies yearning to join. Ben's balls were pulsing as if a single stroke could make them convulse.

Assuming, of course, that the stroke came from a particular female hand.

That's it, he snarled as he grabbed his keys. *I'm getting out of here*.

He could have groaned when he ran into Sally outside his door.

"You're leaving," she said, her fist pressed to the tempting hollow between her breasts. Ben forced himself not to look for her nipples.

"I told you I was," he said.

"I know, but—" She stopped and stared up at him.

"But?"

She bit her lip. "I don't want you to."

If he'd thought his cock hurt before, that was nothing

to the wave of pain that swept through it at her admission. Sweat flashed across his face like a burn.

"Sally—"

"I know it isn't fair." Her hand lightly touched his chest as she cut him off. "I know I'm horrible not to want you to. It's just—" She lowered her voice. "You're going to do to some woman what you did to me, and I can't bear it. Not on top of everything else. Couldn't you—" She swallowed and looked down his front to the evidence of how damn much he needed a release. "Couldn't you . . . satisfy yourself until I get used to the idea? I mean, you were going to do that before, that day I walked in on you."

"Oh, sure, Sally," he said, his sarcasm thick. "Anything to make you feel better. And maybe you could tell me when you might be 'used to the idea' of me having a normal life."

"Ben." She had the nerve to sound reproving. Her other hand came to his chest, her fingertips sending tingles of sexual awareness streaking to his groin. He had to catch her wrists and hold them away so he could breathe again.

"You'll be fine," he said, slow and firm. "Dad marrying Estelle is a good thing, even if you can't see it yet. Go cry into your pillow if you're determined to be miserable. I'm going to get screwed."

"Ben, don't leave like this!" She caught his hand as he pulled away. "I'm sorry, Ben. I truly am."

It was the apology that did it; the rough, real tears that pleaded for forgiveness. He yanked her to him and kissed her, devouring her mouth like a sailor on his first shore leave. She clung right back, her kiss so hot, so open, he honestly thought he was going to die. She was all he wanted. Not other women, her. She'd called herself unfair, but he couldn't even think about her sleeping with another man. The mere idea made him insane enough to shove himself between her legs again. For long, wet minutes he couldn't leave her, couldn't stop himself from tasting her one more time. One more pull of his cheeks. One more plunge of his tongue. One more chance to make her little breasts press closer. If he stopped, his sanity might return. If he stopped, he might realize he mustn't ever do this again.

"Jesus," he cursed, tearing free of her.

Her face was pink from hairline to chin, her mouth swollen like it had been stung. He immediately wanted it sucking his cock. It already looked like it had been.

"We can't do this," he said "We. Can't. Do. This."

"But, Ben—" The words were panted. "I can't think about anything else."

Graham's friend Cecil had rooms in Westminster, not far from Parliament, where he worked as an aide to a senior clerk. For the past few days, Graham had been holed up in them, drowning his various agonies in Cecil's endless liquor supply. He'd be drowning them still if Cecil hadn't burst out with his big confession over their last cocktail.

Cecil was in love with Graham, and had been since they'd met at school.

Graham hadn't had the faintest inkling how to respond. He hoped he hadn't been cutting, but he knew he'd sat there for a full minute in Cecil's overheated bedsit with his mouth gaping like a trout.

His stuffy old friend Cecil. In love with him.

Graham didn't think anyone had ever been in love with him before.

That the first was Cecil was unnerving, to say the least—and worse because it came on top of a host of other unnerving happenings. It made Graham guiltily glad he hadn't confided in Cecil, in spite of how soused he'd been. Cecil had assumed Graham's troubles were with some girl.

Once he'd recovered from Cecil's bombshell, Graham had forced himself to his feet and told his friend he had to be going. He'd hugged him, an idiotic backslapping sort of thing, and tried to say something that wasn't cruel. *That isn't what winds my clock*, he thought he'd slurred. *But I wish you the best with it.*

He'd left Cecil stammering that he hadn't meant it, that it had just been the gin talking. *Ha ha. Just a joke, old boy*—which Graham was too drunk to even pretend to believe.

Christ, he thought now. What a sorry old world this was! He was tramping stolidly north, on his way back to Bedford Square. He could have taken the Tube home; all the alcohol in his veins was causing him to shiver from the cold, but riding the train wouldn't have given his head a chance to clear.

He'd been hiding from what he had to do long enough. Like it or not, Graham had people to protect.

Heaven's Lake, Manchuria

Back in Rome, Aimery's wife was organizing a farewell banquet, one that Auriclus—the guest of honor—had no plans to attend. Though well intended, the event struck him as maudlin and unnecessary. Auriclus had warned Aimery what he meant to do because his passing would affect the shapechangers, not because he wanted anyone to fuss. He'd always preferred to love his people from a distance.

So he was in Manchuria this frigid half hour before dawn, standing on the mountainous shore of a lake so still, so abandoned by humankind that its silence was as palpable a presence as the breath-stealing cold.

Heaven's Lake had long been one of Auriclus's favorite spots on earth. Formed by a volcanic crater, its crystal clear waters were pure enough even for *upyr* to drink. Tonight, the sky stretched like obsidian above its frozen surface, the fathomless blackness broken only by pinpoint stars. With the coming of the Russian railroad and, lately, the invasion of the Japanese, more humans had discovered this area's remote beauty. Happily, the snows of winter sent them home: the trekkers and the tourists and the Kazaks with their cheerful yurts. The white-frosted pines and peaks were Auriclus's now, his to contemplate as he looked back over his long life.

He rested his back against a tall gray boulder, aware of the cold but not discomfitted by it. His weariness rode him lightly, so familiar a companion it had become as much a part of him as any organ of his body. It amused him that he knew no more of what came after death than a mortal. A long life taught one about life, not what transpired on the other side. For all the systems of belief he'd seen come and go, this was no less a mystery to him than to anyone.

He smiled, his fangs running out with pleasure. His ears, sharper than any listening device yet invented, picked out the deep, coughing roar of a Siberian tiger, warning rivals off a recent kill. It was a sound he hadn't heard for some time. The world's great predators were dwindling—even his beloved wolves.

For a moment, he thought, *You could stay, try to protect them.* But interference was not his way. Packs still hunted these mountains. He had to have faith that they would survive. In any case, no one could stop the world from changing. The planet itself had been designed for it. Volcanoes, earthquakes, fires, and floods—what were these but nature's changing of the guard? To everything there was a season, and Auriclus's season had reached its end.

A hint of pearl began to lighten the horizon above the eastern range of the Changbai Shan. This dawn would not reach Rome for many hours, a fact that Auriclus was counting on. The sharing of his tremendous power would come as a shock to some, but they would have the safety of the night to absorb and adjust to it.

He lifted the shiny modern pistol that had hung in his relaxed right hand. Its magazine was loaded with iron rounds, fashioned for him by a human he had thralled. The man had also shown him how to operate the weapon, assuring him it would function in the cold. An *upyr* as old as Auriclus would take a good while to burn. Far better to die quickly, then let the sun dispose of anything that remained—a safety net, as it were, in case the bullet was not enough.

Shapes were beginning to take form around him: the sharp white crags of the mountains, patches of mist clinging like ghosts to the lake's surface. Tears burned his eyes at the loveliness of the scene, the droplets turning to ice almost as soon as they rolled onto his ivory cheeks.

Life has been good, he thought. *Life has been good to me*.

He cocked the hammer of the gun as the mortal had instructed him and pressed the muzzle tight to his temple. The metal was the exact same temperature as his skin. So faintly he wondered if he'd imagined it, the mournful howl of *canis lupus* rose and fell behind him.

The sound came from the west, from the ancients' fabled Kingdom of the Shades.

Perfect, he thought, his immortal heart giving one last beat.

With neither regret nor hesitation, he pulled the trigger.

Bedford Square

❦

Estelle didn't argue with Edmund's reluctance to display his fangs . . . or she didn't argue in words. Rather, she stepped back from him and pulled out her hairgrips, allowing the gleaming waves to fall section by section to her strong, feminine shoulders. When all the silky lengths were down, she ran her fingers through them and shook her head. With this simple act, she transformed herself from woman to seductress.

"Come closer to the light," she said.

Her voice was husky, a siren's song. Edmund's feet began to move.

"I shouldn't do this," he protested.

"Shh," she said. "It will be all right."

There was an old glass sconce set into the wall beside the head of his bed. The fixture had burned gas for a previous generation of humans, but now it held an electric bulb. Edmund stepped into its circle of illumination, unable to resist the lure of her interest in his alienness. His heart felt like it was going to pound through his ribs. This was such a knife edge she was treading—without even knowing it.

"Relax," she said, her shining gray eyes on his. "I'm just going to pull back your upper lip."

She took it between her finger and thumb. A tremor shook his shoulders, a shudder that turned into a more delicate vibration. Her mouth was parted for her hastened breathing as she examined his now fully extended fangs.

"They're sharp," she commented.

"Don't touch the points," he said too quickly, too breathily. "I don't want you to prick yourself."

Her gaze slid back to his. She wet her mouth. His blood began to roar in his ears. He could barely hear her when she spoke again. "And if I touch you here?"

She ran her index finger gently beneath his upper lip, drawing the pad along his gums. The whorls of her finger's pattern tickled the smooth, wet skin. Some instinct or intuition—or, hell, maybe his pupils dilated—told her to press harder at the throbbing base of his fangs. His breath rushed out as she did, then abandoned him altogether when she curled her finger behind his eyeteeth and stroked from the other side.

He literally couldn't move. She might as well have been fingering his glans; the nerves beneath his fangs were that connected to his sexuality. His skin flashed hot and cold by turns, his prick punching out from his body with a force that frightened him. His trousers were open, and the air hit his tip. He could feel the little eye oozing the fluid of extreme lust.

"Does that feel good?" she whispered. "Does it feel like when I rub your cock?"

She read him too well. Edmund caught her wrist and then caught his breath. "It makes me want to bite you, to sink my teeth into your neck and drink."

A fresh flush swept up her face. "Are you certain that would be a mistake?"

"Don't," he said, the sound as hoarse as any he'd uttered. "This is hard enough. I don't need you pushing me."

She looked at him, then dropped her eyes. She seemed contrite, but her lashes fluttered with excitement.

"You're right," she said, "and I'm sorry. Maybe you should tie me up."

Lord, she was killing him. He laughed, shakily, because her faux innocent suggestion actually sounded like a good idea. For the first time in their relationship, he thought she might be a bigger threat to him than he was to her. But maybe it didn't matter. He knew he wasn't walking away from her tonight.

"Climb onto my bed," he said, the order hard enough to make her body jerk. "On your knees."

She obeyed him, which was arousing by itself. She wore her work clothes: a crisp cotton shirtwaist with a pointed collar and a narrow calf-length skirt. The tweedy wool imprisoned her thighs, hampering her movements. Careful to hide his reaction to that, he took a long brocade tie from one of the four-poster's hangings, swinging it from his fingers as he prowled slowly around the bed. Her eyes followed his progress as if she were hypnotized.

Deciding it *could* get more painful, Edmund's cock kicked like a mule. Another spurt of sexual fluid dampened its crown.

"Spine against the pole, Estelle. You'll want something to lean against while I'm taking you."

She shivered, but tried to speak normally. "Shouldn't I remove my clothes?"

"I'll take care of that," he promised.

He could feel the danger gathering inside him, and so could she—the beast that wouldn't be denied what it craved. He hadn't played dominance games many times. Perhaps he'd have played them more if they'd affected him as strongly with others as they did with Estelle. She was the partner he wanted to own, the woman whose safety ought to belong to him. Her body was trembling, her nipples hard as currants behind her tailored blouse. Just roughly enough to give her a taste of what was coming, he pulled her arms behind the post and bound her wrists snugly. His wolf loved her little signs of trepidation, loved that this was a sort of competition. She could probably get loose if she called on the strength of her strange right arm, but from the way her breath had gone ragged, Edmund doubted she'd want to.

He pounced onto the mattress in front of her, the motion one no human could have performed. The most primitive corner of his nature thrilled to her startled gasp.

"Are you wet?" he rumbled from all fours. "Is your lust for me running from you yet?"

"Edmund . . ." she murmured, but he didn't give her a chance to say more.

In one long motion, he ripped her clothes down the front of her. They all fell away—blouse, skirt, underthings— peeling back from her curves like leaves. She gasped again, more loudly. Naked, she was almost too lovely to bear: her womanly breasts and hips, her long, tremulous thighs. Those thighs gleamed with sexual moisture. She was wet enough to satisfy the most insecure of men, and Edmund was hardly that.

The scent of her arousal was a heady cloud in the air.

With a growl that was more wolf than man, he shoved his face against her mound, into the heart of that delicious aroma. As he lapped her, she lurched in her bonds, crying out his name and rocking her hips forward. His tongue was too much for her to hold up under, too quick and clever and strong. He forced her quivering knees wider, latched his mouth onto her bud of pleasure, and made her come.

"Edmund," she groaned. "Don't make me scream in your house."

He couldn't remember why he ought to listen. She was trying to close her legs, maybe to hide her secrets or maybe just to clutch his head closer. Either way, he wouldn't let her. She was his to do with as he pleased. Keeping her spread with his hands, he pushed his tongue inside her, shuddering with triumph when she moaned. Her taste was nearly as sweet as blood. He took her up to the edge and left her hanging there.

She was hotter now than if she'd never come at all.

He chose then to back away and remove his clothes, piece by teasing piece. He knew she loved his body. As he stripped, he made his muscles flex and bulge for her. Her beautiful naked breasts heaved in reaction.

His trousers were the last to go. He stood on the mattress to ease them down. His cock thrust high and thick, the head swaying a finger's breadth from his navel. This was a young man's erection, big and brutishly eager. Edmund reveled in showing it off to her. Because she was kneeling, her view was dead on. His balls had drawn up with excitement, and the little slit was weeping steadily for her.

"Edmund," she breathed—part awe, part admiration. "Good Lord."

"Suck it," he ordered, as autocratic as a king.

She wet her lips and lowered her head to him. He didn't give her more than the bulbous crown; that was quite enough for her to handle. Handle it she did, though, tonguing him with a thoroughness and a skill that tightened all the tendons in his neck. When a moan threatened to squeeze past them, he pulled out.

"Now," he said, his voice harsher than normal. "Why don't we see if I can catch you up to me again?"

"I don't think that's necessary," she confessed, her cheeks so pink they looked hot. "I really liked tasting you."

She didn't yet realize this wasn't about what was necessary. He kissed her mouth until she wriggled, his fingertips playing lightly through her creamy folds. No matter how generously he spread her moisture, more flowed out from her core. Her clit was throbbing like a little heart. He pinched it just hard enough to make her jump.

Then he licked her, the way his wolf had always wanted to—the beads of sweat on her temples, the sensitive bend of her neck, the fragrant channel between her soft, full breasts. Her nipples were candy to his *upyr* senses, smooth as satin on his tongue and pulsing with her excitement. He wanted to sink his fangs into either side of the heated peaks, wanted to drink from her as he suckled.

Aching to do so, he fondled her sex instead, tugging its folds and swellings, stroking its wet channels. This was not to keep her motor ticking over—though it certainly did that—but because he simply couldn't resist touching the evidence of what he did to her.

"Lord," she gasped, struggling against the ties at her wrists. "I wish I could put my hands on you."

He straightened and ran shaking palms down the graceful curve of her back. She arched as if even that simple caress felt good, the muscles in her thighs shifting restlessly. He tried not to look, but he couldn't keep his gaze from sliding to the pulse beating quick and hard in her throat. There was more candy if he wanted it. She wouldn't even fight him taking it. The room had been shadowed when they began. Now, with the temptation that coiled inside him, his aura flared so high he lit her up.

He licked his fangs involuntarily.

"I've never seen you like this," she said. "So wild and excited."

"This is me, Estelle, as I truly am."

Their eyes met and held. He could feel his cock bobbing weightily at his groin, jerking with the strength of his desire for her.

"I'm not afraid, Edmund. I've never been afraid of you."

His breath came harder, his heart out of control. "Do you want my cock inside you now?"

"Yes."

"Do you want all of it?

"Yes, Edmund. Every inch."

"Do you want it hard?"

He didn't know why he was delaying, only that he craved her answers. She settled her knees wider, the bedsprings creaking with the shift. Her voice was throaty and determined. "I want your cock as hard as you can shove it in, as far as it will reach inside of me. I want to find out if I'm as strong as you think I am."

The danger didn't matter. Edmund couldn't hold back when she was like this. He took her hips in a good, firm grip, tilted his pelvis to the needed angle, and plunged his whole hard length into her sex.

The moan that tore from him was that of a tortured man. Taking her was a bliss of the highest order. She was so wet he could have drowned, so hot he could have gone up in flames. He had to pull back and push in again to see if the second penetration was as good. He grunted, because it was better: hotter and tighter as her inner muscles clamped down on him. He couldn't stop then. Pleasure layered over pleasure as he thrust and thrust, a joy not just of his body but his emotions. He loved her so much, and her trust was a precious gift. He cried out each time their hips struck each other—sounds she echoed as if that sleek, wet friction felt just as wonderful to her.

"More," she said, her head falling back to bare her gorgeous neck. "I want more of you."

He reached behind her to grip the hands he'd trapped together with the brocade tie. He didn't offer to release her; her helplessness felt too good, her lush breasts pressed and joggling against his chest. She seemed to agree with his opinion. Their fingers tangled together and clutched tight.

"More," she begged. "*Please.*"

He dug in his knees and gave her all of him.

He hadn't known how badly she wanted him to use force. Her first scream of climax was muffled against his shoulder. Her second, mere heartbeats later, was accompanied by the nip of her teeth into his skin.

That was too much for Edmund's already shaky control. He shot toward his own release like an arrow loosed. He couldn't have forestalled it even if he wanted to. He needed this, needed her, at a deeper level than conscious thoughts could explain. He thrust into her with almost all his strength, reaching her end, pounding his sensitive tip against a hot, wet cushion. Some women didn't like that, but she urged him on with whimpering, eager cries. The need to come screamed through him.

And then he heard it: a distant rumble like an avalanche. Images flipped unbidden through his mind. A frozen lake in a ring of mountains. A silver pistol. A ray of sunlight piercing a snowy pass. *My children*, said a deep, soft voice he vaguely recognized. *Accept my gift and my blessings.*

His climax broke, propelled by the wave of power that was rolling through him without warning. The size of the wave astounded, deafening without a sound. The boat that was his body seized, his blood on fire in his veins. He hadn't known what wanting was before. Hunger thrust through him, like every craving he'd ever felt piled up and multiplied. He had no chance to control it; it was too overmastering. No snake had ever struck its prey as hard as he struck Estelle's neck. His fangs sank deep as he pulled on her like a starving man. The first swallow made him groan, instantly crazed for more of her sweetness. She was so good, and he'd been so hungry for so long. The richness of her life rolled down his throat, warming every cell of his body. Tears of adoration and pleasure squeezed from his eyes. He came again and again, his testicles contracting long after he was dry.

Estelle moaned, too, but it wasn't quite a sound of ecstasy.

He pushed back from her so fast he almost fell out the other side of the bed.

He grabbed the post to save himself, but it was her he should have been worried about protecting. Her head was lolling. Slowly, she lifted it. He saw she'd snapped her restraints.

"Edmund," she said, reaching dazedly for him. "Why did you stop?"

I stopped because I was afraid I'd kill you. Because I'm afraid I might kill you yet. He couldn't say it out loud. He licked his lips without thinking and tasted her. The awful hunger still beat inside him, monstrous and alive. He hadn't taken time to heal her, and two red lines trickled down her neck, drawing his gaze like magnets. As a rule, his kind couldn't drain a human, not without help, but just then he thought he might be able to.

Worrying about her free will seemed inconsequential compared to that.

Without warning, his aura swelled again—a bright, white fire with too much fuel to burn. Frightened, he gripped the post until his knuckles ached. The glare of his energy filled the room like the sun.

Good God, he thought, the pieces coming together. *That was Auriclus in the mountains. He killed himself and shared his power. I'm becoming an elder.*

Estelle turned her hands back and forth as if the sight of them was perplexing her. "Edmund," she said. "I think I'm glowing, too."

She *was* glowing. It wasn't simply the reflection of his increasing power. Her right arm was the brightest, but her eye and ear glowed as well. The light was snaking through her veins as if it had replaced her blood, until she hardly looked human anymore.

Edmund's heart gave a thump of horror.

"I have to get out of here," he said. "I can't hurt the people I love."

He could feel the power reaching out from him, searching for more bodies to remake in its own image. Now, at last, he knew the secret to changing humans into *upyr*, and all he wanted to do was curse. Humans thought drinking vampire blood would turn them into his kind, but it was this—the deep penetration of an elder's aura—that was the true elixir of immortality.

No one in the house would be safe from his flare-up. Not Ben. Not Sally. Not Graham, whom he could sense just inside the house's entryway. His eldest was on his knees, arms wrapped around his stomach as if it hurt. Edmund didn't know if his runaway aura would kill or merely alter them, but either way he couldn't let this happen to his children. He was going to destroy everyone he loved before he figured out how to tame this thing.

"Don't try to follow me," he begged Estelle—all he had time to say.

He leapt away from her as she cried "no!" He was barely thinking as he grabbed his clothes and crashed his shoulder through the bedroom window, barely breathing as he bounded down the steepness of the roof. He had one chance, and he was going to take it.

For all their sakes, he had to disappear into the isolation of the night.

They'd been turning away from each other. Sally had been letting Ben convince her they ought to. And then suddenly neither could stop themselves. Greed tore through them like a train whose brakes had been sabotaged.

"Hurry," Sally gasped. "Just open your trousers."

Her hands fought his to get to the fastenings, his cock pounding painfully behind the cloth.

"Your knickers," he demanded, shoving her "help" away. "Take them off."

She yanked the bits of silk and lace down her legs.

He had his erection gripped in his hand, rubbing it because it needed attention so badly. Sally didn't seem to notice, or if she did, she felt the same. She hiked up her skirt and climbed him with one leg, not even waiting for him to remove his fist before she pushed her sex over him. She was hot and wet and clung to him like a sucking mouth. They faced each other in his open doorway, and it seemed the perfect place to be. Halfway to heaven, he braced the sole of one work boot on the frame behind him. Leverage assured, he released his hold on his shaft, and pushed his sex into hers.

Sally was so ready, he entered her like a knife into warm butter.

Her head rolled on the wood as she felt his full length sink in. Her hands were slapped to either side of the wall behind her. Only the leg she'd crooked around his hip held him.

"Oh, yes," she said, tightening her calf. "That's what I need."

He'd never been so glad for his experience with women. He found the spot inside her sheath that made her cry out when he thrust over it, the one that swelled and got juicy and felt so good to rub his tip over. She clutched his back instead of the door so she could grind her button against his root each time he went balls deep. She wasn't talking anymore, just making guttural, hungry noises that rode like sparks down his nerves.

Her speechlessness was fine. He knew what she wanted, because it was exactly what he did. *More. Faster. Harder. Deeper.* Heaviness spread through his groin, delicious warning of the peak to come. He knew she felt it, too, and that drove him to still more effort. Sweat flew off him as he rolled his hips with greater and greater force. Far from complaining, Sally met his thrusts with abandon.

God help me, he thought, his throat too tense with sexual straining to say a word. She really was the perfect erotic match for him.

Her nails dug into him through the back of his sweater-

vest, the doorframe thumping her bare bottom with every
thrust. This was a life-and-death orgasm they were reaching for. They both uttered a strangled sound as their pleasure spiked closer to the tipping point. They hung on the
edge, snarling at each other as they humped desperately.
They had to go over, had to break this terrible tension.
White flashed across Ben's vision like a photographer's
exploding bulb, his sexual nerves firing in one huge volley.
He knew his body wasn't going to let him pull out. He was
going to flood her with his jism, going to pour it all into
her. He couldn't hold back his shout of relief as he spilled
into her hard and long.

He couldn't have pulled out even if he'd wanted to. Sally's hands were clamped on his arse, holding him in a death
grip as she gushed over him.

"Yes," she growled, her eyes screwed shut. "Yes, yes,
yes."

Ben was always a bit oversensitive in the moments after
he came, but just then it didn't matter. Loving her pleasure,
he ground into her for as long as she shook. He wanted to
stamp the shape of his prick into her pussy, wanted her
never to be the same. When her orgasm finally ended, he
took what felt like his first complete breath in hours.

"Oh. My. Lord," she said, her eyelids managing to open
on the second try. "I got you all wet."

He looked down between them, his cock spent and slipping slowly from her sweet body. He was dizzy and unsure
what had just happened—besides the obvious. The front
of his corduroy trousers was indeed dark, but considering the volume of seed he'd shot out, he couldn't swear the
wet spot wasn't his doing. Jesus, though, if it had been her
who'd drenched him . . .

Wrong though it was, dirty though it was, the possibility
made him want to start fucking her all over again.

Maybe she wanted to as well. She touched him gently,
running her thumb down a dark blue vein. A soft, warm

tingle plucked his exhausted nerves. Muscles twitched deep inside his groin. "Ben . . ."

He'd never know what she meant to say, because they heard someone groaning loudly down in the entryway—not with pleasure but with intense pain.

"Bugger," Sally muttered. "I think that's Graham."

Graham was dying. It was his punishment for playing drunken sot with Cecil, instead of doing what duty demanded. He deserved to die. He would any second. His skeleton felt like it was trying to tear itself apart.

Except he wasn't dying. The pain was just getting worse, wave upon wrenching wave that had him curling into a ball on the entry floor. Forget hunching over on his knees, he was toppled on his side like a fallen tree. Cold sweat all over. Panting like a dog so he wouldn't retch from how bad it hurt.

He screamed outright when the pain jumped another level, a baby squalling for attention. He couldn't help himself. He was panting like a dog. No, he'd thought that already. He'd—

A hole seemed to be ripping inside his gin-soaked mind. His fear climbed uncontrollably. His body was shifting, joints grinding and crunching as they tried to change shape. It was like a horror film he'd seen at the cinema. He could feel the hair tearing through his skin. No, he could see it. Thick silver gray wolf hair. His muzzle was lengthening, his fingers getting stumpy and turning into paws. They scrabbled on the linoleum in a cold panic.

Somehow the professor was turning him into a wolf, was making him a monster like he was. He must have realized Graham would come back to save Ben and Sally. This must be his plot to make Graham just as eager to hide the truth. Graham was so outraged he wanted to tear something's liver out and eat it raw. The blood would roll hot down his throat, the chewy gobbets of meat . . .

Graham shook his head and moaned. He had to fight this, had to stay human.

He forced his thoughts to his shoes, to his smart charcoal gray trilby. He thought of cricket and crisps and nice opposable thumbs. He was human. He was British, by God. No sodding vampire was getting the best of him!

He blinked to find the floor cold beneath his sweaty face: his face and not a muzzle—as if he'd hallucinated what came before. The backs of his hands had no more hair than usual. His shoes were on his feet, still tied, though his hat had rolled to the base of the oak coat stand. Two pairs of feet were standing near it, just past the first riser of the stairs.

"Graham?" Sally said in a small, scared voice. "Are you all right? You were thrashing on the floor."

"We thought you were having some kind of fit," Ben added.

Graham pushed the upper half of his body shakily upright. The more orderly part of his mind noticed his siblings were unusually flushed, and Ben's shirttails were hanging loose over his trousers. He pushed his curiosity from his head. Had he actually begun to change into a wolf? Had Ben and Sally seen it but denied what their eyes had been telling them? He wasn't sure it mattered at this point. This was his chance to make things right. He cleared the throat he'd roughened with his screams.

"I'm fine," he said. "But I have to tell you something you're not going to want to believe."

Nim Wei's Lair

⁂

Nim Wei's desk was an extraordinary *bureau plat* that had been constructed for her by the famous French cabinetmaker, André-Charles Boulle. Generally speaking, it wasn't her habit to allow herself to become attached to possessions; if she wasn't careful, time too easily took them away. Even so, she'd been so enamored by the Frenchman's creations—with their ornate tortoiseshell and brass veneers—that she'd warned him he'd better make *this* piece to last forever. The mortal had been flattered enough that she didn't have to bite him to enforce her will. The resulting desk was a masterpiece. Two hundred years later, she still loved it—not that two centuries meant much to her.

Come to think of it, her head of security was about that age.

Entertained by the parallel, she flicked a glance at him. Frank Hauptmann guarded the inside of her office door tonight. He was handsome and blond and stiff—in the manner Germans seemed to pull off better than anyone. Frank was staring blankly at the medieval tapestries that softened this room's stone walls, seeming to think of nothing as she completed her correspondence. Even with her new telephone, letters needed to be written: to her various human brokers around the world, to the high-ranking *upyr* who ruled other cities on her behalf. Nim Wei could have delegated the task, but she liked to see her orders flowing out with the ink, and liked to know her subordinates were reading them the same way.

Putting one's wishes in black and white had its uses.

She smiled to herself, savoring the sensuality of her task. The feel of the desk beguiled her, the smell of the paper, the near silent scratch of her fountain pen. There was so much pleasure to be had in exercising control, far beyond the pleasures most people thought of. Over the years, Nim Wei had learned to appreciate them all.

Her nerves came alert as Frank shifted his weight slightly.

"Bored?" she asked archly, capping her pen with a small, satisfied snap.

His icy eyes jerked to hers. She knew very well he wasn't bored. He'd been standing before her door sporting an enormous hump of an erection for the last quarter hour. Among his other assets, Frank had a fondness for violence, both giving and receiving it. Nim Wei's next appointment wasn't for a while, and she wasn't hungry enough to hunt tonight. She saw no reason why she shouldn't indulge her security chief's predilection for being treated violently by her.

"No, my queen," he said, recovering from his surprise. "I could never be bored in your company. I await only your pleasure."

She bet he did. She was aware that Frank had a regular bed partner, one of the nest's younger *upyr*. Nim Wei had made the chit immortal as a favor to him, for his many decades of service. On her own, Nim Wei wouldn't have chosen to change the girl. Despite her talent as a pianist, she'd been a bit of a brat. Thought if the world didn't bow down low enough to suit her, there must be something wrong with it. Nim Wei would have released Frank from the erotic aspects of his job if this had seemed likely to cause problems, but Frank's new sweetheart appeared not to have cured his yen for his queen. Nim Wei wondered about that occasionally, then decided the girl's probable annoyance wasn't her concern. She wasn't going to deny herself a rather spectacular lover for no good reason.

After all, Frank's gifts as a cocksman were what drew Nim Wei to him in the first place. Back when Bach had been a sensation, he'd been the eldest son of an old Hamburg family. In what was undoubtedly the start of his musical fixations, he'd fancied himself a violinist—to his merchant father's dismay. Frank hadn't been awful, but he hadn't been good enough to live up to his aspirations for himself. Running away to study in Vienna had earned him only the reward of tumbling into Nim Wei's arms. Alas, even the change hadn't made him a virtuoso. He'd been disappointed, but Frank was a man who knew how to look to his main chance. He'd honed his other talents in the absence of his heart's desire. Now he was ruthless, resentful, and cool as ice—at least until he got a chance to burn up someone's sheets in bed. Then his old passions came to the surface, a transformation Nim Wei enjoyed.

Breaking down other people's control would always amuse her.

"Why don't you get my paddle?" she said to him now. "I think you need reminding how to respect a queen."

The tiniest shudder crossed his broad shoulders.

"The leather one," she specified as he began to move. "So I can thrash you just as hard as I please."

He missed a step but regained his balance. The only sign that she'd affected him was an incremental increase in the mountain at his groin.

"As you wish," he said, bowing a trifle stiffly due to its size.

Nim Wei stilled as an ephemeral something tugged at her mind, distracting her from the game to come. *Edmund.* Her old lover's name slid into her consciousness without warning, bringing with it the sense that he was in danger.

She pushed to her feet behind the desk, no stranger to mysterious awarenesses. She'd been born in a time, in a culture, where magic was commonplace. Indeed, it had been her small abilities as a seer that had led Auriclus to become her sire.

Her maker's name was another unexpected trigger. She caught an image of icy mountains and an even icier handgun. The pistol felt like it was in her hand, lifting toward her temple. She saw a flash, heard a bang, sensed a soul slipping its moorings. Auriclus was dying. He was feeding his power down his bloodline, leaving it to them as a parting gift. Nim Wei was of his bloodline, strictly speaking, but he'd cut her off long ago. She wasn't wholesome enough for him. Wouldn't dance to his self-righteous tunes. She'd become her own line, but that old rejection seared her heart anew. Evil Nim Wei. Too ambitious to trust with the secrets of the shapechangers.

"Mistress?" Frank said, seeing the strangeness of her expression.

Nim Wei fought to focus on the here and now. The strength of the link between her and her sire surprised her— between her and Edmund, for that matter. She could feel her former lover's panic as Auriclus's power rushed into him in a seemingly endless flood. He was being shoved into elder status without the slightest preparation to handle it. He was terrified for his family, his loved ones. He didn't know how to protect them.

Frank dropped the leather paddle onto her desk, steadying her shoulders between big, hard hands. Nim Wei looked at him and blinked.

"I have to get to Edmund Fitz Clare. He's in trouble. I need to help."

Frank's whole body jerked with his flinch. She sensed something flare and shiver in his mind, something that shouldn't have been there. Whatever it was disappeared like a rat diving for a hole before her gift for reading thoughts could pin it down. Any other time, she would have stopped to torture it out of him. Tonight she had other priorities.

"I thought Fitz Clare was your enemy," he said.

She didn't dignify that with a response. Nim Wei had plenty of enemies she didn't actually want to see destroyed.

"Cancel my meetings," she called over her shoulder. "I'm going to his human family. He's running away. They'll need my help finding him."

Frank made some protest that she ignored. She was already yanking open the nearest tunnel door.

Frank ordered himself not to run down the corridor from Nim Wei's suite. He didn't want to attract the attention of the other guards. He was gripping the pocket watch Li-Hua had given him in his right hand, the charm it contained his sole protection against mental intrusions. Sweat chilled his skin as he struggled not to crush its chased silver case.

We're not doomed, he told himself as he turned briskly into the hall that led to his own apartments. *Where there's life, there's hope*.

Despite his efforts to calm himself, he entered his rooms in the grip of a breath-strangling dread.

Li-Hua was sitting naked on his bed, painting her toenails pink. As always, Frank's heart squeezed with love and fear at the sight of her perfect, delicate beauty. She was so alive, so fierce—but also so fragile compared to an *upyr* like their queen. From the moment he'd first seen her on-stage at her concert grand, pounding her human passion into the keys, she'd been all he cared about. To care at all had been a shock to one whose soul had grown as cold as Frank's. To love had been a terror he still shook under.

He might desire his queen, but he'd do anything to keep Li-Hua.

His pulse gave a painful jolt when she looked up at him.

"Pack," he rasped, the order harsh. "Nim Wei is going to Edmund's house. He's in trouble, and our queen fucking wants to help."

Li-Hua jumped to her feet so quickly the bottle of pink nail lacquer tumbled to the floor. "Is Graham Fitz Clare there?"

"I don't know." Frank pulled two long canvas duffels from beneath his bed.

"If Graham is home, Edmund will discover our queen is not the Nim Wei who's been running him for MI5. The moment she says her name, our game will be up. She'll kill us—and probably very slowly—as soon as she knows we tried to get Edmund to destroy her." Sick with horror, Li-Hua flattened her hand across her mouth. "I suppose it's too much to hope he might do the deed anyway."

"*Scheiss*," Frank cursed, because he knew it was. If Edmund Fitz Clare had been inclined to impulsive violence, their ruler would have been dead twice over. He dumped the contents of their shared bureau drawers onto the floor. Whatever seemed useful, he began stuffing into the smaller of the two duffel bags.

"Frank—"

"I know," he said. "We have to get out of here. Collect the weapons. They're more important than clothes anyway."

She went obediently to the locked steel cabinet. They kept their forged passports in there as well. Frank didn't remind her to retrieve them. He knew she'd remember. "What exactly did Nim Wei say about Edmund?"

"That he was in trouble. That he was running away, and his human family would need her help finding him."

"Running away? Why would he . . ." She trailed off in the middle of tossing an extra ammo belt onto the bed. "I wonder if the shapechangers' founder finally did what he's been threatening. Maybe Edmund Fitz Clare wasn't ready to become an elder."

"Maybe." Frank zipped the overfilled clothes bag and lifted his eyes to her.

Li-Hua's gaze was frightened but very hard. "If we can find him before our queen does . . ."

"Yes," he said. "If we can find him first, we have a chance of salvaging our dreams."

"Plan B," she said.

"Plan B," he agreed.

When her face split into a wild, white grin, he lost his heart to her all over again.

Bedford Square

Graham heaved himself off the entry floor and ushered Ben and Sally into the library. After he'd toed a pile of yellowing periodicals aside, he shut the door. Whatever the professor had been doing when Graham collapsed, Graham didn't want him interrupting this discussion. When his siblings were settled—Sally in *his* favorite chair and Ben in Edmund's—Graham filled his chest with oxygen. Unable to relax, he perched on the edge of the couch cushions. He had a feeling this was going to be awkward.

Because there was no way to tie a bow around the truth, he said it flat out. "The professor is a vampire."

Ben burst out laughing.

"No," Graham said. "I'm not having you on. He really is."

Ben's face sobered haltingly. He took in how unamused his big brother was. "You're serious. You really think our father is a vampire. Graham, you do realize you're telling us this while smelling like the bottom of a gin bottle."

"He's a vampire," Graham repeated stolidly. He knew he was sober now; too sober, to be frank. Maybe if he said the awful truth often enough, it would sink in for him. "The man who rescued us from the orphanage is an evil, will-stealing blood drinker. He has an animal form as well. With my own eyes, I've seen him change into a wolf. I think that's why I was thrashing on the floor. He was trying to turn me into a beast like him."

"Graham." Sally had her legs tucked under her on the seat. Looking like an earnest mop-haired cherub, she grabbed the chair's worn leather arms and leaned forward. "I don't think this is the way to break up Daddy and Estelle. They announced they were engaged at dinner."

"Engaged?" Graham's breath went out of him. He shoved up from the couch and began to pace one of the clear paths on the carpet. "He's moving faster than I thought to deepen his hold on her."

"Graham," Ben said. Apparently, his siblings thought if they kept using his name, he'd retract his outrageous claims. "You're drunk. And probably upset about losing Estelle. I understand strong feelings can cloud a person's judgment, but—"

Graham cut him off. "In your whole life, have you ever seen our guardian eat? I mean, really take a bite in your presence and swallow it?"

"His delicate stomach . . ." Sally said.

"Is nothing but a Banbury tale to fuddle us. He has to change into his wolf form if he wants to eat human food. That's why he always has Mrs. Mackie take his trays up to his study. If that doesn't convince you, think about his strange allergy to sunshine. Suspicious, don't you think? Up all night, asleep all day. Sort of reminds you of a vampire, doesn't it?"

"He drinks too much," Sally said unsurely. "He oversleeps."

"He barely drinks at all!" Graham exclaimed. "Think back, and you'll realize you've never seen him take more than a sip. He let you believe he was a sot because it suited his purposes. We've no idea what the professor's life was like before he adopted us. No idea how old he even is."

"But Graham—" Sally's brow furrowed at the way his voice had risen. He knew she wasn't used to seeing him emotional. "Vampires aren't *real*."

Graham ground his teeth in frustration. "They're real," he said, low enough for it to be a growl. "MI5 established an entire section to watch his kind. His Majesty's Secret Service considers them a danger to the realm."

"A danger to the realm . . ." Ben shifted in Edmund's chair. "Graham . . ."

"I've seen his true face," Graham insisted, fisting his hands as he spit it out. He felt like he was being torn in two, trying to convince his siblings of facts he scarcely wanted to accept himself. "I've woken him during the day and watched him struggle to keep his eyes open. He can spin illusions. He can worm his way into our heads and make us see him as an older man. His true face isn't any older than yours or mine. He's a monster, Ben, and he wants to control Estelle. He wants to drink her blood!"

Graham's fervor had pushed his brother back in his chair. Ben's face was pale, his expression less sure than it had been before. "You're serious about this."

"As serious as death. Ben, you know me. I wouldn't say this unless I was convinced. We're all in danger from him."

"*We're* in danger?" Sally said. "Graham, that's going too far."

"Could he—" Ben stopped and scrubbed at his disordered hair. His gaze went to Sally, a dark look Graham couldn't interpret. "You said he could spin illusions. Could he, maybe, affect our behavior in other ways?"

"Oh, Ben," Sally said. "Don't try to blame that on anyone but us."

"But maybe—" Ben lowered his voice, directing his words to her. "Maybe what we did wasn't our fault."

"What did you do?" Graham asked, confused by their manner but hoping the explanation would increase his chances of swaying them.

He'd never know if they would have answered. The library door burst open to reveal Estelle. She looked like she'd been blown in by a storm.

"Thank God," she breathed from the threshold. "I need your help. Edmund's run away!"

Heat prickled in waves across Graham's skin. Her news was a shock, but it wasn't the reason for his sudden spike in temperature. Estelle was disheveled: her hair windblown, her shapely body wrapped in one of the professor's custom-tailored shirts. She was tall enough that the garment didn't cover very much of her. Inappropriate though it was, he couldn't help noticing her legs were spectacular.

Ruthlessly ignoring his reaction, Graham thrust out his arm and pointed a finger at her.

"Ask her," he said. "Ask her if her lover isn't a vampire."

Criminy, Estelle thought, too taken aback to guard her expression. For the last little while she'd been calling through the bedroom window for Edmund to come back, without achieving anything beyond half freezing. When she'd given up and come down here to find his children, this was not the reception she'd been hoping for.

"Good Lord," Sally said, "Estelle thinks the professor is a vampire, too!"

"He *is* a vampire," Graham huffed in exasperation. "Look at those bite marks on Estelle's throat."

Estelle slapped her hand over the forgotten wound. She needn't have bothered. Sally was off and running on her own track.

"What do you mean, he's run away?" she asked Estelle angrily. "What have you done to my father?"

"I haven't done anything. Something upset him. He said he was afraid he was going to hurt the people he loved."

"He is going to hurt them," Graham said. "He already has."

"That isn't true!" Sally cried.

"*Quiet*," Ben ordered in such a hard and penetrating tone that everyone fell silent and gaped at him. "Wait," he said to Sally. "We're going to sort this out."

He came to stand before Estelle. "Lower your hand."

Estelle swallowed and let it drop from her neck. Ben took her jaw between his fingers, lifting and turning it to examine her.

"Jesus," he said. "Those do look like fang marks."

"I told you!" Graham burst out.

"Hush," Ben said but without heat. Estelle tried not to wince as he searched her eyes. His were green with tiny gold striations. She wasn't sure she'd ever seen them this close up. They were pretty, but she'd have forgone the pleasure to avoid this questioning. "Tell the truth, Estelle. Is—" Ben sighed and began again. "Is our father a vampire?"

Estelle would have lied to Sally and maybe to Graham as well; he had obviously prejudged what his father was. But Ben was simply trying to ascertain the truth, and Ben was one of the most evenhanded people Estelle knew. Of them all, he was the likeliest to give Edmund a fair shake.

"He is," Estelle said reluctantly. "But he isn't evil, not like Graham seems to think. He'd never hurt any of you. I think he was having some sort of accidental increase in power. He jumped out the window because he didn't know how to control it, and he didn't want to harm anyone."

"He *is* a vampire then," Ben repeated, clearly having trouble accepting this. "He told you so to your face."

"He told me, and he showed me. Graham isn't mistaken about that part."

She glanced at Edmund's eldest. He stood next to Ben

now, his brows beetled above his nose as if he didn't trust Estelle not to try something. Her truthfulness seemed not to have softened him. He turned to his brother.

"You have to get Sally away from here," he said, causing Ben's eyes to widen. "A chance this good might not come again, and you don't want to be anywhere near the house when Edmund returns. You don't know how to fight a being with his abilities."

"Edmund loves you," Estelle pleaded. "You don't need to fight him. You need to help me find him. I'm afraid of what he'll do out there alone, of what might happen. He looked so tormented when whatever it was overcame his control."

Graham folded his massive arms. "Would this have been before or after he fucked the sense out of you?"

Estelle could only gasp in shock at that. She doubted Graham had ever used that word against a woman before.

"I don't understand," Sally said. "Why are you both lying about this?"

"We're not," Estelle and Graham snapped in unison.

"Hey!" said Sally. "Don't pick on me."

Ben pushed from his chair and went to stand by hers, his hand squeezing her shoulder protectively. She looked up at him, her expression begging him to straighten out the others. This, however, wasn't the support Ben had to offer.

"I don't think they're lying," he said. "I think the professor may be what they say. Whether he's dangerous . . ." He shook his head as if he couldn't believe they were having this discussion. "Until we know for sure, perhaps we'd better err on Graham's side."

"No!" Estelle cried. "You know your father. You know how much he cares for you."

"I know Graham, too," Ben said quietly. "He's not a liar, and he's not given to dramatics."

"And I am?" Estelle could have torn out her hair— though of course that wouldn't have bolstered her position.

Slowly, she released her breath. She'd gain nothing by losing her temper. The Fitz Clare children closing ranks was to be expected. Even Sally wasn't looking as though she wanted to argue anymore.

"Fine," Estelle said. "I'll search for Edmund on my own."

This, at last, made Graham unbend. "You can't," he said, catching her elbow. "Being around him isn't any safer for you than it is for us."

"Graham," she said in warning just as a pounding sounded on the front door.

"Don't," he said when she tried to go answer it. "We don't know who that is."

He had her by the left arm, so she used her right to firmly pry away his hold.

"I don't care who it is," she said, "as long as they're willing to help."

Unfortunately, the person behind the door seemed more in need of help than able to give it. His fist still raised to knock, he was swaying slightly on the stoop—a tall, fair-haired man whose skin was as pale as marble under a full moon. He wore dark dress trousers and an unbuttoned wool overcoat. Beneath them, he was bare-chested and shoeless. He looked familiar, though Estelle could not recall meeting him.

"Oh," said Sally, "It's Mister . . . Mister . . ."

Before she could remember, the man toppled forward toward Estelle.

She caught him, but his weight drove her to her knees; he had to be six feet tall, and while he was lean, he was no feather.

As she struggled not to go sprawling, she found herself wishing she had more than Edmund's shirt to cover her.

"It's Robin," she barely heard the fallen man gasp. "Robin Fitz Clare."

The name snapped through her, explaining why he'd

seemed familiar, but she didn't have time to return the greeting. Edmund's natural son began to convulse right there on her lap. As he did, sparkling waves of light chased across the too white planes of his chest and face. The effect lit up the entry like a flickering electric bulb. Whatever had happened to Edmund seemed to be affecting Robin as well, though—luckily—Estelle's funny hand and arm weren't glowing in response. She knew she wasn't ready to explain that to this crowd.

"Sorry," Robin apologized through chattering teeth. "Glamour's shot to hell. Not used to all this new power."

"Stay back," Estelle barked when Graham would have approached. Her arms circled Robin protectively.

"He's a vampire, too," Graham objected. "I saw him and the professor turn into wolves."

"He's the professor's *son*, and you can damn well wait until he recovers before you sharpen your stake."

"His son!" Sally exclaimed.

"Oh, Lord," Robin sighed as his convulsions eased. "I see all sorts of cats are being let out of the bag tonight." He sat up slowly, testing whether his muscles were really calm, then patted Estelle's arm to let her know he was all right. "I take it my instincts weren't misleading me: My father really has flown the coop?"

"I'm afraid so," Estelle said. "Do you know what happened to him?"

Rather than answer, Robin turned cool, narrow eyes to Graham. "Help me up," he said, extending his hand to Edmund's other son. "I'll talk once I'm sitting in a real chair."

Graham complied, if warily. They all trooped back to the library, where Robin pulled a seat close to the fire as if he were cold. None of them could take their eyes off him. He was still glowing—though less than before—and still lovelier than any human being could be. For once, Sally was absolutely struck speechless. Ben was cuddling her against him on the couch. Estelle and Graham had each chosen chairs . . . not next to each other.

"You've been told what I am," Robin began, "after a fashion, so I'll start with what matters now. The founder of your father's and my line of vampires—shapechanging *upyr*, we call ourselves—committed suicide tonight and divvied up his power among his children. The more senior the *upyr*, the more energy they received, and the man you know as the professor got quite a bit. He's been pushed to a new plateau and has become an elder: a master vampire who can change humans into what he is."

Robin paused to rub his forehead, then looked at them again. "I have a theory that my father should have become an elder long ago. He had concerns about his ability to handle the responsibility that comes with power, and I suspect that—unbeknownst to him—he's been holding himself back. When this step-up hit him, I think his unconscious dam crumbled. As a result, he's jumped farther than he knows how to handle, and he's justifiably afraid he'll hurt someone."

Ben spoke up. "Won't he be all right if we simply let him stay away from us long enough to regain control?"

"Normally I'd say yes, but he and I believe he has an enemy, a vampire from a rival bloodline who could take advantage of his vulnerable state. I need to find my father before she can. If you have any idea where he might have run, now's the time to say."

"You can't just sense where he is?" Estelle asked, remembering how Edmund found her when she was attacked at Harrods.

Robin shook his head ruefully. "Unfortunately not. My supernatural sensors are a bit haywire. Overloaded, I expect. I knew my father was in trouble but not where he was. I'm feeling lucky to have put one foot in front of the other to get myself to you."

"This is all well and good," Graham interjected, "but

why should we trust you? You're the same kind of creature that he is."

"The woman you've been working with could kill Edmund, Graham. Whatever you think about what we are, is that really what you want? The man who raised you dead? Believe me, Nim Wei is closer to being a monster than your father ever was."

"What are you talking about? My handler is human. My handler works for the government."

"Your *handler*?" Ben's eyes rounded at the term. "Graham, what have you gotten yourself mixed up in? Is that why you mentioned MI5 before? Are you working for those spooks?"

"Graham is a spy?" Sally said. "Oh, really, *that's* just not possible."

"Fuck," Graham cursed, his face gone red with frustration—and perhaps a little with insult. "I am *not* discussing this with you."

"I think you'd better," Ben countered, beginning to lean forward. "Considering you want us to leave the professor swinging in the wind."

"You don't under—"

The debate was cut short by another banging at the door. Robin came to attention like a hunting dog. Estelle had the distinct impression that he was sniffing the air.

"Shit," he said. "It's her."

Sally shrieked as he shot out of his chair so fast the movement was a blur. Estelle felt a bit like shrieking herself, though she'd seen Edmund do similar things. They all leapt to their feet as a crash exploded outside the room. As one, they ran to the library door, which was the first opening to the left of the entryway. They shrank back with a concerted gasp when they saw what was happening there.

The vampires were grappling at superspeed—and superstrength as well. Giant cracks were opening in the plaster

and the lath as they smashed back and forth into various
walls. The action was hard to follow, but Estelle thought
Robin had his hands around the female's neck. Edmund's
former lover was wearing something pink, but other than
that Estelle couldn't tell what Nim Wei was doing to defend
herself.

What she was saying, on the other hand, was perfectly
clear.

"Jesus Bloody Christ," she swore. "I'm here to help, you
puling little shit!"

The railing tore off the stairs in a trail of splinters as the
blurs streaked there.

"I won't let you hurt his family!" Robin roared.

The shape that belonged to him bent its knees and then
shot upward, dragging the other one. As luck would have it,
the pair crashed headfirst into one of the ceiling's main support beams. The house shuddered with the impact, but the
wood did not break. Instead, both vampires plummeted to
the entry floor, dazed enough to have slowed to human veloc-
ity. To Estelle's dismay, Nim Wei sat atop Robin now. Her
hands gripped either side of his head as she smacked it over
and over into a patch of not-yet-decimated walnut parquet.

The fact that her fangs had run out made what she was
doing twice as alarming. Ben started forward, instinctively
wanting to help Robin, but Graham more sensibly caught
his arm. Estelle couldn't disapprove. Ben might be fit, but
he didn't have the strength to stop the vampiress.

"I'm here to help," she was saying in rhythm with her
blows. "I'm. Here. To. Help."

She let go when Robin's arms went limp.

"Are you done being an idiot?" she asked, still not getting up.

Robin's eyes were closed, a trickle of blood matting his
impossibly golden hair. He groaned what could have been
a *yes*.

"Good," Nim Wei said. "And don't worry about healing

that crack I put in your skull. In case you hadn't noticed, you've become an elder, too—though you're not, of course, as elder as I am."

Only mildly out of breath, Nim Wei rose and swatted the plaster dust from her clothes. She was wearing a very pretty silk kimono robe—not pink, after all, Estelle saw, but white with dark red blossoms. She was startlingly small, as short as Sally and even slighter in build. Her ebony hair settled around her shoulders like a cape being smoothed by invisible maidservants.

Even having seen it happen, it was difficult to believe this slip of a woman had reduced her male opponent to a moaning heap.

When she turned to face her quartet of gawkers, Estelle had to suppress a gasp. Apparently, she'd lost control of her glamour during her battle with Edmund's son. Without its shield, her beauty was unearthly. It wasn't hard to see that she and Robin were the same kind of being. The perfection of their features was frightening.

"Well," the woman said, seeming a little awkward now that she wasn't occupied with pummeling Robin. "I suppose I ought to introduce myself. I'm Nim Wei, the vampire queen of London. A long time ago, your father and I . . . knew each other."

She extended her hand to Graham, who was staring at it as if it were a snake. Estelle was about to nudge him—offending this creature absolutely did not seem like a good idea—but then he pulled himself straight and spoke.

"I don't care what you say your name is," he declared, hard as iron. "You are not my Nim Wei."

Graham wasn't sure how he'd lost control of this situation, but he didn't like it one bit. In less time than he'd thought possible, Edmund's son dragged himself onto the bottom tread of the stairs. The hall looked like a hurricane had blown through it, but Robin had recovered sufficiently to start interrogating Graham—if not to look particularly sprightly doing it.

"You're saying that this woman here, whom I know to be the only *upyr* by her name, is not the woman who told you your adoptive father is a vampire."

Graham shot a look at Robin's attacker. The vampiress appeared smugly pleased to see someone else in the hot seat.

"They're both Oriental," he answered, unable to repress his frown, "but other than that, they couldn't be less alike. For one thing, *my* Nim Wei is human."

The female vampire snorted through her button nose, her deceptively slender arms crossed beneath her breasts. She was leaning against the fractured wall opposite the rest of them. She did look a little like his Nim Wei, but Graham wasn't in the mood to admit that.

"If your handler isn't a vampire, I'll eat toast," she said scornfully. "You've been cozened, boyo. Thralled to within an inch of your puny human life."

"Edmund read *your* face from Graham's memories," Robin pointed out. "That's why we thought you were involved."

The female vampire shrugged. "You know some of our kind can plant illusions in human minds."

"But that would mean someone who knew you well was trying to frame you."

"Just getting there?" the female vampire mocked. "Not only was someone trying to frame me, I expect she was trying to manipulate Edmund and his brother into killing me on her behalf, probably to clear the path for someone more to her liking to take over. The succession would never unfold the way she thinks, but most rebels are stupid that way."

Robin narrowed his eyes at her. "You know who it is."

"I've a fair idea, seeing as there's only one female in my nest who could pass for me. Don't you worry, though. As soon as I get home, I guarantee the chit and whoever helped her will never get a chance to back the wrong horse again."

Graham fought a shiver at the chilly confidence in her voice. Whatever else she was, this woman was a killer; he could not have a single doubt of that.

"Did you murder Martin Walser?" he asked point-blank.

Nim Wei—he supposed he had to call her that—turned only her head to him, as if her neck were made of machine parts instead of flesh. If the question rattled her, it didn't show. "I am not familiar with that name."

"Martin Walser was my previous handler at MI5, before the woman calling herself Nim Wei brought me into X Section."

She didn't get a chance to answer, because Robin cleared his throat.

"Er, Graham," he said in a tone of faint embarrassment. "Maybe you ought to know: Walser was your father's associate. They worked together to found X Section. Whoever pretended to be your new handler probably killed him. Edmund knew there weren't any X Section operations targeting him and that your handler had to be a fake. He simply thought the fake was her."

He waved his hand toward Nim Wei, who rolled her eyes. Graham felt his head start to spin. Could this possibly be correct? Could the woman who'd revealed the truth about his father be a murderer? Could she have drained every drop of blood from his former boss? Graham's fists clenched with his longing to deny it all.

"Why would my father be working with MI5 to spy on his own kind?"

Robin shot an even less comfortable glance toward Nim Wei. "He was worried that some members of the *upyr* might try to interfere in mortal affairs, the world situation being what it is. He thought it best if he helped you humans keep an eye on them."

"Oh, charming," Nim Wei drawled. "I wouldn't have thought it possible, but I'm feeling even more ridiculous for wanting to help that bastard."

"You've interfered in human politics in the past," Robin reminded her. "I heard you were once extremely fond of the beds of kings."

Graham ignored their sniping to address Estelle. "Did you know Edmund was working with MI5?"

She shook her head, wide-eyed. "I didn't, but I'm not sure we should worry about that now. He's out there some-where, and even if *this* Nim Wei isn't his enemy, I'd feel a great deal better if we got him back." She looked toward the two vampires. "Edmund isn't truly a danger to us, is he? He only thought he was because he wasn't accustomed to his new power."

"Probably not," Nim Wei said grudgingly, "though with Auriclus involved, who knows? Your heads just might explode if you're close to him." She leveled a cool gaze on Robin. "For all his goody-goody talk, your line's founder had an uncanny knack for letting people down when they needed him."

"Oh, and your leadership is so much better. You'd prob-ably have fit in one last torture session before you killed yourself."

"Stop." Estelle hunkered down to lay her hand on Rob-in's knee. His bristling lessened at her touch. "This won't help us find Edmund."

"I'll get my coat," Ben said, pushing past her into the hall.

Graham couldn't believe what Ben had just done: used four small words to join the other side from him. Maybe Ben was right to do it, but the hurt Graham felt was com-plicated and intense. "You're going to take their say-so on all this? Just like that?"

Ben stopped and turned back to him. "I think we have to, Graham. We owe the professor too much not to give him the benefit of the doubt. Crazy as it sounds, their explanation fits the man I know better than yours does."

"I'll get my coat, too," Sally said.

"You will not," Ben retorted immediately.

"I have to," Sally said. "If I don't, you know you'll want someone to stay at the house with me. Graham doesn't trust the others, but he won't stay himself, and if he goes, *you* need to watch out for him. And don't say Estelle can protect me because—" Sally's face struggled just a bit. "Estelle has to join the search. Daddy loves her. If he's really upset, she's the one he'll listen to."

Ben gave her his hardest look, but couldn't argue with her logic. To Graham's surprise, their squabble was over almost before it began. "You girls promise to stay back if we find him? In case he is dangerous?"

"I do," Sally said. "Cross my heart."

"If you humans are coming," Nim Wei interrupted, "you'll need to carry something iron. That will help fend off the effect of his power if it flares again."

Ben took this piece of intelligence with aplomb, turning on his heel and striding into the library. Moments later, he returned with the full complement of fireplace tools. When Graham accepted the poker, Ben met and held his stare.

"I know what you're thinking," he said—though Graham wondered if he did. "We have to be careful. It's just, if the professor isn't a monster, I can't turn my back on him."

"Don't imagine this was easy for me," Graham said, his eyes gone hotter than was comfortable. "I didn't want to turn against him."

"You didn't turn against him." Edmund's other son had risen from the bottom stair, the gentleness of his voice an eerie echo of the professor's. "You were thralled to think the worst of him."

His kindness did nothing to ease the terrible storm

building inside Graham. If what Robin said was true, if the woman he'd known as Nim Wei had tricked him into thinking Edmund was evil, that only meant Graham was weak and wrong. Being right wouldn't have made him happy, but the idea that he'd been mistaken sickened him.

He remembered how he'd dragged Edmund from his bed and held him in the sun until his skin blistered.

If Graham had done that for no good reason to the man who'd saved him, who'd saved them all, he didn't know how he'd live with himself.

Hampstead Heath

On some level of awareness, Edmund knew where he was running: not just away but to, not just escaping but trying to reassert the truth of himself. When Hampstead Heath appeared before him, cold and misty and quiet, he knew he could stop at last.

He and Robin had hunted these gentle slopes many times. They'd howled at the moon. They'd performed the wolfish version of breaking bread. They'd collapsed naked on their backs and laughed over nothing more than the pleasure of being alive, laughed so hard that tears had rolled from their eyes.

Sons didn't do that with fathers they despised.

Maybe more to the point, fathers who could be true monsters didn't care either way.

Edmund let his head drop back on his buzzing spine. The grass beneath his feet was crisp with frost, reminding him he'd grabbed a shirt and trousers but no shoes. Auriclus's deathbed gift continued to course through him, causing his skin to shine faintly—though this no longer seemed frightening. Edmund was absorbing the energy, tucking it away in corners he hadn't known were waiting to receive it. He'd explore them later; go through the new skills and knowledge they contained. As it was, feeling the pieces of Auriclus's intelligence slide into his brain was like watching a stock market ticker while half awake. Though he knew the symbols had meaning, he couldn't yet crack their code.

I will make sense of this, he thought. *I'll find a way not to be a danger to those I love.*

His galloping heart rate slowed, finally approaching a speed more natural to his species. He began to walk toward the lake where he suspected he and Robin had first been seen by Graham as wolves. Mist churned sluggishly over the water's surface, a rime of ice crackling its edges.

Even Graham loves me, Edmund thought. *No matter what he's been told.*

Edmund realized he had everything he'd ever been jealous of his older brother for. A family who loved him. Respect. A woman he wanted to share the rest of his life with. And now he was an elder, too. He had choices that had been closed to him before. Those choices might test his conscience, but he thought—just maybe—he wasn't going to be ashamed of how he'd handle them.

He smiled at the hope flaring in his heart. If Estelle had been there, he would have hugged her. She had helped him find this faith in himself. In her eyes, he'd always been a good man.

He hadn't told her he loved her nearly often enough.

She'll be worried, he thought, a pang of guilt in that. He'd heard her calling after him for quite a distance; heard her love and fear as she pleaded for him to return. He glanced over his shoulder, in the direction of Bedford Square. He'd go home as soon as he had enough control to reconstruct his glamour. He had time. Dawn was a little while off yet.

When he turned back to the lake, he received an unpleasant shock.

"How nice," said a figure who hadn't been in front of him before. "Our newly minted elder drops conveniently into our laps—and in one of his favorite haunts. I love it when our kind behave the way I expect them to."

The *upyr* who'd taken him by surprise was a slight Oriental female dressed in dark clothes, from her knitted cap to her sailor's peacoat to her diminutive army boots. She was young. Edmund judged her as having lived less than a hundred immortal years, and maybe as few as fifty. Her youth was compensated for by the deadly looking machine gun whose wooden stock she'd braced against her slim shoulder. As a historian, Edmund followed developments in military technology. This gray steel model looked German made. It was belt fed, probably capable of firing a thousand rounds per minute. A human her size wouldn't have been able to support the heavy weapon without its bipod, but she held the thing as if she could happily point its muzzle at him all night.

Somehow Edmund didn't think that was her plan.

"Ah, ah, ah," she scolded as his muscles tensed to retreat from her. "My partner is covering your back. We've been lying in wait for you."

Edmund's head jerked around. A man stood behind him now, perhaps a meter away. Dressed to match his partner, he was a small giant—as muscular and tall as Graham, though he carried his size with more élan than Edmund's son. He held a smaller machine gun than the woman: a "gangster gun," Edmund believed Americans called it.

"Brass shells," the man informed him, "with iron projectiles inside. Mine only shoots seven hundred rounds per minute, but we think it'll cut a nice swath in you."

"Who are you?" Edmund demanded. "Why are you doing this?"

He returned his gaze to the woman, unable to decide

who was the more dangerous. He couldn't read either of
their minds, which was strange in and of itself. Despite
their relative youth, determination radiated from the pair
as clearly as the cold, hard tang of their weaponry. Edmund
knew they'd kill him if he stepped wrong.

He hadn't yet, apparently, because the woman smiled
at him, smug and cool. She felt safe with her gun in hand,
secure against his "newly minted" elder power. Edmund's
mind raced for some way to capitalize on that.

"We're doing this for our freedom," she said. "Because
we refuse to spend another minute under that bitch's thumb.
As for who we are . . ." Her smile broadened. "This is my
true love, Frank, and I'm Li-Hua, once celebrated by all of
London for my skill at tickling the ivories."

"I'm afraid I don't know you," he said politely.

Her manner turned arch. "Your son, Graham, knows me
very well. Of course, he thinks my name is Nim Wei."

Edmund almost rushed her in the sudden rage that
burst in his veins. The pieces flew together with a silent
click. *This* woman had bitten Graham and thralled him.
This woman had tried to make his son hate him. At the
last second, he stopped his muscles from launching his
weight at her. He wasn't certain he could leap faster than
both their guns, wasn't absolutely convinced his new elder
status would enable him to survive being torn apart by iron
bullets.

Li-Hua's smile slanted into a grin when she saw him
restrain himself. Edmund could tell she was enjoying the
excitement of this standoff.

"It truly is a shame," she said, tutting mockingly. "You
could have spared yourself this trouble if you'd just killed
our queen as we'd hoped. Your brother is the head of the
shapechanger Council. *You* wouldn't have been executed
for meting out justice."

"Maybe I can kill her now," Edmund offered, prepared

to promise anything that would help him get out of this. "I have become an elder, after all."

"Such a liar," Li-Hua said an instant before her finger squeezed the trigger.

Her thoughts had given him no warning that his negotiating time was up. Edmund was too stunned to run, and then he lost the ability. The pain blazing through him swallowed his will. *A thousand rounds per minute* became more than words; it became hundreds of balls of superheated iron punching into him. The air sounded oddly like paper ripping as the force of the impacts threw him back and onto the ground. His eyes remained open, but his body was paralyzed. His *upyr* gifts were screaming, swelling, streaming outward from the holes in his flesh in golden rays of light. Edmund knew his power was trying—fruitlessly, it seemed to him—to heal the terrible damage wrought by the one metal his kind were weakened by. Normal bullets would have been shoved out, but these could not be.

As if his power were giving up, the light show snuffed out.

The female vampire stood over him, not shooting now but ready to resume. A pool of spent brass lay smoking on the ground around her.

"That's enough," her lover said. He'd moved beside her. His hand was smoothing up and down her back, soothing her. "He'll be helpless for a while. We don't want to do irreparable damage to our ace in the hole."

Edmund feared they already had.

Don't die, he ordered himself as his blood soaked too fast and from too many places into the earth under him. He thought of his family, of Estelle and how much joy loving her had brought him. He had so much more to give her, to give everyone. It almost seemed as if her voice were speaking furiously in his mind.

Don't you die, Edmund Fitz Clare.

* * *

Estelle didn't cry until she saw the bullet casings littering the grass, until she saw the giant patch of blood on the ground. The heath was matted with it, the soil stained dark. She hadn't let herself give in to fear before that; hadn't wanted to believe Edmund was in real danger. He couldn't die, not when they'd finally discovered what they meant to each other.

Sadly, that wasn't the story the evidence before her told. The little iron scuttle she'd been carrying for protection dropped from her numb fingers.

"Oh, my God," Sally said, her voice rising. "Is that what I think it is?"

Outwardly calm, Robin crouched down to rub a bit of blood-soaked dirt between his thumb and fingers. He brought the scent to his nose. "The blood is Edmund's, and he's still alive. I can sense that much."

"Yes," Nim Wei agreed, her slitted gaze turned away from them and toward the eastern horizon. The sheerest wash of gray was lightening the sky. "His captors don't want to kill him. I feel two of them, both *upyr*. They've taken him to some sort of delivery van—black or maybe navy with dark windows." She shook her head. "That's all I'm getting. Li-Hua is young, but she has a gift for hiding her thoughts. I think she's shielding the others, too."

"But you can track them?" Estelle fought back a sob. Helpful though Nim Wei was being, Estelle suspected the vampire queen had no patience for the pitiful. "You can discover where they're taking him?"

"They've ingested something," Nim Wei said. "Cocaine, I think. To keep them awake. They're planning to travel by daylight."

"That's fine," Estelle said, "but where have they gone?"

Nim Wei turned to her, her face a cool and beautiful carving. "I'm sorry. I don't know. There are many vans in this city, and I cannot tell you how to discover which belongs to them."

"But they have Edmund. *They have Edmund*!"

Ben put his arms around her as she lost control of herself. Graham looked as if he wanted to comfort her, too, but didn't feel he had the right. Edmund's absence was an aching rip in her heart. She wasn't supposed to lose him, not like this, not before they'd even had a chance to grow accustomed to their happiness.

She hadn't told him she loved him nearly often enough.

"You must know something," she begged Nim Wei. "Why they've done it. What they hope to gain."

Something that could have been compassion flickered through Nim Wei's eyes. "I don't know," she said again. "I believe I'm lucky to have read what I did."

When Ben spoke, his voice was rough enough to draw another sob into Estelle's throat. "We'll find him, Estelle."

"*I'll* find him," Graham corrected.

Sally went to Graham and took his hands. Hers were small enough to be swallowed. "Not alone, Graham. No one thinks you have to do that. No one blames you for this."

He opened his mouth but couldn't speak. Starlight glistened on the tears running down his honest English face.

"Not alone," Sally repeated. "We all love Daddy. We'll all help find him."

"Oh, God," Graham choked out, as if he wasn't sure her offer was a good thing.

Wanting to laugh in spite of everything, Estelle held out her arms to him. With a muffled cry he came to her and held her, so tightly she almost couldn't breathe—though the last thing she wanted was to let go. She knew this must be tearing him apart. Everyone who'd ever been close to Graham thought of him as a decent soul, someone who truly wanted to do what was right. Estelle suspected he was just now realizing how much that image meant to him.

Knowing his brother even better than she did, Ben joined the embrace, and then Sally, too. Caught between the people he loved, Graham began to weep harder, his big, broad shoulders wracked by sobs.

For whatever reason, his falling apart helped her feel stronger.

"All of us," Estelle promised softly. "All of us will save Edmund."

Will the Fitz Clares be able to rescue Edmund?
Don't miss the next book in the Fitz Clare Chronicles
by Emma Holly

BREAKING MIDNIGHT

Available July 2009 from Berkley Sensation!